A DEATHBED OF ROSES

The Fourth Jess O'Malley Mystery

The creek behind the derelict cottage

JINNY ALEXANDER

ISBN Paperback: 978-1-916814-06-6

ISBN ebook: 978-1-916814-07-3

Cover Design: Wicked Good Book Covers
Map of Ballyfortnum: Jinny Alexander and Dewi Hargreaves
Chapter heading artwork: Jinny Alexander

Visit www.jinnyalexander.com

This book is dedicated to Morag, Paul,
Graham, and Shirin.
The world is smaller without you.

A note to my American-English readers

I'm so glad you're here! I'm a British author, living in the Republic of
Ireland, and all my books are set in Ireland or the UK. As such, I use
British English in my writing so you'll notice different spellings and a
few extra letters – **U**s after **O**s, for instance, and **L**s that come in pairs.
I make up for these extras by using fewer **Z**s…

I hope you'll enjoy my natural English voice and immerse yourselves
fully into my UK and Irish settings and characters, but if you're still not
convinced, I recommend a nice cup of tea.

Over here, a nice cup of tea fixes *almost* everything.

Love, Jinny xx

PRONUNCIATION GUIDE TO IRISH NAMES IN THE BOOK

In the Jess O'Malley Irish Village mystery series, several characters have Irish names. It's not always obvious how these names are pronounced, so I hope this pronunciation guide will help.

Please note, there are variations of many of these pronunciations. I've given the one that represents how I hear that character's name in my own head while I write about them.

FIRST NAMES:
Colm = Cuh-lum
Deiric = Derek
Kieran = KEER-uhn
Seamus = SHAY-mus
Siobhan = Shuh-vawn
Sean = Shaun, Shawn

SURNAMES:
Geraghty = geh-ruh-tee
Docherty = DOK-uh-tee
Shaughnessy = SHAW-nuh-see

(Some of these names only get a passing mention in this book, but you never know when they may reappear later in the series!)

IRISH WORDS AND PHRASES

CÉAD MÍLE FÁILTE (Kay-od mee-leh foyle-cha): A hundred thousand welcomes.

SLÁINTE (slawn-che): Cheers!

CRAIC (crack): an enjoyable social activity; a good time

BAILE (boll-ya) = Town. The English names of many Irish towns begin with Bally because it's the Anglicised version of the Irish word.

This sketch is based on my own tumbledown sheds, smothered with ivy and roses, in my back garden in a small Irish village similar to Ballyfortnum. Many old houses have similar sheds, where typically, turf would have been stored.

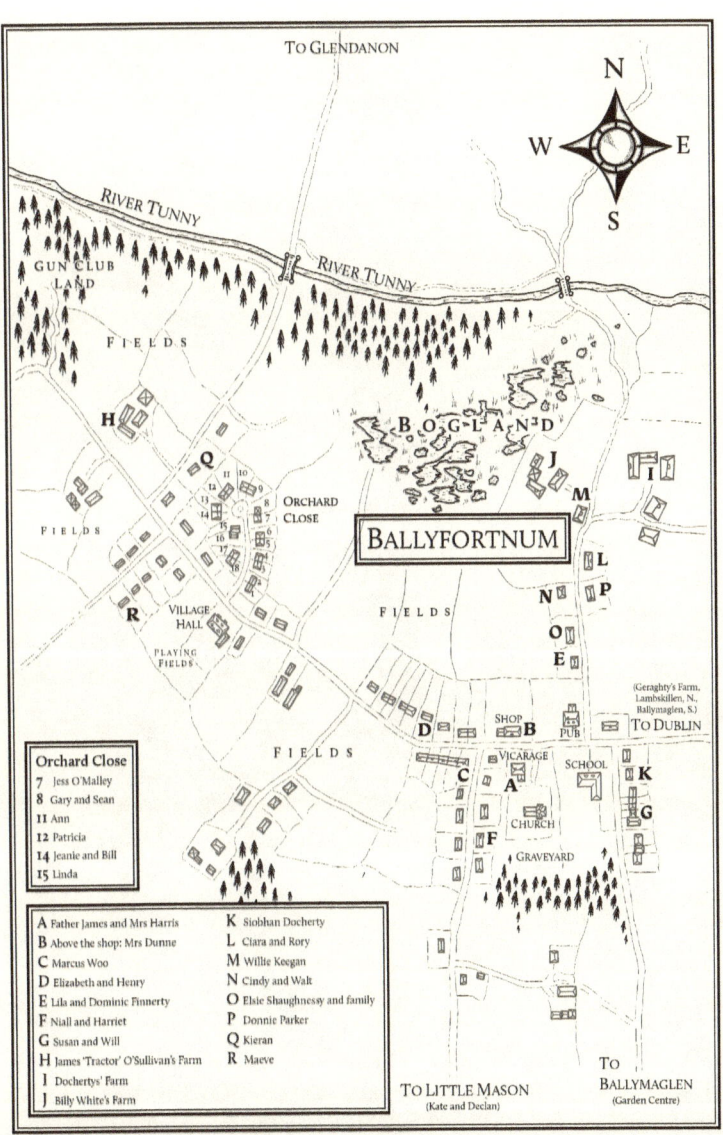

To Glendanon

N
W E
S

River Tunny

Gun Club Land

River Tunny

Fields

H

Q

Fields

B·O·G·L·A·N·D

J

M

I

Orchard Close

BALLYFORTNUM

L

N P

R

Village Hall

Fields

O
E

Playing Fields

(Geraghty's Farm, Lambskillen, N., Ballymaglen, S.)

Shop B

Pub

To Dublin

Fields

D

Vicarage

School

K

C

A

G

F

Church

Graveyard

Orchard Close

7 Jess O'Malley
8 Gary and Sean
11 Ann
12 Patricia
14 Jeanie and Bill
15 Linda

A Father James and Mrs Harris
B Above the shop: Mrs Dunne
C Marcus Woo
D Elizabeth and Henry
E Lila and Dominic Finnerty
F Niall and Harriet
G Susan and Will
H James 'Tractor' O'Sullivan's Farm
I Dochertys' Farm
J Billy White's Farm

K Siobhan Docherty
L Ciara and Rory
M Willie Keegan
N Cindy and Walt
O Elsie Shaughnessy and family
P Donnie Parker
Q Kieran
R Maeve

To Little Mason
(Kate and Declan)

To Ballymaglen
(Garden Centre)

Chapter One

With judging for the Tidy Village Award only a week away, Ballyfortnum buzzed with anticipation. Throughout most of the village, gardens bloomed in full colour that could easily compete with Joseph's technicolour dreamcoat. Jess wouldn't mind if Jason Donovan popped in, now she thought of it ... maybe he could be a guest judge. Was he still playing Joseph on stage? Probably not.

"Ouch!"

Jess O'Malley's reverie was broken by Father James. On his bike. Going too fast for these narrow country lanes. Again.

"Oh," she said, as she disentangled her ponytail from the thorny hedgerow she'd backed into. "It's you. Should've known. Hello. Get down, Fletcher!" She tugged the excited Labrador away from the priest, before he, too, was knocked into the hedge.

Father James, refreshingly young for the priesthood, with fading Irish-ginger hair and wearing most un-clerical Lycra cycling shorts, jumped from his bike and held out his hand to pull Jess from the hedge. "I'm sorry." He flashed his boyish smile and looked only slightly abashed.

"I thought Mrs Harris had put a stop to all this." Jess gestured at the bike, trying not to point too obviously to the tight-fitting shorts.

"She did try," he agreed, "but I was getting fat. Too many—"

"Scones." Jess finished the sentence for him and they both laughed. "Well, since you have once again almost killed me, yes. I think scones would be a perfectly acceptable apology. Shall we?" She waved a hand in the direction of the village and brushed a scattering of leaves from her shoulder.

Father James swung the bike around and fell into step beside her, heading back the way he just come, towards the centre of the village.

"Well," he said, "it just so happens that Mrs Harris made a fresh batch this morning. She was just taking them out of the oven as I left. You can tell me how things are shaping up for Tuesday. A business meeting."

"I will, but do we *need* an excuse to eat scones?" Jess raised her eyebrows and he grinned.

Jess's black Labrador, Fletcher, daft as ever, twined around Jess's legs, Father James's legs, and the errant bicycle, while simultaneously sniffing at every blade of grass he passed.

As they neared the village centre, the hedges and fields that divided the park and Orchard Close from the main part of the village gave way to neat gardens. Jess and Father James settled into their usual easy chat, stopping from time to time to admire a particularly bountiful display of flowers.

"Henry's done us proud." Father James nodded towards a spectacular display of flowering shrubs, late spring bulbs, and early summer bedding plants, all perfectly placed for maximum impact from both the gate and the front windows of Henry's and Elizabeth's house.

"Of course! He's by far the best gardener around. Besides, imagine if the head of the Tidy Village Committee let the side down."

"The standard is better than ever, I think. I don't know how you all do it. The parochial garden would be dead if it were left to me." He threw a sidelong glance at Jess.

"Good thing we're onto you, then." She grinned. "It's been fun, to be honest."

Since Jess had found herself on the committee, thanks to cajoling from Father James, Henry, *and* her new friend Lila, she'd surprised herself by just how much she'd enjoyed becoming so involved with a village activity. Her recently-discovered love of gardening together with her long-standing competitive spirit, made her as determined as any of the Ballyfortnum residents to ensure the village retained its All-Ireland Tidy Village Champion of Champions trophy for yet another year. Ever since the village had first entered the competition, sometime in the seventies, the village had featured high on the leaderboard, usually winning first place in at least one of the contest's many categories. For six years in a row, Ballyfortnum had been the proud recipient of the All-Ireland Champion trophy.

Jess was *not* going to let this be the year they dropped the ball.

She'd also become actively involved in an exciting new nature project on the Dochertys' farm, and what with planning the rewilding of several acres of farmland, including planting new woodland and hedging, and joining the community's efforts to leave Ballyfortnum positively blooming, her days were fuller than they'd ever been since she'd moved into the village a few years ago. She hadn't really had time to spare for the Tidy Village committee, but as the contest sponsors had added several new categories over the past couple of years, Father James, Henry, and Lila had conspired to use that as the excuse to persuade Jess to join them. Nonetheless, she was never entirely certain whether they'd *really* needed an extra person or if Father James had engineered the suggestion to get Jess more involved in village life.

"Here we are. In you go." Father James leaned his bike against the wall, pushed open the heavy wooden door that led into the hallway of the parochial house, and dropped his cycling helmet onto a long wooden table. "Go on through. I'll just get changed. Make yourself at home."

Jess unclipped Fletcher's leash and let him lead the way into the enormous kitchen; bright and warm from the lazy end-of-May sun that streamed through the leaded window panes and cast squared patterns across the huge pine table.

A couple of minutes later, Father James, now in his more usual attire of jeans, shirt, and clerical collar, reappeared in the doorway. He ran a hand through his hair and crossed the kitchen to lift the kettle from its place on the counter. "Tea, then?"

Jess didn't bother to answer what they both knew was only a rhetorical question, but responded instead with one of her own. "No Mrs Harris today? Retired, has she?"

Usually, the elderly housekeeper could be found standing at the stove, stirring something, or bustling at the sink or countertops, preparing something delicious. Not many parochial houses had housekeepers, nowadays, but Mrs Harris had been established in the Ballyfortnum priest's house for far longer than anyone could recall and steadfastly refused to retire. What with her persistent adherence to the old ways and the vibrant youthfulness of their forty-ish priest and his modern take on the church, the running of St Mary's church was often quite the talking point among the clergy, according to Father James. Some of the older villagers deemed him unsuitable for the job, but to the younger generations, he was a breath of fresh air, and the children in the village's school, conveniently situated right beside the church, adored him.

Even the most stalwart protestors to a priest in jeans or cycling shorts couldn't argue with the fact attendance figures were up for the first time in decades, since his arrival.

Besides, thought Jess with a smile she hid behind her hand, it's not as if he takes mass in those shorts, is it? Not that anyone would have the faintest idea what a priest wears beneath his Sunday robes, anyway.

Father James clattered around the kitchen, breaking her thoughts, as he filled the kettle and rummaged in a cupboard. "She's off visiting her niece today. Be back for supper. Scones, then?" He retrieved two pretty china plates and a pair of china cups, all bearing mismatched floral designs. He set the plates on the table, frowned at the cups, and swapped them for a pair of sturdy mugs. "You and I," he said, casting a wry look towards Jess, "are mug people. Get the jam?"

She laughed, nodded, and opened the enormous fridge to root for a pot of jam. "Rhubarb or raspberry?"

Once they were companionably spreading butter and lashings of rhubarb jam onto fresh fruit scones, Jess brought him up to speed with the preparations for the upcoming judging of the Tidy Village contest. He'd agreed to be there, as usual, but after a busy few weeks, had missed the last few committee meetings.

On the coming Tuesday, at approximately nine in the morning, the cohort of Tidy Village judges would arrive with their clipboards and cameras and poker-straight faces, and peer into each and every garden in the village. "Well, not quite every garden," Jess added with a small chuckle, "but a good chunk of them. Not those few the committee have agreed to avoid at all costs." On the whole, though, she and Father James agreed the village gardens were tidy, vibrant, and ready to impress.

Aside from admiring the gardens, the judges would examine the communal areas and amenities such as the shop, pub, school, church, and village hall. This year, for the first time, and as an added extra, they would also be given a guided tour of the Thomas Docherty Nature Reserve. At present, the idea for the reserve was so new, it had nothing more to show than strands of fencing wire strung between posts to mark out the layout, and a large pile of paper covered with maps, plans, sketches, and lists. Nonetheless, the judges had agreed that, while they were in Ballyfortnum, they would wear their 'official judging hats' in the morning, and become 'unofficially happy to help with some suggestions and advice' in the afternoon. Henry, bless him, had pulled those strings. Years of involvement in the Tidy Village contest had won him friendship and favour with many of the long-standing judges, who had got to know him well.

Alongside her new position on the Tidy Village committee, Jess had become thoroughly invested in the plans for the nature reserve. Her experience and contacts in the horticultural college she attended twice-weekly in Kildare, and her experience and contacts in the nearby Ballymaglen Garden Centre, where she worked two afternoons a week, would prove invaluable to the planning process. However, it was her new-found friendship with the Dochertys and Lila Finnerty that had cemented their inclusion of Jess in the discussions about the reserve, and the Dochertys had eagerly invited her on board with its development as they'd all sat around the pub table just a few weeks ago, dreaming up the best way to reverse the damage years of intensive over-farming had caused their land over the years.

"Remind me again," Father James said over a jam-laden scone. "Where are we taking them first?"

Jess pulled her phone from her pocket to consult the emailed minutes from the last committee meeting, which contained the schedule for the judging. "Arrive at nine.

Coffee and welcome in the village hall. Walk around my end of the village—village hall and park; Orchard Close and surrounding—only as far as Tractor's junction, though—" She broke off and looked up at Father James without raising her head. "Do you think we'll ever stop calling it Tractor's junction? It's been almost a year since ... well, you know?" Renowned local playboy and farmer, James O'Sullivan, known as Tractor to all but his mother, had died suddenly the previous summer, and the village was still at some level of disbelief about his demise.

Father James shook his head; his mouth full of crumbly scone. "Doubt it," he said, swallowing down the scone with a swig of tea. "Go on." He gestured at Jess's phone with his mug.

"Back to the village hall for a quick breather. Drive to village. Park here." Jess nodded towards the kitchen window, although the church's main car park was out of sight from where they sat.

Father James topped up their mugs from the heavy parochial teapot. "Okay. I'll get Willie to make sure the graveyard is tidy as can be. And ask him to tidy the driveway over the weekend. We'll spare a few cents for some overtime. He'll grumble, of course."

"Of course." Jess didn't really know Willie Keegan, but he was well-known to the rest of the committee. He might put on a great show of grumpiness, but his hard work and attention to details proved his pride in his work as the church's groundskeeper, and when he wasn't pottering around the churchyard, he was usually out and about with his lawnmower, keeping the village verges neatly trimmed, or tidying up the schoolyard. "So ..." Jess found her place in the schedule again and scrolled down the page. "Park here in the church car park. We'll do the amenities first, since they're together—bar the park, of course. They'll have just come from

7

there. They'll have a look round the church, then we'll take them to the school and back along the other side of the road to the pub and shop. That won't take long. Then we're on to the village-centre houses. We'll go on along past Henry and Elizabeth's; cross over to come back past the workers' cottages, then go a little way down the Little Mason road and turn back just before Charles O'Sullivan's farm." She paused and glanced at her friend to check he was keeping up.

He nodded.

"Then just a little way up the pub lane—at least as far as Lila's."

"At least as far as Lila's. Don't tell Henry, but I think hers is my favourite this year."

"Mine too. Henry's is lovely, but Lila's is … freer? More natural but still gorgeous. I reckon the bishop would approve? Fits well with his initiative."

The priest nodded, "Willie isn't keen, of course."

"Of course," Jess said again, with a quick laugh. The bishop had recently added his support to a nationwide environmental initiative from the Catholic church to return unused church lands to nature, which had appealed to Father James's lack of will for gardening and to Jess's belief that nature was better than over-manicured gardens and an excess of weedkiller. Willie Keegan, meanwhile, was of the camp that preferred mown lawns and low-maintenance gravel or paving, and would complain about the untidiness of nature just as quick as he'd complain about all the work he did to tidy it. His own garden, also on the lane beside the pub, between Lila's flower-crammed cottage garden and the sterile green of the late Thomas Docherty's farm, was mostly given over to a wide concrete driveway, on which he spent any spare hours tinkering on a beloved old rust-bucket of a car he hoped to do up and enter in next year's round of national vintage rallies.

"Lila's really is beautiful." Jess sighed and helped herself to another scone.

Father James made a zipping motion with his hand across his mouth while selecting another scone with his free hand. "No favourites though. Not that we'll admit to in front of the committee. Where next? Is it lunchtime yet?"

"Almost. We'll just walk past the school a little in each direction, to look in at those gardens and suchlike, and that's it. Then the judges will go into the school—Henry and Maeve will go with—meet the children, admire the playground, and then come back here for lunch. Mrs Harris has all that under control, I'm sure."

"Sandwiches and fruit salad."

Jess raised her eyebrows.

"Yes, there will be scones too, but she's saving those for the end. Just before they leave."

"Like a bribe?" Jess laughed.

"Exactly. Leave them with the sweetest taste and greatest memories. Works every time. You didn't think it was the gardens that kept Ballyfortnum on the leaderboard all these years?"

"Will we not bother with the work next year then?" Jess said, her voice teasing as she sat back in her chair and cradled her mug in hands. She smiled at him, savouring the warmth of the sun beating in at the window.

"You'll stay on the committee for next year then?" He flashed her a knowing smile. "Knew once they had you, you'd be invested. Ha!" He raised his mug in a toast. "Go on. Take me through the after-lunch part?"

In the hour or two between lunch and scones on Tuesday, the judges would shed their official presence, leave their clipboards and judging criteria behind, and visit the Dochertys' farm. Jess and Lila, who was also involved in planning the nature reserve, would walk with the judges to meet Anne and Matty Docherty, and with luck, Peggy McCaffrey from the National Parks and Wildlife Service would also meet them there, as long as no emergencies had arisen to hinder her plans. Matty would lead the party around the farmland, doing a 'show and tell' through the still-emerging plans for the reserve, with the hope that the judges might offer some suggestions of their own for the project, and advice about possible funding opportunities.

By the time they'd all trudged around several acres of farmland and back to the vicarage, they would be more than ready for tea and scones.

"So," said Jess, smiling across the table at Father James, "that's the plan. I hope," she added, as she closed the email and set her phone down on the table, "a reporter and photographer are going to show up at some point, too. I suppose I should give them a ring, check they've remembered." She leaned back in her chair to bask in the sunshine as she sipped her tea. "I think we're all under control. Hopefully nothing will go wrong."

Chapter Two

Father James waved Jess off and disappeared back into the depths of the house to call Willie-the-groundsman about doing that last-minute tidy-up of the churchyard.

Jess paused at the end of the church driveway and checked the time. "We'll just walk to the corner, eh, Fletch?" She stooped to ruffle the Labrador's velvety ears before turning right, towards the pub and the school. Outside the pub, hanging baskets bloomed with a vibrant mix of summer-coloured nemesia and trailing lime-hued fronds of creeping Jenny. The picnic tables on the pavement were adorned with matching potted centrepieces, and Paddy—who ran the pub—had also added window boxes to each of the low sills. The nemesia, in all shades of sunset, was warm and cheerful, and the memory of an evening a few months ago popped unbidden into Jess's head. *That's where it all began.*

It had been in the pub, on the same night in early April when the plans for the nature reserve had been hatched, that Lila Finnerty had first suggested Jess join the Tidy Village Committee, although it took Father James's later persuasion to convince Jess the suggestion was a serious one. Jess had only got to know Lila in March, just a few weeks before that evening in the pub, but they'd quickly bonded over their love of gardening and Lila's easy friendliness. The sudden death of a neighbour had strengthened their rapidly-blossoming friendship. One thing had led to another in that way things sometimes do, and here she was: fully involved in village life, on the Tidy Village committee, and enjoying an ever-widening circle of new friends, all largely thanks to Lila's exuberant personality and willingness to invite Jess into her social whirl.

She smiled, and walked on, peering in at the school playground and fields over the functional chain link fence dividing the school from the road. The grass on the playing field was scrubby with bare patches of mud; the grass worn away from football and hurling and whatever other things the children got up to in their PE lessons these days. In contrast, the concrete playground area was neat and tidy, boasting newly-built raised planters combined with low wooden benches—Willie Keegan's handiwork, apparently. Each planter was sown with vegetables, and although most of the plants were still small, young, and sparse, there was a satisfyingly successful row of lettuces varying in shades from pale green through to deep burgundy, and an eye-catching covering of pink and white strawberry blossoms in each of the planters. Orange and golden-yellow marigolds were a cheery addition to two planters, and a wigwam of peas was just coming into flower in the furthest one. Jess nodded in approval. "Looks fab, Fletch. Looks fab."

Around the corner, along the back road to Ballymaglen, the houses facing the school entrance had done their bit too. Most boasted neatly-cut lawns; prettily-planted pots, and colourful flower borders. Even the couple of houses with tarmacked or paved driveways and little colour or planting were neat and tidy.

Siobhan Docherty lived in the second house from the junction. She'd begged a few well-stocked plant pots from Lila and Henry to donate to any of her neighbours who might need a little extra something, or who lacked their own green fingers, herself included. The front of Siobhan's own house, exactly opposite the school gates, was usually slightly scruffy and strewn with children's toys and bicycles. In preparation for the arrival of the Tidy Village judges, however, she'd spent Sunday afternoon edging the driveway with a row of low pots, each one cheerfully spilling over with easy-care lobelia, petunias, and marigolds.

"Had to leave it till the last minute," she told anyone who'd listen, "or the kids would've trashed it. They're not allowed to play out until the judging's done, just in case."

Siobhan was another from Lila's circle of friends who Jess didn't know very well yet but already knew she liked a lot. Jess also already knew her well enough to be quite certain Siobhan was the kind of person who'd have left it to the last minute even if she didn't have three unruly young children to blame.

Overall, though, Jess thought as she surveyed the village from the corner in front of the school, Ballyfortnum was almost ready for the judging. Only one house, old, derelict, and abandoned, let the village down in terms of the imminent contest. It stood on the main village road, on the corner opposite the school and the pub, and was completely unavoidable on the judges' route.

Jess crossed the road and stood in front of its gate. A week or two ago, Maeve had issued instructions—all neatly written into the committee minutes—for 'someone' to cut the grass in front of the cottage, and hack back the worst of the overgrowth. Willie Keegan, being the 'someone' in question, had done his best, and Jess thought it looked quite picturesque, smothered with a timely sprawl of beautiful, pale-pink dogroses. Scattered among the overgrown grasses, tall purple thistle-heads and early spikes of rosebay willowherb added colour to the untamed area beyond the house. Completing the theme of nature's pinks and purples, the huge rhododendron bushes edging the overgrown space behind the cottage were in full magenta bloom; a sight anyone in Ballyfortnum would find it hard to disapprove of despite the plant being non-native, invasive, and increasingly problematic in some parts of the country. Besides, the massive blooms undoubtedly added a good deal of cheer to help disguise the ugly derelict house.

"It's really not too bad, in the sun," she said aloud. "Right, Fletch?"

The Labrador looked at her, said nothing, but lifted his leg and peed up the gate post of the cottage in question.

"Ah, Fletch. It's really not that bad." She ruffled his head and they turned back towards Marcus's cottage, to collect Snowflake and walk on home to Orchard Close.

Just a few hundred yards from the church driveway, and diagonally across the road from the shop, Jess let herself into Marcus's tiny workers' cottage. She greeted Snowflake with a pat and a quick belly-rub before letting him out to join Fletcher in the garden, leaving the door open to let the sun flood into the poky hallway. She kicked off her trainers, and went straight to the kitchen to put on the kettle. As it began to burble, she padded back through the little hallway to Marcus's bedroom, and woke him with a kiss on his forehead and a swish of the curtains, letting light stream into the cramped room. "Come on, Sleeping Beauty. Wakey wakey."

Marcus stirred blearily, groaning as he pulled himself upright from where he'd lain sprawled on top of the bedcovers, still wearing his shirt and trousers, clearly exhausted after a long run of erratic shifts at the Lambskillen Garda Station.

"Thought you weren't sleeping till later, after I took Snow?"

He groaned again, yawned, and rubbed his eyes. "It was only supposed to be a quick nap. What time is it?"

"About half-ten. I brought you a couple of scones from the vicarage. Want them now? Kettle's on."

He nodded gratefully, already rummaging in a drawer for fresh clothes.

Fighting the urge to snuggle into bed beside him, Jess left him to get dressed while she unwrapped the scones she'd pilfered from Father James's stash.

Marcus didn't spend too much time in his own cottage these days, and was edging ever-closer to moving in with Jess permanently, but with Jess's own schedule being jam-packed this week, he'd come home that morning after Monday's long night shift to "air the place and tidy the garden before next Tuesday". The open windows suggested he had, at least, attended to the first of those intentions, but the sight of him asleep on top of his duvet combined with the dead heads on the tulips at the front gate proved he'd not made much progress with the second.

By the time she'd made tea and sorted out the scones, Marcus appeared in the kitchen doorway, shiny and slightly damp from a shower, but dressed in jeans and working clumsily through the buttons on a fresh shirt as he yawned loudly.

Jess set the plate of scones on the small kitchen table, took over with the buttons, then picked up the plate again. "Okay," she said, holding it in front of Marcus as someone might hold a carrot to tempt a horse to move forward. "What if you sit in the garden with this and a cup of tea while I spend half an hour at the weeding for you? But you have to come out and keep me company, even if you are too lazy to help."

Outside, he obligingly sank onto the doorstep, plate on lap and bare feet on the warm concrete path, while Jess dropped to her knees on the grass and dead-headed the flowers.

"Anything exciting happening at work?"

He shook his head, swallowing a mouthful of scone before answering. "Not at all. It's very quiet." His irregular shifts at the moment were largely due to covering some of his colleagues' holiday leave, and would likely continue right through until the end of August, while the workforce took turns to jet off to various corners of the world on their annual summer holidays. "Hope it stays that way. I'm wrecked already, without having any big cases to deal with." He stifled another yawn, and took a large bite of the second scone. "Mmm. Mrs Harris? Or Linda's?"

"Mrs Harris, this time. Don't tell Linda, but they are almost as good as hers, aren't they?"

For the next hour or so, Jess tidied the little cottage garden, helped sporadically by Marcus, as he pulled the odd weed and found Jess the tools she asked for. Fletcher and Snowflake also offered help, although Fletcher's enthusiastic digging in the flower bed earned him only a cross word and got him sent to lie in the shade, panting, dirt-speckled, and sulking, while Snowflake sat at Marcus's feet looking angelic and pristine in his snow-white West Highland coat.

Chapter Three

Ballyfortnum really couldn't have looked much better, Jess thought, as she drove through the village on the following Monday afternoon. Early June was the perfect time for the gardens, with even the hedgerows smothered in drifts of snow-like hawthorn blossom. Dancing plumes of white cow parsley gave a pretty, almost ethereal look to any uncut verges on the edges of the lanes, and golden buttercups added a cheerful splash of sunshine. In the more built-up areas, the verges were neatly mown, except those left for wildflowers or dotted with a sprinkling of daisies.

Most of the gardens were either immaculate, or at least vibrant and cheery. Only a handful of the households had made no effort whatsoever, and of those, most were on the edges of the village beyond the area the judges would assess.

Not bad, Jess thought, *not bad at all*. All they needed now was for tomorrow to be dry and bright, and if the sun could shine, better still. She pulled up outside the shop, two wheels on the pavement and the engine left running, while she darted inside to grab a pint of milk.

Mrs Dunne was busy at the large shop window, giving a last spit and polish in preparation for the big day, and a strong smell of lemon and vinegar greeted Jess as she stepped inside. The counter, unusually, was clear and tidy, the newspapers stacked in a neat pile and the tempting till-side display of chocolate moved onto a shelf.

"You'll lose income if you hide this away over here," Jess joked, selecting a Flake. "Good thing it's only once or twice a year! Your hanging baskets are looking gorgeous."

Mrs Dunne shuffled backwards off the window sill and clambered awkwardly down. "Think I'm about done in. Think it looks all right, do you, love?" She gestured around the shop with the cloth she'd been using on the glass, wafting a smell of vinegar into the air.

Jess nodded. "It looks lovely. The whole village does. It's great to see everyone putting in the effort. Think we'll win again?"

Mrs Dunne snorted. "Course we will! Six years in a row, love. There's no stopping us."

"Hope not!" Jess set the milk on the counter and handed Mrs Dunne her card to swipe. "See you tomorrow," she said, ripping open the chocolate wrapper and taking a large bite, careful not to drop flaky crumbs across the gleaming counter. "We'll be here mid-morning if all goes to plan. Don't forget to give the flowers one last polish," she called with a smile, and let the door swing shut behind her.

A few houses further along the road, she stopped on the edge of the pavement once more, this time cutting the engine before getting out of the car and opening the gate to Elizabeth's and Henry's garden, taking care not to let Stanley or Daisy escape. She bent to make a fuss of the friendly little King Charles. Daisy, an altogether less friendly whippet-cross who had previously belonged to Elizabeth's neighbour, danced just beyond reach, yapping noisily.

Henry greeted Jess on the doorstep, alerted by the barking. He, too, was confident all was as ready as it could be. Elizabeth appeared at his side to offer Jess tea, as Stanley wandered off into the house and Daisy continued her yapping at their feet. Jess refused the tea, wanting to get home, but by the time they'd stood on the doorstep and chatted for twenty minutes, she may as well have accepted a cup.

"I think we have everything covered," Henry said. "I'll see you at eight-forty in the hall?"

"And I'll come along to help with the tea," Elizabeth added.

Jess smiled gratefully at her friends. "Perfect."

In Orchard Close, as elsewhere in the village, many of the neighbours were outside their houses, enjoying the bank holiday weather as they gave one last push to make sure their gardens wouldn't let the village down. At Number 1, a man Jess didn't know but waved at whenever she walked past was busy hosing his driveway. At Numbers 2 and 18, directly opposite each other, the residents were washing their cars; one with a suds-filled bucket and the other with a garden hose. At Number 16, Linda's joined-on neighbour knelt over a flowerbed, trowel in hand and a trug at her feet. Even Sean and Gary, Jess's attached neighbours, were in their front garden. She didn't see them often, what with Sean frequently working away, and Gary having only recently moved in.

"My new lodger," Sean had introduced Gary as, but from their chats over the back-garden fence, Jess suspected Gary was not *just* a lodger.

Even before Jess turned her little red car into her short driveway, she could hear Fletcher barking a frantic greeting from inside Number 7, complaining about having been left behind while Jess was out doing one last check on the state of the village. As she pulled into the drive, Fletcher pressed his nose against the window, stalling the barking for a few seconds. Paws on the sill, and the rest of him balanced on the back of the sofa, his whole body shook with excitement and the speed of his frantically-wagging tail. Snowflake's little white face appeared beside him as the Westie tried valiantly to peer over the sofa and around his bigger, more energetic Labrador friend, almost knocked flying as Fletcher began a new onslaught of frenetic barking.

Jess cut the engine, wagged a finger at Fletcher, and mouthed, "Stop it," even though she knew there was no point. Before she reached her front door, Sean stepped up to the low hedge between the two front gardens, to meet her.

"Want us to do yours, too?" He waved his arm towards the soapy bucket at the base of a step ladder, and towards Gary, balanced precariously at the top, with a squeegee in his hand.

"Ooh, yes! Would you? That would be great." She hadn't a ladder of her own, and didn't much like going up them, either. It was a few weeks since the window cleaner had called, and if Sean's windows were going to sparkle, hers should too. "Thank you. I'll bring you out a cuppa? Or a beer?"

Inside, Fletcher and Snowflake had abandoned their positions on the back of the sofa and now scrabbled at the door, urging her to hurry up and get inside. She unlocked the door and forced her way in, pushing Fletcher backwards with the door as she opened it.

Under Fletcher's unwieldly paws lay a pile of mail. Jess rubbed Fletcher's chest with one hand, simultaneously ruffling his fur and shoving him back so she could retrieve the post. Although it was mostly junk, there was a handwritten letter amongst the flyers. She tore open the envelope to extract a folded sheet of lined notepaper while kicking off her trainers before padding into the kitchen to make Sean and Gary the promised tea, reading the brief note as she went: *Maeve,* confirming in neat cursive that she'd see Jess at the village hall tomorrow at about eight-forty. A reminder to Jess not to be late, more than anything, Jess guessed.

Maeve was yet another of the Ballyfortnum residents Jess had only met for the first time in the last few weeks, since joining the Tidy Village committee. Along with Henry, Father James, Lila, and now Jess, Maeve made up the last member of the committee. She lived behind the park, along the lane almost opposite the road that led towards the river. Jess had passed her house many times, as it lay on the quickest back-road route to Ballymaglen, but she'd rarely given the houses here a second glance. Maeve was, Jess guessed, in her late fifties. She had no-nonsense, short-cropped greying brown hair, and wire-rimmed glasses that added to her default look of one who disapproved of everything. She was bossy, abrupt, and decisive. The kind of person who gets things done, as Lila had told Jess when she'd asked her to join the committee: "She's a bit much sometimes, but she does get the job done, and we'd spend a lot more time getting a lot less done, if she wasn't on the committee." While Henry was officially the Chairman, Maeve was undoubtedly in charge. She seemed to think she'd met Jess before, back when Jess's dad was on the committee. Jess was quite sure she'd have remembered if they'd met, but Maeve was not the sort of person you'd argue with.

Jess smiled at the bossy tone of the note, and dropped it onto the table to make the tea.

Before she could ask the two men now cleaning her living room window whether they took milk, her phone bleeped. Lila.

See you in the morn. 8.40ish x

Everyone, it seemed, was ready. It was mad how seriously everyone took this funny little contest. Aside from in the UK and Ireland, nowhere else in the world seemed to have any notions of awarding national prizes and prestige upon a community just for keeping their gardens and communal areas tidy. Jess wondered if other places didn't need to offer incentives for such a commonsense display of good manners and citizenship, or if, contrarily to that idea, everyone else just minded their own business and didn't care whether their neighbours kept their gateposts polished or not. Nonetheless, Jess had to agree that by entering as many of the categories as they were eligible for in the annual competition, and with the added stakes of fighting to hold onto their trophy, the village was, indeed, usually well-kept and pleasing to the eye, with almost everyone mucking in and getting caught up in the spirit of the contest.

There was some speculation that as the village grew, they would be edged out of the village category and into 'Small Towns'. There had also been the odd joke made about keeping the population down, to ensure Ballyfortnum remained below that crucial number of one thousand residents or fewer. Jess shuddered at the thought—there'd been enough sudden deaths in the village over the past few years without wishing for any more. Presently, they still fell well within the limits of the 'Village' category, but a planned housing development on the eastern boundary threatened to increase the village by upwards of another three-hundred people, and objections, Jess knew, had been lodged.

She put three mugs of steaming black tea on a tray, added the milk carton and a sugar bowl, a couple of teaspoons, and a pack of Digestive biscuits, balanced it on the hall table while she shut an indignant Fletcher and uncomplaining Snowflake behind the living room door. That done, she opened the front door and set the tray on the bonnet of her car, where the tea slopped perilously close to the rims of the mugs. "Here you go. Who takes milk? Sugar?"

Gary slithered down the ladder, with Sean holding it steady until the last minute, when he stepped aside to let Gary off. Sean added a splash of milk to one of the mugs, and two spoonfuls of sugar to another, handed the sugared one to Gary, and leaned against Jess's car to admire their progress. "Reckon we'll keep the trophy then?"

Jess grinned at him. "We'd better. I can only imagine the upset if not, and now I've been dragged onto the committee, I don't want anyone blaming me if we lose it!"

Gary sat on Jess's doorstep and stretched out his legs, tanned and toned in cut-off denim shorts. "You're all mad here," he said, in his American drawl. "I still can't fathom what this nonsense is."

Sean peered over his glasses in the same indulgent manner Jess remembered her grandfather looking at her when he explained things to her when she was small. "I've told you a thousand times. Communities fight to the death to persuade four or five stuck-up Dubliners who've barely seen a tree that their village is always beautifully kept with never a stray piece of rubbish blowing on the street, and every person in the community always keeps their garden spotlessly clean and totally weed-free while simultaneously encouraging a diverse range of wildlife and native flowers." His voice was even and deadpan, and Jess snorted into her tea.

"That pretty much sums it up," she told Gary.

"Yep. Still don't follow." He leaned back against Jess's blue-painted front door and tipped back his mop of dark curls, his bearded face turned upwards to catch the sinking rays of the sun as it dropped slowly beyond Linda's house, facing them on the opposite side of the close.

Sean and Jess exchanged a look, laughed, and slurped tea. Sean had lived at Number 8 for as long as Jess had lived in the village, but while they sometimes exchanged pleasantries over the garden fence, or when passing on their doorsteps as they rushed to and from their cars, he frequently worked away and she hadn't got to know him very well. Mid-sixties, counting down the months until retirement, he was a quiet, easy neighbour. Only since Gary had moved in about a month ago, and Sean now travelled less, had Jess began to chat to them more often. Gary, younger than Sean by at least a decade, possibly two, was bubbly and chatty and far closer to Jess in age than most of their other neighbours in Orchard Close. Gary was seemingly enthralled by rural Irish village life, after living in Dublin since moving to Ireland for university to study literature, way back in the late nineties. He worked online, and he and Jess often shared a gossip over the garden fence on her days at home.

Her dad would be pleased to know that, after living here alone, sad, and hermit-like, for the first year or so after his death, she was now finding a good network of new friends in the community, and, after all this time, really settling in. She raised her mug in silent salute to her dad, and said aloud, "Here's to Ballyfortnum taking home the gold again."

"Cheers!" Sean clinked his mug on hers.

"To the win!" Gary held his black tea aloft, but didn't get up from his suntrap-seat on the step.

"Think the weather will hold?" Jess asked, squinting up at the cloudless sky. June so far, had been blazing, but they were only four days in, so that didn't mean much.

Before her neighbours could answer, her phone vibrated in her pocket, and the trill sound of her ringtone pierced the quiet street. She lifted her bum from the car bonnet, fumbled for the phone, and checked the caller ID.

"Elizabeth? What's up?" A prickle of worry chilled her neck. Had something happened to Henry? Elizabeth never called her. "Is everything okay?"

Chapter Four

Elizabeth must have caught the panic in Jess's voice, as she was quick to reassure her. "No, no, everything's fine. Henry asked me to give you a ring. He's just outside washing the cars, and he didn't want to stop. He just took a call from Don Hennessey—you know, the judge. One of the judges for tomorrow. One of the other judges has been taken ill."

"Is—" Jess began to speak but Elizabeth cut her off, pre-empting the question.

"No, no, the rest are still coming. But they've got someone else to replace Jim—he's the one that's taken ill. It's a shame, but it doesn't change the day for us, Henry says to tell you, but he asked if you wouldn't mind letting Maeve know. He can't get her on the phone and didn't want to leave a message—she's not keen on voice messages and you know how she hates to be caught unawares. Give her time to digest it before the morning?"

Jess groaned. "Must I?"

Elizabeth held her silence.

"Oh all right. I need to walk the dogs anyway. I suppose I can take them round there now. I didn't need dinner anyway. But if she shouts at me ..."

Elizabeth laughed. "She's not that bad. It's just that Henry thinks it better to let her know tonight, rather than catching her with something unplanned tomorrow. She does like—"

"To be prepared. I know, I know. Tell him it's okay; I'll go tell her. See you tomorrow." She hung up the phone and rolled her eyes at Gary, who pulled himself to his feet, dumped his mug on the tray, and picked up the bucket of soapy water.

"Go on," he said. "I'll clean your front door while you're gone. A treat for when you get back." He smirked at her through his beard. "If you do," he added in an ominous tone.

"You don't even know the woman," Sean protested.

"True, but from the sound of it, that's no bad thing." He gestured Jess towards her own front door. "In you go; get sorted. Sooner you go, sooner you'll be back, right?"

Ten minutes later, with Fletcher's lead wrapped tight and short around one hand, and Snowflake's looped loosely over the other, she rapped on Maeve's front door.

Maeve, as predicted, was unimpressed by the late change to the plans. She huffed and mumbled a string of unsavoury words, many of which were directed to the poor unknown unfortunate who would be stepping in to replace the original adjudicator. The fallen comrade, Maeve explained with some drama, was well-known to her and Henry, and had become a good friend over the years. "I do hope," Maeve blustered, her face a little pinked, "this will not affect the standards and consistency of the judging."

"I'm sure they've chosen the replacement with due care." Jess had absolutely no idea how they'd have gone about choosing a good replacement at such short notice. "The village looks lovely, and we've done all we can. Everyone says everything looks better than ever." She reached out to pat Maeve reassuringly on the arm, hoping to placate her fellow committee member, but Maeve stepped back a fraction and Jess let her hand fall to her side, Snowflake's lead still hooked over her wrist. "Try not to worry. I'm only telling you now so it doesn't take you by surprise in the morning."

Maeve pulled herself together with a deep breath in and out and a determined stiffening of her back. "You're right, I'm sure. We must just be sure to keep them well away from those scruffy Farrells. And the Hegartys. And maybe not go too far down the Little Mason Lane. Or up towards Harris's ... To be frank with you, Jessica, I am beginning to wonder if this is far more trouble than it's worth. Maybe it's time we put a stop to it. Quit while we're ahead, as they say."

"Maeve! Stop fussing! You know full well we have the route planned out and we already said we'll avoid all those." Jess sighed. "Do you want to go over it one more time?" She gestured to her bag. "I brought my laptop, just in case."

Maeve gave a thin, fractured laugh. "I'm worrying about nothing, amn't I? You know what I'm like."

Jess smiled gently at her committee colleague. "I know how important it is to the village, but do try not to worry. Let's go through it one more time, just to be sure."

Maeve's porch had a low half-wall, with wooden pillars supporting a pretty gabled roof, reminiscent of the little Lych gates Jess had seen in old English churches in her childhood. She pinned the two dog leads under her foot, set her bag onto the wall, and extracted her laptop. "It'll just take a minute to start up. Fletcher! Do sit still. Hang on, I'll tie him to the gate." As the computer came slowly to life, Jess closed Maeve's front gate and secured Fletcher firmly to it. "Sit there quietly and try to be good." She patted his head, looped Snowflake's lead through the gate, too, and left them to it.

Maeve disappeared in through the still-open front door, and returned a few minutes later with a tray bearing two tall glasses of water, a saucer with an assortment of biscuits, and Maeve's phone, which she tucked into her pocket once she'd set down the tray. "It's too hot for tea, don't you think?"

Jess picked up one of the glasses, helped herself to a Bourbon biscuit, and didn't voice her disagreement: it was never too hot for tea. She drank the water gratefully, and keyed at the buttons on the computer until the agenda appeared on the screen. She pulled up an annotated map showing their planned route through the village, and dragged the two open pages to sit side-by-side on the screen. "Here, see." She traced the routes with her finger, cross-referencing each path to the time schedule they'd agreed on, much as she had done with Father James the Tuesday before, when she'd read him the emailed notes detailing the day's schedule. "We'll turn before we get here—" She jabbed at the screen with her finger. "—and the only places we really can't avoid passing—here, for example—" She indicated the derelict cottage opposite the school. "—we'll have to use some distraction; chat about the weather or something, but honestly, Maeve, nowhere is really untidy this year. I really do think it will all be fine. We've all chipped in to help the less interested or less able, after all. Look how much you've done yourself." She poked her finger at a few different locations on the route, where she knew Maeve had spent hours with a trowel and trays of bedding plants. "And here, too." She pointed to some communal stretches of grass, where she knew Maeve had sent a grumbling Willie Keegan, insisting he tackle them with his lawnmower. She'd heard all about it from Mrs Dunne, when she'd popped in for a loaf of bread last week.

Maeve nibbled at a custard cream and nodded slowly. "I'm sure you're right. And I'm quite sure she'll be perfectly capable of the job. I've worried for nothing, I expect."

"Or he? Elizabeth didn't say. We just need to be confident. If we act as if we are proud of the village, they'll believe it too. And," Jess added through a bite of biscuit, "we *are* proud, and rightly so. Everything looks amazing. We've got this." She laughed and closed her laptop. "Listen to me! I've only been on this committee five minutes and I'm as invested as the rest of you. Besides, it's not in my interest to let this be the year the village doesn't win; you'd all blame me!"

For a second, Maeve looked as if she was thinking this over, weighing up whether it would, in fact, be Jess's fault if they lost the trophy, but then her whole posture loosened and she smiled properly, making her look altogether younger and kinder. "We wouldn't have asked you if we didn't think you could do the job. Thank you for reassuring me. I will see you at eight-thirty tomorrow morning."

"No later than eight-forty, anyway," Jess grinned. "I'll be there. Get a good night's sleep. We'll be walking miles by the time we've covered the whole village."

She stashed her laptop back in her bag, and, hungry now it was getting so late and she still hadn't eaten, plucked another biscuit from the saucer, and went to release the dogs from the gate. "Bye, Maeve, sleep well. And don't fret!"

Chapter Five

J ess was up early on Tuesday, making sure she had plenty
of time to give Fletcher and Snowflake a good walk before
shutting them in for the morning. Linda had agreed to pop
in around lunchtime and let them out for a pee, if Marcus
wasn't back by then. He'd worked another long nightshift,
but should be home by nine, if all went well in the Garda
station through the night. He'd sleep for a few hours, once
he got home—his own home or Jess's—but at least it was his
last shift for a few days and he wouldn't need to work again
until Friday.

By eight-twenty-five, Jess had eaten three slices of toast
and marmalade, walked almost to the river and back, thrown
one last critical look at her own tiny patch of front garden,
blown a kiss to Number 8 in thanks for Sean's and Gary's
efforts last night—her front door gleamed and the windows
shone—and set off out of Orchard Close in her car. She
wouldn't usually drive to the village hall, less than five
minutes' walk away, opposite the entrance to Orchard Close,
but today she'd decided to leave her car there to make her
garden look better when the judges walked around the close
in an hour or so. A shiny, newly-washed car in a car park, she
reasoned, was not any kind of blot on the landscape. Cars
blocking shiny, newly-washed front doors; not so useful.

In the village hall car park two minutes later, she stood beside her car and looked back across the road towards her neat little *cul de sac*. Only eighteen houses, but according to the Tidy Village criteria, enough to qualify for the 'estate' category. The entire close had been built at the same time by the same builder, so the houses were complementary and uniform in appearance, although not boringly identical.

The wide patch of grass to the left of the entrance boasted a handful of fruit trees, most of which bore promising clusters of baby apples, just beginning to develop. On the other side—the patch in front of Number 1—a vibrant array of wildflowers put on its best show, and the colourful mix made Jess smile every time she walked past. A couple of handmade signs announced PLEASE DON'T CUT US DOWN! THE BEES NEED US! in a child's careful lettering. One sign was bordered with a pattern of yellow-and-brown bees; the other with cheerful red poppies. The signs were a project the older schoolchildren had embarked on, and there were similar signs dotted around the village at other strategic points. Jess and Lila had procured a few to stick in the ground outside some of the scruffier gardens in the village, united in their opinion that 'Tidy Village' must not mean 'Weed-killed and over-manicured'.

This was a view increasingly shared by the sponsors of Tidy Village contest, and over the last few years, categories such as 'Best Natural Area', 'Pollination Plants Award' and 'Climate Action Award' had been added to the list. This, combined with the Bishop's new rewilding initiative, had worked wonders to increase of awareness of a need to encourage pollinators, especially among the older generation who typically filled the church pews every Sunday. Some of the residents, of course, still believed in shorn green lawns and regimental planting, but many of the gardens—Lila's being the best example—were embracing the organic cottage-garden look that Jess loved.

The only thing marring the entrance to Orchard Close was a tractor, stopped on the road opposite the village hall's gateway. The driver appeared to be deep in an animated conversation on his phone, and the tractor and its trailer entirely blocked Jess's view of the little cluster of fruit trees. Jess glared at him, hoping he'd pick up on her silent message: *Move! And hurry up about it!*

As Jess shoved aside her annoyance about the tractor and stood momentarily lost in her appreciation of Orchard Close and the efforts of her immediate neighbours to keep it tidy, two cars pulled into the car park, followed by Father James whizzing along the road on his bike as if chased by demons. He was, Jess was pleased to note, not wearing his Lycra. Instead, he was dressed in smart-for-him chinos, a short-sleeved black shirt, his clerical collar, and his bicycle helmet, which he unfastened as he took the corner into the car park. His face was red from the exertion, and his hair, when released from the helmet as he spun around that final corner, was a comical mix of hat-squashed and flyway curls. Overall, though, he'd scrubbed up well enough. Surely even Maeve would approve of his efforts to 'look more like priest' for once—something she'd raised frequently at their committee meetings in the run-up to judging day.

"Thought I was going to be late," he panted, skidding to a halt in front of Jess, helmet now dangling from his wrist. "Was waiting for Willie to turn up so I could ask him to cut back a briar that must've sprouted from nowhere ... did it myself in the end ... expect he was busy straightening some grass somewhere ... didn't answer his phone ... don't know why he has one ..." Father James propped the bike against the wall, still panting. "Right fed up with the contest, so he is.

Maybe he's gone into hiding for the day." According to the committee, Willie Keegan was *always* fed up with the contest, and prone to non-stop grumbling in the lead-up, then proud as anyone once it was all over and they'd won the trophy yet again.

"You're fine," Jess said. "We've heaps of time. Unless they turn up early."

The two cars that had come in ahead of the priest parked neatly alongside Jess's car. Henry and Elizabeth emerged from Henry's sparkling Vauxhall, and beside them, Lila scrambled out of her cheerful blue Mini. The wedged-open door to the village hall suggested that Maeve was probably already inside, getting organised before anyone else could arrive to organise her.

Flanking the door were two large troughs of bedding plants, matched by the flowers in the window boxes. 'Best windows' was one of the many categories Ballyfortnum had entered this year, and one in which the village had been awarded Gold for the last few years. Jess was optimistic this year would be no different, but receiving Gold in any single category was only part of the battle. For the ultimate prize of All-Ireland Champion of Champions, villages were judged on an accumulative points system. While any number of villages could win a Gold award, only one could achieve All-Ireland Winner in each category. The more points a village collected throughout all their categories, the more chance they had of claiming the All-Ireland Champion of Champions, netting the main prize and prestige. It was this award that Maeve, and the rest of the committee, had their sights firmly set on. *No pressure,* thought Jess, not for the first time. *No pressure at all.*

Father James tucked his bike around the side of the building, and the committee members, minus Maeve, traipsed through the lobby and into the dim main hall, in search of their unofficial leader.

Elizabeth, as promised, made straight for the kitchen, where she would fill the kettles and arrange teas and coffees, ready to greet the judges. Jess followed, carrying the tin of shortbread the committee had begged Linda to make for the occasion.

"Just leave that here; I'll find a plate for it. Go on out there and check that Maeve is happy." Elizabeth shooed Jess away to rejoin the others in the large, echoey main hall.

In the corner of the hall nearest to the kitchen, Maeve had pushed together a couple of tables to make one larger table, over which she'd put a crisp white cloth, each dangling edge an equal length. She'd set chairs around the table, all neatly tucked in, and added a pair of small vases to the table, each holding a beautiful arrangement of summer flowers.

"Yours?" Jess asked Lila, nodding to the flowers.

Lila shook her head. "Hers, I think. Lovely, aren't they?"

After one final assessment of the room, Maeve sat down at the head of the table; the cue for the others to sit, too. There was a general scraping of chairs and scuffling, immediately undoing Maeve's efforts to present neatly-aligned chairs to the judging team, as Henry, Lila, and Father James took their places around the table, leaving empty seats scattered between them for the judges.

"Best to spread them out. Don't want them huddling together and plotting," Father James said with a laugh, still puffing a little from the exertions of his rapid pedal from the church to the village hall.

Jess retrieved the printed agendas from her bag, and set them on the clean white table cloth, one in front of each seat, before pulling out the empty chair beside Lila and sinking onto it.

Elizabeth emerged from the kitchen with two plates of Linda's shortbread. "Don't touch. Not 'til they're here."

"Think we're ready," Lila said, with a wide smile. "Let's knock 'em dead!"

"Ooh, let's not." Elizabeth shuddered and Jess laughed.

"Yeah, maybe not! We've had enough of that around here, thanks."

Lila nudged Jess in the ribs. "You know what I meant."

"It's five to," Maeve said, in the kind of voice that suggested this was a problem. "I do hope they are not going to be late."

Minutes later, there was the sound of the front doors swinging open, a gaggle of voices, and the judges entered the hall, suggesting they had either travelled together from Dublin in one car, or arrived separately but waited in the car park until the full cohort was present.

A united front, Jess thought. *Unswayable and incorruptible. As if anyone would!* She'd heard rumours, though. Henry had many uncorroborated stories of attempted bribes—buttering up; drinks in the local, a passing of small, sealed envelopes behind surreptitious hands. Jess hadn't believed a word of it, and Henry's twinkling eyes said neither did he.

There were four of them. The first to enter the main room was a neat, short woman in stocky shoes; serious-faced and clutching a clipboard, who looked immediately more approachable as her face broke into a wide smile when Henry stood to greet her.

"Lydia! How are you?" He kissed her cheek, and pulled out the vacant chair to his right, which she obediently settled onto, and the two engaged in that kind of 'catching-up' chatter of people who know each other well but see each other little.

Maeve, clearly familiar with two of the others, shot Henry a glare before taking over the host duties and introductions.

"Donald. Patrick." She shook each man's hand in turn, then turned to the group around the table. "Donald Hennessey and Patrick Murtagh. You know most people. Not Jess, I think. She's our newest committee member."

Elizabeth coughed daintily. "You'd remember her father. George O'Malley."

The two men's heads swivelled in unison towards Jess, whose face warmed under the sudden scrutiny. The woman Henry had called Lydia stopped her chat with Henry to turn, too, to Jess. "George's daughter! How lovely. Nice to meet you, Jess." Her smile was warm and genuine, and Jess liked her immediately.

The men Maeve had introduced as Donald and Patrick echoed Lydia's words, shook Jess's hand, and told her how much they'd liked her dad, and that they thought they might have met her briefly, a couple of years ago, and Jess, her face still a little warm from the attention, smiled back, remembering how much her dad had enjoyed the committee and being a part of the Tidy Village efforts each year.

"Don," the taller of the two men said. "Not Donald. And this—" He gestured to the slim, elegant woman who stood quietly beside him. "—is Frances. Frances Monaghan. Some of you have probably met her before?" He shot a smile at Maeve but didn't wait for an answer. "She's kindly stepped in for Jim." He turned back to Maeve, encompassing Henry, Elizabeth, Father James, and Lila as his gaze swept around the table. "I haven't spoken to Jim, but his wife has sent his apologies and best wishes. She said to tell you 'Good Luck', too. Now he is off the panel for this year, he can't be accused of bias when he says he hopes you hold on to the title!"

A low ripple of laughter rippled around the table and the two male judges sat; both immediately helping themselves to a piece of Linda's shortbread.

Maeve nodded stiffly at Frances, who hovered awkwardly for a moment until Elizabeth gave the chair beside her a gentle shove, gesturing for the replacement judge to sit. The woman did so, accepting a cup of tea and a piece of crumbly shortbread with a grateful smile.

Jess, seated across from the pair, leaned forward. "So we're both new," she said, plucking a slice of shortbread from the plate. "Have you been to any of the other villages yet, or are we your first?"

Ballyfortnum, Frances said, was her very first stop in her newly-appointed capacity as a Tidy Village judge. Jim, apparently, had only been taken ill on Saturday, and there had been no judging scheduled for the weekend, or the Monday bank holiday. "But I'm not a total beginner," she added, with a quick glance at Maeve. "I've been involved in the Tidy Villages for some time, behind the scenes. And, I'm from Abbeydare; far side of Ballymaglen."

Although Jess knew the village Frances named, she wasn't sure what it had to do with not being a novice in the Tidy Village judging.

Father James, eavesdropping from Elizabeth's other side, chipped in with a boyish smile. "You know, our arch rival village! Silver medal last year ..." He winked at Frances, who chuckled and held up her hands in defence.

"Nothing to do with me, I promise. I haven't lived there for years. It's pretty, sure it is, but I can't take any credit! My mam and da are still there, but I have to be impartial."

"Plus, she's been Secretary for years," Lydia said, smiling at Frances.

Frances returned the smile with a small nod.

"Aye, she's been well-vetted and she knows the criteria, so no better person. We're very grateful she was able to step in at such short notice, aren't we?" Donald directed the question to everyone, and received a volley of nods and murmurs of agreement and support in reply.

Jess, feeling quite sorry for Frances as she coloured under the scrutiny, offered her a second piece of shortbread and asked her if she knew of the Ballymaglen Garden Centre, explaining that she'd done a course there and now worked there twice a week, offering a distraction of smalltalk while the attention moved from Frances's judging credentials to other topics.

After a few more minutes of chatter about how good the shortbread was; how good the weather was; how each other's families were, and how they all hoped Jim would make a quick recovery from his illness, Maeve made a show of looking at the large clock on the hall wall, and got to her feet.

"We should get started. It's almost nine-thirty already. We won't get it all done if we don't keep to schedule." She tapped her fingers on the sheet of paper in front of her and glared pointedly at Henry, until he, too, got to his feet, albeit with a little less enthusiasm than Maeve.

"Hope the replacement can also be bought with tea and scones." Lila threw a meaningful grin at Frances.

Frances drained her tea, wiped a sprinkling of crumbs from her blouse, and smiled back, visibly more relaxed now she'd sampled Linda's shortbread and had a cup of tea.

From the depths of Lila's overstuffed bag, her phone burst into a lively rendition of the summer's current radio-favourite tune, and she scrambled to retrieve it, pulling it free from a tangle of knitting.

"You thought you'd have time to stop and knit?" Jess said, incredulous, gathering tea-and-biscuit detritus to stack and clear.

Lila muttered a quiet obscenity into her phone, shoved back her chair, and moved away from the table, although Jess, being nearest, caught a thread of the conversation.

"Yeah. Yeah. Okay. Will try to stall them. Keep me posted." Lila disconnected the call, returned to her chair but stood behind it, clutching the back of the seat as if it was holding her up, and threw Jess a look of sheer panic.

Jess pushed back her own chair, and stood facing her friend, keeping her back to the table and blocking Lila from view of the others.

"I need to talk to you." Lila whispered almost inaudibly; her brow wrinkled with worry. "There's a problem."

A prickle of fear chilled Jess's neck. "You okay?" she mouthed, and Lila slowly shook her head.

Jess turned back to face the table. "We'll just clear this away into the kitchen before we start out," she announced brightly. "Anyone want a refill, or shall we get tidied up? Give me a hand?" She thrust the almost-empty shortbread plates at Lila and gestured her friend towards the kitchen with a nod. "Chat amongst yourselves while we get finished up here and then we'll get going? We'll just be a few minutes; won't be long." She was garbling, but something had upset Lila, and Jess needed to find out what was wrong before they headed out into the village and the sunshine. She collected up as many empty cups as she could carry, ignored Maeve's impatient tutting, and followed Lila towards the kitchen, calling over her shoulder to the judges and committee, "Be right back."

Chapter Six

L ila wedged the door with her foot until Jess had carried her load of dirty cups into the kitchen, then followed her in and stopped in front of the pair of still-gently-swinging doors.

Jess, her arms still full of cups, turned to face her friend. "Wha—Don't!" She lurched forwards towards Lila, certain she was about to lean back against the door to block anyone else from coming in. "They swing," she added unnecessarily, gesturing to the doors with the pile of crockery, as she imagined Lila falling through the doors in an ungainly heap.

"Oops." Lila offered a weak smile and stepped forward to offload the crumb-scattered plates onto the counter. "That wouldn't have helped. We've trouble enough."

"Out with it," said Jess, setting down her own dirty dishes and turning to face her friend. "What's up?"

"That was Siobhan. There's ... there's been ..." Lila waved her arms about as she grappled for the words.

Jess's stomach flipped. *Not a death. Please not another death. Especially not today.*

"Sabotage!" Lila clutched her chest theatrically. "Someone's gone and sabotaged us!"

Jess, mindful of the others waiting just beyond the kitchen door in the main hall, pulled her friend further into the kitchen, as far from the doorway as possible. She turned on the tap to disguise the sound of their conversation. "You what?" she whispered. "Quick, before someone else comes in."

"That was Siobhan," Lila said again. "She just dropped the kids at school, said someone said there's loads of flowers cut down, and some graffiti, and ... and I don't know what, I didn't take it in really. She went to look, and they've managed to get a few people together to try to tidy it up as fast as they can, but she's not sure it'll be enough, or quick enough."

"Where?"

"Up near the school. Pub. That old cottage, you know, the one with the roses?"

Jess nodded, dumbstruck, questions jostling in her mind.

"Some of the other mams from school are with her. Matty's on his way. Colm, Billy, Anne, anyone she could get hold of. She said can we hold off going that way as long as possible?"

Jess stared at Lila without seeing her, as she tried to process the news. "Who? Who would—? Never mind. That can wait. We need a plan, and fast. Let me think ..." She shifted her gaze to the small window, facing out onto the car park and the entrance to Orchard Close, as if the fruit trees or the row of neatly-parked vehicles might give her some answers. *At least the tractor's gone*, she thought, incongruously. She spun on her foot to face Lila. "How bad is it?"

"Not really sure. Shuv was rambling; thinking on her feet, you know? Panicking a bit?"

Jess nodded.

"Right," she said decisively, after a moment of silence. "Go tell Elizabeth we need her for a sec. Tell her we need her to switch off the water boiler or something. Something to get her to come. Henry or Father James too, if you can. Elizabeth can finish clearing up in here while we come up with something. I'll make a couple of calls, see who else we can rally to help clear up the mess. Go on." She gestured to the door with a nod of her head, already pulling her phone from her jeans pocket and scrolling for the number of her elderly opposite-neighbour.

"Linda, it's me, Jess. There's been some vandalism in the village. Can you run over the road and see if Gary is home? I don't have his number. Sean'll be at work, I'd reckon?"

Linda began to speak, but Jess interrupted. "Hang on. I'm in a hurry. Listen carefully. Gary's practical. Send him up into the village—the school, shop, thereabouts, he'll know where to go when he gets there. Tell him to do whatever he can to help. Take cleaning stuff; I think there's paint to clean off."

Linda, always good in a crisis, was economic and efficient. "All right. What else?"

"Can you come over here to help Elizabeth wash up, so we've extra hands? In case Elizabeth needs to go?"

Jess ended the call, confident that Linda would spring into action, and dialled Marcus.

"Come on, come on ..." She glared at the screen as if it would make him answer quicker. "Where are you?" She checked the time. He should be just about home by now; either at her house or his own. "Come on!"

It went to voicemail.

"Marcus, where *are* you? Something's happened in the village. Call me?"

She hung up as Elizabeth, followed by Lila and Father James, bustled through the swinging doors, but as she went to stuff the phone back into her pocket, thought better of it and typed out a text, remembering how she'd worried Marcus only a couple of weeks earlier with a panicky-sounding message when she'd found a dead buzzard on a farm track and he'd been certain she'd found a human corpse.

Noone's died, btw, but sounds like someoens vandalled the viallge. Help. Judges almost ready to judge it. need to stall them will do best xxxx

Not bothering to fix the typos, she hit SEND, hoping he'd work it out. Of course, she thought, pocketing her phone, he was probably there already. He'd have seen Siobhan and whoever she'd managed to pull together—other parents dropping off their children at school, at least, from what Lila had said—and whatever it was she'd found, as he'd driven through on his way home, probably. Hopefully.

"What's up?" Father James interrupted her thoughts of Marcus as the doors swung closed-open-closed behind him, eventually staying shut and sealing the four of them into the relative privacy of the community-centre kitchen. "I'm pretty certain you know exactly how to turn off the boiler, and it doesn't take four of us."

Lila, a little calmer now she'd had time to catch her breath, filled them in, Elizabeth's eyes widening in shock and disbelief, and Father James his usual unruffled self.

"Okay," he said, barely missing a beat, "we'll adjust the plan slightly. We're doing this end first anyway, right?"

Jess, Lila, and Elizabeth nodded.

We've all memorised the schedule, at least, Jess thought, with a flash of out-of-place satisfaction.

"So we'll go slower, for starters. That'll buy some time. How much of the village is affected?" He glanced at Jess, then Lila, who looked at each other and shrugged.

"Not exactly sure," Lila said. "I'll call Shuv back, shall I?" Even as she spoke, she'd pulled her phone from her pocket, already bringing up the number.

Siobhan answered immediately, and the sound of garbled chatter emanated from the phone. Before Lila had a chance to say much, or stem Siobhan's excited flow of chatter, Father James held out his hand for the phone

"Let me," he said, taking it. "Siobhan? Father James. Slow down. What's the problem?" He listened for a moment, nodding, but not speaking, while Siobhan's tinny voice echoed from the phone, Jess, Lila, and Elizabeth all straining to hear.

"Okay. Can you get someone to do a quick drive around? Check the Little Mason Road, up towards the O'Sullivan farm? We can go there first too, to give more time, if it's clear?" He paused for a moment, to allow Siobhan to process the instructions.

"Okay." Siobhan's voice was clearer now she'd calmed down, but quieter too.

Jess, Lila, and Elizabeth edged closer to Father James, trying to listen.

Father James frowned, waved them off with his free hand, and took a small step backwards. "Then check the other roads. Yours, for example, and then up to Lila's and back ... although, if Matty and Colm are with you, they'd have come from there, so they'd have noticed if there was anything?" He fell silent again for a moment as Siobhan, her voice muffled once more, seemed to be talking to someone else.

The three women crowded closer, straining to hear.

"Back off," Father James mouthed at his audience. "Tell you in a min. It'll be okay." He held up a hand: *Wait*. "Go on," he said into the phone as Siobhan's voice became clearer again. She spoke rapidly for a minute or so, fragments of her words carrying into the kitchen.

"Okay." Father James nodded at the trio; one sharp tilt of his head to emphasise the word. "Okay. Call Lila with updates after. Talk soon. Thanks Siobhan." He disconnected the call and passed the phone back to Lila. "So," he said, taking in each of the women in turn. "Plants spoiled at the pub, shop, and verges; paint on windows and some on the pavement by the school, church, and pub. Probably one person acting alone, maybe two. Whoever it was seems to have vanished. Given the tight window of time it must've been done, hopefully the mess is contained to that area, but Colm's taking Anne off to do a recce of the other key areas on our list. One of them will call you back in about ten minutes. Now," he said, taking a breath, "will we tell the others?"

Again, there were a few moments of silence as everyone considered the question.

"Ideally," Jess said after a minute or two, "we'd tell the committee but not the judges?"

Elizabeth disagreed. "We should tell them all, surely? They'll be understanding?"

"Sympathetic," Lila added. "Unless they think we did it *for* sympathy..."

"What if we continue as planned, for now, show them this end of the village, regroup here for a breather, as planned, and decide then?" Father James suggested, ever the voice of reason.

Jess nodded slowly as she realised his proposal was most the sensible.

"We'll try to let Henry know," he added, glancing at Elizabeth, who nodded her agreement.

"But not Maeve?" Lila said.

"Not Maeve," Jess and Father James said in unison.

"No point in worrying her," Jess said. "Not unless we have to. You know how she hates changes to plans."

The others nodded.

"I'll tidy up in here," Elizabeth said. "Won't take too long. You carry on as planned."

"Linda'll be over to help you in a few minutes," Jess told her. "Then you can scoot up to the village too, see what's what?"

She turned to the priest. "Shall we split up? We don't all need to show them this end of the village? Divide and conquer?"

"Without stressing Maeve out?" Lila grinned at Jess; her initial shock already replaced by a 'can-do' determination.

"Actually, that's easy enough," Jess said. "I deliberately hadn't put on the schedule that we'd all go everywhere, to allow for last-minute emergencies. I should think Henry and Maeve could handle this end of things quite well by themselves. Elizabeth stays here to tidy up, and once Linda arrives, they can brew up more tea and rustle up enough extra biscuits to stall them for another half hour, I should think ... Although I doubt we've enough shortbread. They've polished most of that of already." She glanced at Father James.

He smiled guiltily and held out his hands in acknowledgement of her unspoken accusation. "It's so good. What can I say? And yes, good idea. By the time they've had another cup of tea, used the facilities, chattered some more, we can easily fill a good thirty minutes or more. I'll see to that. I'll go with them; you and Lila head on into the village?"

With the new plan agreed, Jess, Lila, and Father James rejoined the others in the main hall.

"Let's get this show on the road, shall we?" The priest addressed the judges breezily, and there was a ripple of agreement as bags were gathered, schedules shuffled, and feet got to. Father James winked at Jess, out of sight of the others.

She took his cue: "Yes, you go off with Henry, Maeve, and Father James. The rest of us will meet you back here in about—" she glanced at the clock on the hall wall. "—forty-five minutes? Say about ten-twenty? Thereabouts? It's hot enough out, so you'll not be wanting to rush about quite as fast as we'd planned, and you'll be grateful for another cup of tea by then? And a bathroom break. Then we'll regroup to do the next bit." She was pleased to hear her voice sound level and normal, and when Maeve picked up her clipboard and ushered the judges towards the door without a murmur of dissent, Jess knew she'd pulled off the last-minute change of plan unnoticed, even managing to add on an extra quarter of an hour as if it was nothing unusual at all.

Chapter Seven

F rom the village hall doorstep, Jess and Lila waved off the judges, Father James, Henry, and Maeve. They watched for an impatient few minutes while Father James, bless him, ushered them as fast he could to the corner of Maeve's road and away out of sight.

"Stroke of luck we had them scheduled to go there first, not Orchard Close," Lila said as they stood waiting until the coast was clear. "We'd have been stuck here forever. Come on, they've gone. Let's go!" She grabbed Jess's hand, and together, they dashed across the car park and into Lila's Mini, fastening their seatbelts as Lila started the engine and hurtled towards the village centre faster than either the speed limit or the narrow country lane deemed sensible.

As they passed Henry and Elizabeth's house on their left, then Marcus's cottage on the right, all seemed as it had been when Jess had driven through on the previous afternoon. The gardens were neat and tidy; the pavements swept and litter-free; the flowers nodding in the slightest of summer breezes, but as they approached the shop and church, the damage became apparent.

"Shite!"

"That's putting it mildly." Barely slowing, Lila swerved the little car into a parking space, pulling her seatbelt off with on hand while applying the handbrake with the other.

Jess, having undone her own seatbelt as soon as they'd swung haphazardly into the church driveway, leaped from the passenger seat and was dashing across the road towards the shop by the time Lila's car door clunked shut behind her.

Between the shop and the school, there was a buzz of frantic activity. It seemed as if half the village was spread out along the road between the shop and school. Some were armed with brooms, buckets, and an assortment of garden tools; others appeared to be giving little practical help but plenty of commentary and advice.

The hanging baskets that had looked so colourful just that morning now held only bare earth scattered with the odd green leaf. Jess imagined that had she arrived a little earlier, the pavements would have been strewn with flower heads worthy of a procession or wedding, but the gathered villagers must have swept them into the black rubbish sacks a couple of them held, or into the cheerful yellow wheelbarrow someone had left on the pavement up by the old cottage. Despite anyone's best efforts, flower heads could not be reattached, and Jess's eyes prickled with disappointment and fury as she gazed in horror at the destruction of the beautiful planters they'd put so much effort into. *Who could have done such a thing?* Even the terminal complainers like Willie Keegan and Maeve were so proud of the village, and put so much effort into getting it ready for the competition. Jess didn't believe for a minute that they really meant it when they complained about how much work it was, or that either would do anything to sabotage it.

She walked slowly to the shop; knowing she was under great time pressure but somehow unable to hurry, her feet leaden as she approached the forlorn figure leaning on the shop door frame with tears streaking her face while a man Jess didn't recognise balanced precariously on a chair and scrubbed at the windows.

Jess, never having seen Mrs Dunne so upset, took the last few yards in long strides. "I ... What ... I ..." She gave up, unable to find the words, and embraced the shopkeeper in a hug.

"Oh Jess, love, how could they?" Mrs Dunne's voice was soft but shook with anger as she trembled in Jess's arms. "How *could* they?"

"All our work," Jess said eventually. Uselessly. "All that work. Did you see who it was?"

The man jumped down from the chair in front of the shop window; a cloth dripping in his hand and a bucket of soapy water at his feet. "Think that's all off now, eh?" he said, taking in Jess and Mrs Dunne with his question.

"What was it?" Jess asked. "Paint?"

"Aye. Just thrown, in a hurry, like. No words; nothing obscene, like. Just a right old mess. Came off easy enough, so it did. I'd say they're having a harder job of it up at that old cottage." The man nodded towards the pub and beyond, to where the derelict cottage stood in its tangle of dogroses and rhododendrons. "Made more o' a mess there, so they did."

"Suppose they'd more time up there without no one seeing them." Mrs Dunne pulled free from Jess's arms and sniffed. "Although what with school an' all, I'm surprised no one saw the feckers. They must've been mighty fast about it all."

"What else have they done?" Jess asked, stepping off the pavement and into the road, to see more clearly as she looked towards the school and the empty cottage the man had mentioned.

"They left the church—dunno if that's tellin' ye something about the kind of people they are." He shrugged, as if the culprits might be well-brought up Catholics who attended mass every week and wouldn't dream of vandalising the church but thought nothing of desecrating the rest of the village.

"For speed, more like?" Jess suggested. "They knew they had to be quick if they didn't want to get caught? No time to run back and forth across the road?"

The man shrugged again. "Mebbee. Could be on to summat, come to think. All the mess's this side o' the road, now ye say it ... Same at the pub as here, then a good douse of paint over the cottage an' all the flowers pulled from here to there and back again. The gobshites." He spat into the gutter and picked up the bucket in one hand and the chair in the other. "I'll set this back in fer ye." He didn't move, though, as if worried he might miss out on something if he disappeared inside the shop.

Jess stepped back onto the pavement as a car came by. "Hmm. Maybe two people then, wouldn't you think? One for the paint and one to trash the flowers? I'll go look. You'll be all right, Mrs Dunne?"

She nodded, huffed, and sighed. "I'll come on down with you; get Paddy to make us up some tea. Mind the shop, eh, Mick?" She nodded again, taking in the man with the bucket, the shop, and Jess in one glance. "No one'll be comin' in for now, shouldn't worry."

Mick set the chair down on the pavement again and settled himself onto it to light a cigarette, and with that, Mrs Dunne started down the road towards the pub, Jess striding along beside her.

At the pub, the scene was much the same: the hanging baskets and window boxes stripped from their flowers, and a stubborn smear of red paint staining the wall as Billy White scrubbed at it with a soap-bubbled broom.

"Well Jess," he said, stopping as they approached and wiping his forehead with a sudsy hand.

"Ah, Billy," was all she could manage, and the two exchanged a sad smile. Jess didn't know Billy all that well—they'd only met properly for the first time a few weeks ago when she'd been walking Fletcher down by the Gun Club lands Billy helped manage, but he was friendly with the Dochertys and she liked his easy manner and quick wits.

"Paddy inside, is he?" Mrs Dunne didn't wait for an answer, but disappeared into the gloomy interior in search of the landlord.

"They'll be wanting something stronger than tea," Billy said.

"I'd say we'll all be drinking as soon as the judges are gone," Jess agreed. "But for now, tell them to stick to tea?" She gave Billy a wry grin. "For now. I'll keep going; catch up with Lila, see what we need to decide about the judges? See you in a bit."

She crossed the farm track that led to Billy's farm, Lila's house, and the Dochertys' farm, and joined Lila, Matty Docherty, Siobhan, and Jess's neighbour Gary in the front garden of the derelict house on the corner across from the pub and the school. A couple of the mums from the school rocked toddlers in pushchairs, and another couple Jess vaguely recognised were sweeping plants from the pavement and road into the large yellow wheelbarrow—a tangled heap of pale pink dog roses, already wilting on their thorny stems, Jess noted with a pang of sadness.

Where just yesterday afternoon, the derelict cottage had been covered prettily with chocolate-box worthy roses, now the years of decay were evident to all. Most of the windows had rotted long ago and some were boarded with paint-smeared plywood. The door hung skewed on rusting hinges, also daubed with splashes of orange-red paint. Matty and Gary were trying to remove the Pollock-style splatters; Matty with a stiff broom and Gary with a scrubbing brush, but they didn't seem to be making much progress.

"Jess." Gary held up the scrubbing brush in greeting. A trail of soapy ran down his arm. "We're wondering whether to try a pressure washer, or if that'd make everything too wet. What d'ya think? Paint, or water."

Jess looked at the sky. Although it wasn't yet ten o'clock, and the front of the cottage still in shade, the sun was climbing fast and the day already hot. "Try it," she said, making an uncommonly quick decision. The sun'll soon dry it off and it has to be better than that?" She gestured at the paint splashes. "Have you got one? Bill has one if you need? At Number 14. Next to Linda?" She'd seen him out power-washing his car and garage door often enough. Besides, Bill was her go-to neighbour for most things tool-wise. She'd procured his ladder for weeks on end when she'd decorated the inside of her house last year, and he was always happy to take his lawnmower around the close whenever he felt it needed a trim, not only in preparation for the Tidy Village contest. Orchard Close's equivalent of Willie Keegan, Father James had joked at a recent committee meeting, and it seemed to be true from what Jess had learned of Willie in recent weeks. She pulled her phone from her pocket, scrolled for a number, hit the button, and passed it to Gary. "Here," she said, "ask him to bring it?"

To his credit, Gary looked only slightly bewildered, and rallied quickly to introduce himself to his opposite neighbour on Jess's phone.

While Gary talked to Bill-at-14, Jess turned back to Matty and Lila. "What will we do? We'll have to tell the judges, won't we? There's no way we can tidy all this up."

"It's not as bad as it first looks," Siobhan said. "If we work fast, we can replant the hanging baskets and all that—they're mostly just uprooted out, not cut as we first thought. Loads of people came to help. Some actually *were* a good help. Others just stood about and got in the way." She gave a low chuckle. "One of the farm lads did more in five minutes than some of the wagons who just wanted a good look so they've something to gossip about." She shrugged. "Ah sure. We've gathered everything into a couple of wheelbarrows, to get it off the paths, but actually, most of it is probably salvageable, if we're quick. Look." She went to the yellow barrow, grabbed it by the handles, and gestured Jess towards the back of the cottage.

Jess obediently led the way, glad that Willie or someone had trimmed back the worst of the brambles, leaving the path to the sheds at the back almost clear.

"We've been shoving it all round here out of sight," Siobhan said, parking the barrow in front of a shabby open-fronted lean-to shed. "Cleaning up seemed more urgent, then we can see what we can fix?"

Jess turned and smiled weekly, nodding her agreement. "Good idea." She stepped forward to the first bay of the rickety three-sided shed and peered into a battered metal wheelbarrow that looked like it had been abandoned with the house and was in equal disrepair. "Oh, I see what you mean."

As Siobhan said, the hanging basket plants and flowers had been tugged up by their roots, most with large clumps of soft brown compost still clinging to them. Some, of course, were crumpled and wilting, but someone had had the foresight to pour some water into the base of the barrow and park it in the shade of the cottage's old woodshed. Many of the flowers were, indeed, salvageable. If only they had time. Jess groped in her pocket for her phone, then remembered she'd given it to Gary. "What's the time?"

It was five to ten. Twenty-five minutes before the judges would regroup at the village hall. Hopefully another twenty or thirty while they had more tea. Maybe forty-five minutes in total. She counted up the hanging baskets in her mind, then the window boxes and displays from the picnic tables on the pavement in front of the pub. Then the people available who might be able to work gardening magic and reassemble the arrangements. Her. Lila. Siobhan. Anne. For starters. How much could she and Lila manage in twenty minutes and still get cleaned up and back to the hall as if nothing had happened?

"It might be doable," she said aloud, as she walked back towards the front of the house. "Matty, can you go and get all the hanging baskets? And the rest? The window boxes, and everything. Bring it all, because any we don't get done, we can leave round here out of sight anyway. Be quick. Has Gary gone for the power washer?"

Gary appeared from the doorway of the old cottage. "Nah, I'm here. Bill's on his way. Was just hoping I might be able to get in and see if the water's still turned on." He shook his head. "I can't. It's boarded up from the inside."

"Look round the back," Matty called out. "Someone got water from somewhere; for the plants and this." He gestured at the almost-empty bucket he'd been using to scrub at the paint. "Might be a tap?"

"First, though," Jess said, stopping Gary with her hand on his arm, "can one of you go and ask those women with the prams if any of them are handy with plants? We need all the help we can get if we're going to get the displays replanted—Marcus!" She broke off and ran across the road to fling herself into Marcus's arms, leaving Matty to approach the huddle as Gary disappeared round the back of the house in search of water. "Thank God you're here. What's happened? I mean ... who? And ... well, just who, I suppose. The *why* part seems obvious. Sabotage. Where have you been?"

He held her tight to his chest for a moment, kissed her forehead, and then gently pushed her away a little so he could talk, still holding her hands as he spoke to her. He'd been into the school, he said, asking if anyone saw anything, what with the timing coinciding with the morning drop-off. "Someone must have seen *something*," he said, with a sigh.

"And did they?"

"Yes and no. You know how children are. If I listened to them all, I'd be looking for a ten-headed monster, a team of black-and-white striped robbers in balaclava, a man with a machine gun, and a *really* bold boy."

Jess laughed, already reassured and calmed by his presence, and anchored by his hands still holding hers. "Good luck with that. I think you're looking for at least two people, but probably not a whole team, and probably no machine gun."

Chapter Eight

"Marcus—" Gary's unmistakable American twang cut through Jess's conversation with Marcus. "Glad you're here. Got a minute?" He gestured towards the rear of the cottage. "Something you should see."

Marcus flashed Jess a quizzical glance.

She shrugged, shook her head, and followed Marcus and Gary as the American led the way towards the shed where Siobhan had parked the yellow barrow neatly beside the metal one. He ignored the first half of the shed and pointed instead to the second bay of the tumbledown building, divided from where the barrows stood by a crumbling stone-and-concrete wall.

"Don't think you ..." Gary put out a hand to stop Jess, but she ducked around his arm.

"Oh!" She stopped in her tracks after all, not halted by Gary's hand or by his words, but by what lay on the hardened-earth shed floor in front of them. She clasped a hand to her mouth, not wanting to go further, and discover who the boots belonged to. Hard-wearing, toughened brown work boots. Leading to a pair of stiff blue jeans, creased by an iron but stained with patches of oil, or dirt. A pair of well-worn jeans trying to look smart, she thought, forcing her thoughts away from knowing what the denim-clad legs must lead to, still hidden by the shadow of the dividing wall.

Marcus stepped forward into the small shed.

Jess, too, took a tentative step forward, and another, until she could make out a checked lumberjack-pattern shirt, then another, as Marcus dropped to his knees beside the prone figure of Willie Keegan.

The groundskeeper lay motionless on the dirt floor, on a tangle of ivy and roses. His head lay about two feet from the shed's back wall, and his legs stretched out towards the bright sunshine, all under the cover of the shed's corrugated metal roof, its open side framed by picture-postcard tendrils of pink dog roses and shiny green ivy leaves.

Gary, behind Jess, rested his hand on her shoulder, but said nothing.

"Oh shite. Is he ... is he ...?" Jess couldn't form the words. Surely there couldn't be another suspicious death in quiet, peaceful Ballyfortnum. Surely there couldn't. And, she thought incongruously, especially not *today*.

Marcus bent over the still body; rested two fingers on the man's neck while lowering his face to Willie's, checking for breath. He said nothing for a moment, watching for the rise of the man's chest, or waiting to feel the soft movement of air against his cheek.

"There's a pulse," he said, without looking up. "Call 999. Ask for an ambulance. He's breathing. Just about."

Jess thrust her phone towards Gary for the second time that morning, but shoved it back in her pocket on seeing that her neighbour was already tapping at the screen of his latest-model iPhone. She sank to her knees beside the groundskeeper, wincing as the thorns of dog roses and brambles pierced her jeans. "What do you need me to do?" she asked Marcus, touching the injured man's face gently with her fingertips.

As Marcus had said, Willie Keegan was breathing, although his pulse and breaths were weak. His head appeared cushioned by a dark clump of ivy and a few straggling stems of rusty-pink roses that must have pushed their way into the dim interior of the shed through the cracks in the walls. His arms lay outstretched at his sides, also reaching towards the light outside the shed, but not quite parallel to his body. Where at first glance, Jess had seen shadows on Willie's checked shirt, now she was nearer she realised the darker patches might be blood, most likely from the large, brown-red gash on the side of his forehead.

"Head wound," Marcus said, economically. "Something to pad it with? And recovery position—you know how?"

She threw him a glance that said of course she did, already gently rearranging the man's limbs so she could roll him carefully onto his side. "I've nothing I can use," she said, looking around for something she could use as a dressing, then throwing a desperate glance at Gary and Marcus.

Gary, talking rapidly into his phone, giving meticulous directions to whoever had answered, was in no position to strip off his T-shirt. He met her eyes for a second, then turned away, concentrating on the call.

Marcus, still kneeling beside her, undid a few buttons on his shirt, tugged it over his head without bothering to undo the rest, and folded it into a thick, soft pad.

For the briefest of seconds a flutter rose in Jess's chest at the sight of Marcus's bared chest; smooth and toned. She took the shirt from him and held it tentatively against a large cut, oozing slightly just below Willie's receding hairline. "It's not too bad, I don't think. Seems to be almost stopped." She slowly, carefully, lifted the shirt from the wound and went to tuck it gently under Willie's head to cushion him from the hard ground. "Marcus? Look." Partly under Willie's head was a dark-coloured, rolled-up piece of cloth she hadn't noticed as she'd turned him onto his side, too focused on arranging him correctly. "What's that?"

Marcus leaned in to look. "Don't touch it, will you?"

Jess nodded and pushed Marcus's scrunched-up shirt under the side of Willie's head where the dark piece of cloth offered no cushion since Jess had rolled him over. That done, she sank back on her heels, jiffled on the gravelly earthen floor until no sharp stones were jabbing into her legs, and sighed heavily. *Thank God the man was alive.*

Marcus bent onto one knew to examine the wound, brushing dirt from Willie's balding head with gentle fingers. "You okay?" He shot a look at Jess, who nodded. He touched her lightly on the upper arm, his fingers lingering for a second before giving her a reassuring squeeze. "Watch him carefully for any change. I'll call for backup."

He rose to his feet, moving carefully around Jess and Willie in the cramped space to get out of the shed, and called one of his colleagues at the Garda station, bringing them up to speed. "Yes, ambulance is on the way—"

Gary nodded confirmation. "Twenty minutes, maybe less."

Jess groaned inwardly, willing it to hurry. The hospital, and nearest ambulance station, was in Lambskillen, a good thirty minutes' drive for an average journey. With blue lights and sirens, an ambulance might manage in fifteen. Hopefully Willie would start to come around before then, rather than take a turn for the worse.

"What's up?" Lila's voice carried from the corner of the cottage to where Jess, Marcus, and Gary huddled around the tumbledown woodshed. "Oh! Oh no ... Is he ..."

Her words tailed off as she, like Jess just moments before, was unable to voice the thought that Willie might be dead.

"No," Jess and Marcus answered together.

"He's breathing," Jess added, flicking a quick, wan grimace at Lila as she echoed Marcus's words. "Just about."

For a moment, Lila said nothing. Matty, presumably alerted more by the silence than the drama, rounded the corner to join them, carrying a power washer.

"Power washer," he announced, unnecessarily, then stopped as he too, took in the scene, dropped the power washer to the ground, and repeated the whole "Is he dead?" palaver.

Lila pulled out her phone. "I'll have to call the others. We'll have to call off the judging now," she said, her already-pale face draining further of colour. "We can't hide this from them. It's too much. Henry? Henry? Can you hear me? It's me, Lila."

Jess, having agreed to stay with the still-unresponsive Willie until the ambulance arrived, rearranged herself on the dry earth, jiffling for a more comfortable position in the cramped space.

Just outside the gloomy woodshed, Marcus scanned the scene. Using the camera on his phone, he took a series of photos of Willie, the ground he lay on, and the area in general.

"Shove over a bit, can you," Jess called softly. "It's dark enough in here without you blocking the light."

He frowned at her, already wearing his Serious Policeman face, and moved away, the fading volume of his voice on the phone plotting his path towards the front of the cottage.

As soon as he had gone, Jess wished she hadn't asked him to move. She shivered in the dull, sunless shed and willed him to hurry back. *Please don't die, Willie. Please don't die.*

Almost out of Jess's straining earshot, in what had once been the front garden of the long-abandoned cottage, she guessed he was questioning the onlookers—Matty, Gary, a handful of others who had been in and out of the cottage's untidy garden since the discovery of the vandalism—trying to piece things together as he waited for his colleagues to arrive from the

Garda station. Every now and then a snippet of conversation would reach Jess's ears, but never enough for her to make out anything useful.

With Willie still unconscious, and little to do except check his breathing every few minutes, Jess got to her feet again, shaking the pins and needles from her ankles as they came back to life. She eased herself from the shed, and careful not to trample anywhere that hadn't already been crushed by the footfall of the last few minutes of activity, scrutinised the surroundings with a critical eye, hoping to find some kind of clue to what had happened. Was the culprit still hiding nearby? Was there a weapon tossed carelessly into the overgrown roses or under the gnarly stems of the rhododendrons that surrounded the property with that thick, magenta hedge? Could the perpetrator be hiding in the rhododendrons? She shuddered again.

Hope not.

The rhododendrons were overgrown, sprawling, and large enough that there would be cave-like spaces under the foliage; a shady hideaway beneath those fist-sized blooms and glossy green leaves. A long-forgotten image flashed into her mind of a place her parents had taken Jess and her siblings often, when they were children ... before Alice had got ill and they'd hardly gone anywhere anymore ... a large park, or perhaps the grounds of an English stately home ... picnics and ducks and squirrels and hide-and-seek games, climbing in, and hiding under, huge, thick rhododendron hedges. Her mum loved rhododendrons, Jess thought, with a pang of wistful longing for her childhood. She shook away the thought, but not before making a mental note to text her brother and sister later.

Lollipop Club.

As her and Eric's childhood detective club popped into her mind, she turned back to Willie with a small smile. "Are you another case for our silly little Lollipop Club, Willie Keegan?"

He lay quiet and unmoving in the long-disused woodshed so she turned away, allowing her thoughts to drift back to her siblings. She should've got Alice to come down this week. She'd have loved the parochial fuss in the lead up to the Tidy Village contest; laughed about it in a way that managed to sound both disparaging and enthralled.

Glancing warily at the thicket of rhododendron bushes once more, in case they *did* conceal a mystery assassin, she tugged her phone free and snapped a photo, sending it to Eric and Alice with a quick message. *Remember that place we used to go to? With all the rhododendrons? Also... call later ... mystery! Xx*

Feeling guilty for thinking of mysteries and sleuthing with her siblings while Willie lay injured beside her, she turned her focus to snapping more pictures of the scene, trying to cover anything and everything that may help Marcus and his Gardai colleagues find the culprit, or anything Marcus may have missed with his own series of snapshots.

It was unlikely anyone could be hiding in the rhododendrons. The brambles between the sheds and the rhododendrons were thick and thorny. There was no freshly-trampled path through; no easy way to reach them from the weed-smothered patch of concrete between the house and sheds, where she stood.

Back towards the road, between the cottage and the neighbour on the opposite side from the double gates where she'd entered the garden, a thick cluster of old fruit trees huddled together like gnarled old men bent over a game of chess in a park. They were tied together by cleavers, briars, and yet more ivy. Where grass managed to force a way through, it was almost two feet tall. There was a faintly-worn path almost up against the side of the cottage, perhaps made by a fox or badger, but it looked like no one had been near the fruit trees for years. The brambles made the former back garden quite impenetrable aside from the path someone—Willie?—had cleared from the double gates to the sheds. Whoever had tidied up the grounds had largely focused on making the front look presentable—focused only on what might be seen from the road, if the judges were paying attention. They cleared from the gates to the concrete in front of the sheds but not ventured any further into the back garden. *Goats. Goats would clear this up.*

"Where did *that* thought come from?" she said aloud. She knew nothing about goats, and while everyone always said they ate anything, she had no idea if that was really true. For all she knew, all this would poison them. She gave herself a little shake, forcing her mind back to the job at hand. She didn't need imaginary poisoned goats to worry about too, not when she already had a real-live human victim to think about.

She needed to find clues. Evidence. Anything out of place. Aside from an unconscious man lying on a bed of wild roses, a tangle of briars, and a few stray lumps of turf. The shed Willie lay in had evidently been the fuel store for this poor, sad, unloved cottage, and the other bay of the shed presumably the tool store, but other than the barrows and a few tools in the first and the smattering of turf crumbs in the second, there was nothing in the sheds.

Nothing except an unconscious man with a head wound caused by a blow from something heavy …

And if, as it seemed, whoever had caused all the destruction in the village, and attacked poor Willie had left in a hurry so as to not be seen, then would they have taken that 'something heavy' with them? *Not likely. Not likely at all, Jess.*

She checked on Willie again. The poor man still lay motionless, but his breathing was stable and the wound on his head clotted and drying. Jess retraced her steps towards the corner of the cottage, careful to stick to the cleared stretch of concrete.

Marcus, shirtless and tanned in the sun, stood by the gate, talking into his phone.

Gary, Matty, Lila, and a cluster of other concerned neighbours stood in a huddle on the pavement. A man with a large, expensive camera stood amongst them, gesticulating wildly as he spoke.

"The reporter?" Jess wondered aloud. "Just where we *don't* want him. Dammit."

Chapter Nine

Somewhere in the distance, the welcome sound of a siren promised the impending arrival of help, although whether it was the ambulance, or Marcus's colleagues from the Gardai, she couldn't tell. Both, perhaps, arriving together as a cavalry.

Marcus glanced over at her, lifted a hand in acknowledgement of her presence, but remained focused on the phone call. She nodded at him—*everything's fine, just checking if there's any update here*—and he flashed her a quick smile that made her insides flutter, and held up five fingers: *I'm on it. I trust you to look after the casualty. Won't be long now. Five minutes, perhaps.*

Jess nodded again and turned back to the scene behind the cottage. With Willie still peaceful and breathing gently on his bed of dry earth and dying roses, she could take the time to look for that weapon.

Was the overgrown garden a little trampled there, leading away from the concrete in front of the shed in which Willie lay? She walked to the corner of the shed and looked again around the wilderness beyond. The grass was distinctly flattened, but only at the edges of the scrubby stretch of concrete that joined house and sheds. The trampled edges were probably from when she, Marcus, and Gary had gathered around the shed when they'd found Willie's fallen body. Nothing conclusive.

She spun around slowly, scanning the ground. A smear of dark red-brown stained a patch of the concrete where the weeds hadn't taken hold, and the straggles of buttercup and grass around it were flattened and wilting. Likewise, the tendrils of roses and ivy on the ground poking around the open side of the shed appeared to have been disturbed, marking a distinct trail towards where Willie lay.

Besides, when she and Marcus had checked his head wound, and when she'd put him in the recovery position, she'd found that pad of clothing under his head. Someone had move him; maybe even tried to help him. Had he been hit outside the shed, then dragged inside to hide him, just in case anyone ventured into the garden? She looked around her, as if that mysterious someone might suddenly appear, or have been there all along, unnoticed by her, Marcus, or Gary.

She peered again into the back of the shed, blinking as her eyes adjusted to the change of light. She squinted at the space beyond Willie and the floor around him. Had those twisted strands of ivy and rose stems been dragged in? She moved her gaze upwards. The few thorny stems that had pushed in under the roof were long, straight, brittle and brown. They bore no flowers, or only the odd feeble brown-coloured, dead head, its petals crisp and papery. The roses on the floor, then, must have been pulled in from outside, caught on Willie's clothing as he'd fallen or dragged in by whoever had left him there.

She stepped backwards and dropped to her haunches to study the earth at the entrance of the shed, but the floor was hardened from years of feet traipsing in and out of the shed, and even if there had been any scuff marks left by the attacker's footprints, they'd have been smudged away by her or Marcus or Gary, as they'd moved in and out to attend to Willie. *Nothing conclusive here either.* She took a few more photos anyway, shook her head, and entered the shed to check on Willie again, still unmoving except the tiny, fragile, in and out of his breathing. *What next?*

She backed out of Willie's half of the shed and sidestepped so she could see into the almost-identical lean-to shed joined onto it; the one where the barrows of uprooted plants had been pushed into the shade beside a newish-looking strimmer, a pair of garden shears, and a garden rake, all leaning haphazardly against the side wall. A couple of buckets stood at the corner, outside the shed, recently-used, judging by the millimetres of water in the bottom of each.

Like its neighbour, this half of the shed was shaded and dim, and while the dog roses and brambles clambered over the roof, twisted amongst a glossy canopy of ivy, only a few browning strands had poked their way inside, through any small gaps between the corrugated metal roof and the crumbling stone walls. A clump of straggly ivy filled an empty window frame, the glass presumably long-gone, and some tenacious rose stems probed through cracks in the stonework, but largely, both halves of the shed were equally empty, dingy, and musty, with the same beaten-earth floors.

Aside from the wheelbarrows, the strimmer, and the couple of newer garden tools, the first bay held a small selection of rusting metal tools hanging from equally rusted nails on two of the walls. Also on the side wall, a wooden shelf, crumbling with woodworm and grey with age and cobwebs, clung to the stonework; probably held up by sheer determination and dust. A couple of filthy jam jars on the shelf concealed unidentifiable contents and had clearly not been touched in decades. Higher up, more rusting hooks and nails had been battered into the wooden beams that held up the sagging tin roof. An old leather bridle and other horse-related paraphernalia dangled dried and stiffened from a single crooked nail. On another, a large metal hoop hung, perhaps the rim of an ancient cart wheel.

Could any of those things have been used to hit Willie over the head? The strimmer and rake didn't look as if they belonged to the old house—had Willie himself left them there? Neither was covered with tell-tale splatters of blood. Or paint, for that matter. She touched the top of the strimmer, but it was, unsurprisingly, cold to the touch and gave nothing away as to how recently it had been used. Was anything obviously missing? However would she be able to tell? There were no tell-tale lighter or darker shapes—cartoonish outlines of a missing tool where the surrounding wall had faded or darkened to a different shade of dusty-grey concrete, to mark out a clear clue to a missing weapon. There were no broken strands of ivy or other foliage trailing, newly-broken, across the floor.

In fact, a few rogue strands of ivy twined in and out of the rusty implements, effectively tying them together. If one tool was missing, the ivy would have been pulled from the wall. She knew better than to touch anything and mess with a potential crime scene, but she was fairly certain the ivy would have adhered to the old stone, and if she tugged it, it would pull loose a small shower of stone and concrete. Ivy could do a lot of damage to a wall; she'd seen it before when they'd cleared a part of an old walled garden in the grounds of the horticultural college she attended twice a week. She squinted hopefully at the floor beneath the tools, but there were no piles of freshly-crumbled stone or pulled-away stems of ivy. *Nothing to see here.* She went back to the other shed.

On the ground beyond Willie's head, there lay only the scant remains of a turf pile. A few crumbly half-bricks had fallen loose from the pile, scattered randomly to lie wherever they'd toppled. She imagined the smell of a turf fire, smoke wafting from the cottage's chimney, the residents huddled by an open fire or around a stove in the tiny kitchen. She'd never been inside the cottage, but it was easy to imagine it as similar in layout to Marcus's little worker's cottage on the opposite side of the road, although Marcus's stood at the end of a row of joined-together terraced homes and this derelict one was detached, and a little larger.

She pressed her face to the filthy glass of the nearest window, but couldn't see through the dirt. Another of the windows was broken, and one of the planks used to board it had fallen away, but ivy had filled the gap, hiding the edges of the broken shards. A small hole in the twisted stems suggested birds had made a home in the ivy, or in the empty rooms of the cottage, but it was far too small to have admitted anything larger than a robin or blackbird. Jess shuddered at the thought of all the small creatures that may be nesting behind the walls, and moved hurriedly away from the broken window. The back door was also boarded-up. Nothing here looked as if it had been disturbed in years. She smiled as she remembered how her friend Kate had once insisted on shoving a flyer for her Get Slim group through the battered letterbox in the front door, "Just in case the builders are interested." No builders had ever shown up, as far as Jess knew, and she wondered if the leaflet still lay there, in a pile of years-old junk mail merging into a slowly-rotting floor.

Towards the side of the house, almost opposite where Willie lay, an outside tap was fixed to the wall. A damp patch of concrete beneath it suggested Matty had been right—someone had got water from here. She washed her hands in a stream of cool water, then ducked her head under the flow to take a drink, before turning her back on the unloved house to face Willie; still and quiet in the gloom.

What now? She snapped more photos on her phone, encompassing the sheds, their dim interiors, the stained and scuffed marks on the concrete where she suspected Willie had been dragged, head-first, into his hiding place in the shed, and the trampled edges of the grass. When she'd exhausted angles to photograph, she walked again the edge of the concrete, changed the camera setting to video, and swept it inch by inch across the garden, searching for any giveaway dips in the weeds.

Seeing nothing more than the narrow animal track between the cottage and the gnarled fruit trees, she turned her attention from the old orchard to take a slow panoramic video of the swathes of feet-high grass and the impenetrable bramble thicket to the rear of the property. This time, as she moved the phone steadily from left to right and back again, something glinted in the sunshine, to the back right-hand side, in a tangle of blackberry briars.

She stood frozen in the sunshine, trying to make out what was causing the glint, and debating to herself whether to go closer and investigate, or wait for Marcus.

The screech of rapidly-approaching sirens interrupted her dilemma, and she turned from the garden to make her way to the front of the house just as an ambulance pulled to a halt on the road, closely followed by a Gardai car containing two of Marcus's uniformed colleagues. The cavalry was here.

Chapter Ten

With Willie safely handed over to the capable hands of the paramedics, and Marcus, now wearing the slightly blood-stained and very crumpled shirt, deep in conversation with his colleagues from the station, Jess made her way through the dispersing throng of onlookers to Lila and Matty.

They'd been joined by Anne and Colm, returned from their recce of the rest of the village, and Gary, who had abandoned any notions of pressure-washing, following Marcus's instructions to leave everything exactly as it was, and was chatting animatedly in the midst of the group. The man with the camera was still amongst them, still gesticulating animatedly, his camera swinging from a strap around his neck.

Jess shot him a glare and tugged Lila aside. "Is he the reporter? He'd better not make *this* his feature."

"Sure, he's grand," Lila said. "That's Deiric."

Jess had no idea who Deiric might be, other than a nosy reporter, supposed to be capturing the *good* about the village, not this drama and upset. She cast him another quick glance, shrugged, and decided whatever the reporter did or didn't decide to report was her least pressing problem, and one someone else could worry about. She allowed Lila to pull her back into the midst of the group for a hurried discussion about what to do about the judging.

Has anyone talked to the others? Henry, or Maeve?" She shuddered at the thought of Maeve's reaction to this new threat to the Tidy Village judging, before remembering that Maeve, so far, knew nothing of the first stage either.

"You'll have to tell them now," Anne said to a round of fervent nods and agreeing noises.

"Let them decide what they want to do," Matty said with a shrug. "No point standing around here and second-guessing it. Go on back and find out. Let us know."

So, after a quick check-in with Marcus, who gave her a quick hug and the promise to come and find her as soon as he could, Jess and Lila traipsed back across the road to Lila's Mini.

"Hopefully, they've got the tea ready," Jess said with a heavy sigh. "We need a cup of tea, after that. I can't believe it."

"Me neither." Lila started the engine and turned slowly out of the church car park at a far more sedate pace than she'd driven them to the church less than an hour ago.

"Stop!"

Lila gave a high-pitched squeal and jammed her foot on the brake. "What?" she said, panic edging her voice as the car skidded to squealing halt almost level with Marcus's cottage. "What's wrong?"

"I'm sorry," Jess said. "It's okay! Nothing's wrong. I just thought I should grab poor Marcus a fresh shirt before we go? He's really not the type to want to stand abut half-naked, but it can't be very pleasant, wearing a shirt covered in Willie's blood?" She threw an apologetic glance at Lila. "Sorry. I didn't mean to scare you. Nice emergency stop though. Do you mind if I just run in?"

Two minutes later, with Jess clutching a fresh shirt pulled from Marcus's wardrobe, Lila expertly reversed the few hundred yards back to the derelict cottage, now marked out with billowing police tape tied across the front gates.

"That was quick," Lila said, swerving backwards across the road to stop alongside Marcus and a couple of uniformed Gardai.

Jess leaned across the car, across Lila, and thrust the shirt through the open driver-side window. "Thought you'd like this," she told a bemused Marcus. "Maybe send the other one off to forensics, in case it's not just Willie's blood on it, yeah?"

Marcus took the proffered shirt, and started to say something, but Jess nudged Lila in the arm and hissed in a faux-whisper, "Go! Drive! He'll only say something about me not telling him how to do his job. See you later!" She blew him a kiss and leaned back against the car seat, resting her head on the headrest and closing her eyes for a minute. "Isn't this supposed to be a quiet village? I swear it was never this dramatic when Dad was alive."

"Or before you lived here?" Lila countered in a dry tone. "How many's that now? I've lost count. Are we into double digits yet?"

Jess groaned. "Don't," she said without opening her eyes. Perhaps if she kept them shut, this would all be some kind of pre-judging dream caused by nerves and excitement, and in a minute, her alarm clock would go off or Fletcher would wake her by licking her face, or Marcus would wake her with a nice cup of tea and breakfast in bed. She opened her eyes. "Besides, Willie isn't dead. Thank God." She knew Lila was referring to the uncommonly high number of suspicious deaths the village had seen over the past two years. *Please don't let him become the latest. Please God don't let him die.* She wasn't religious, and rarely went to mass, despite her friendship with the parish priest, but now, she'd pray her heart out if it stopped Willie becoming the village's latest murder victim.

"What did the paramedics say?"

"Not much, to be honest. I told them his breathing had stayed pretty steady, but that he hadn't moved or opened his eyes or anything. Then I pretty much got out of their way so they could sort him out. Marcus'll know more, later, I should think." She shivered, despite the heat of the June day, longing to be wrapped in Marcus's arms, with him reassuring her everything would be all right. An image of another dead body formed in her mind, and she shook her head to dislodge the image. "Thank goodness I only saw one of them," she said. She gave an abrupted half-laugh. "Sorry, was thinking about the fisherman I found."

Lila took her hand from the steering wheel to pat Jess on the knee. "Tea and biscuits. Come on." With that proclamation, she swung the Mini into the village hall car park, cut the engine, and opened her door. "Good timing, look." She pointed out of the car park, towards Orchard Close, where Henry, Maeve, Father James, and the quartet of judges were grouped under the fruit trees admiring the schoolchildren's wild flower signs.

As Jess and Lila got out of the car, Father James broke free from the group and strode across the road to meet them, his eyebrows already raised in quizzical concern as he approached.

Jess shook her head in an unspoken answer, and he turned his gaze to Lila.

She shrugged. "It's not great. We need tea."

"But I'd say the judging is off," Jess said, her voice flat and low. "Turned out it's not just vandalism. It's—" An unexpected sob caught in her throat and she spun away and started towards the door, rubbing her eyes with her forearm as they filled with tears.

Lila caught up with her at the door and threaded her arm through Jess's to lead her inside, calling over her shoulder to Father James that they might as well tell everyone together as there was no point repeating it over and over. She ushered Jess into the women's toilets, enveloped her in a hug, then disappeared into the nearest cubicle to tear off a wodge of toilet paper. She folded the paper into a thick pad and held it under the cold tap for a few seconds. "Here."

Jess took the soggy wad from Lila and pressed it against her eyes. When the tears stopped, she tossed the paper into the bin, and splashed more cold water on her face. "Sorry. It's just that ... well, you know?"

"Yeah. I know. I'm sure he'll be grand. You said he's breathing, and sure, didn't you say the bleeding had stopped. He'll be grand, just you see. Now, we'd better go and tell them what's going on. Ready?"

Jess took a deep breath. "Ready," she said in a firm, steady voice. "You?" She pulled open the door, held it for Lila to pass through, and followed her into the village hall's main room.

As they entered, the low murmur of chat stopped and all heads turned towards the Jess and Lila, concerned looks mirrored on every face.

For a moment, there was silence.

"You'll be wanting tea first, eh?" Linda, bless her, picked up the heavy teapot from the centre of the table and poured the deep brown liquid into two empty mugs.

Elizabeth added a splash of milk to each. "Sugar? You look like you've had a shock and you've clearly brought bad news."

Jess shuddered. "God, no. No sugar. It's not *that* bad!" She managed a weak laugh and, around the table, those who knew her well enough to know how much she hated sugar in her tea echoed the chuckle. "I'll have a biscuit instead."

"Take two." Father James shoved a plate towards her and she did as he'd instructed, casting him a feeble smile and passing the plate on to Lila, who also helped herself to two.

"I'm really sorry," Jess finally said, after a couple of bites of Rich Tea biscuit. "But there's been an incident in the village and ... and—"

"We think we need to have change of plan for today," Lila finished, equally ineffectively, before dunking her biscuit in her steaming tea.

Everyone began to speak at once, and for a moment or two, no one stopped them, then Maeve, always good in a crisis despite her own dislike of the unexpected, tapped a spoon to her mug and said, "I suppose you'd better tell us what's happened that's left you so shook. Out with it."

For the next twenty minutes or so, Lila and Jess relayed the events that had taken place in the village in the short time between the judges passing through Ballyfortnum village centre on their way to the village hall and the time that Lila had received the call, just as they'd been about to set out to start the judging process.

"So," Jess finished up, "Willie has been taken off to hospital, and he was unconscious but stable, according to the paramedics, but now the whole place is a mess and there are police, and tape, and still some of the paint, and the hanging baskets are all destroyed and we didn't have time to replant them even though we thought we might be able to, and now no one's allowed back into the shed to get them anyway, and I ..." She was rambling. She faltered; took a breath, and finished in a rush. "I just don't see how you'll be able to judge anything now, or how anyone would want to, given what's happened." She sighed heavily and picked up the second biscuit. "It's all just in a terrible mess," she said again, leaned back against her chair, and took a large bite of Rich Tea, trying not to crunch too loudly while everyone digested the news in stunned silence.

Maeve's mouth set into a thin line; her brow furrowed in confusion.

Father James looked like someone had kicked him in the stomach, knocking the wind out of him.

Elizabeth had come to stand behind Henry, and rested an arm around his shoulder. He reached up and took her hand.

Linda, having set down the teapot, sank into the nearest empty chair and fanned herself with one of the printed schedules they'd left on the table earlier.

The four judges looked at each other, each seeming to wait for another to speak.

For a long moment, no one spoke.

"Well," Don said, eventually, breaking the silence. "Well."

"We've not had to deal with anything quite like this," Patrick admitted, pulling an old-fashioned cotton hanky from his pocket and running it across his forehead.

"Do the four of you want to have a chat? Why don't I show you into the meeting room, and you can confer amongst yourselves." Father James suggested, to the obvious relief of the judges. "That'll give us a few minutes to see if we can't come up with a plan, too. See what can be done?" He got to his feet, as did Don and Patrick.

Lydia and Frances exchanged a quick look, nodded at each other, and followed suit, each still clutching a mug of half-drunk tea.

"This way." Father James led the way to the small meeting room at the front of the building. The four bewildered Tidy Village judges meekly fell into step behind him much as Jess imagined sheep following a trusted shepherd in the priest's Sunday sermons. Not that she'd heard many of them, but that was a fairly standard one, wasn't it?

As soon as the door closed behind them, the babble started. Maeve, true to form, swore a bit, then rallied with a call to action and the formulation of a new plan. She snatched up her clipboard and a pen, and peered over her glasses exactly as if she were a disgruntled headteacher in a convent school, or perhaps a very stereotypical librarian. "It's just the village centre, you say?"

Jess leaned back in her chair and sighed with relief. Maeve was back in control. Everything would be all right.

For the next ten minutes, with the judges out of the way, the committee batted ideas back and forth, debating whether the judges would be happy to see the rest of the village as planned, while ignoring the drama around the pub, shop, and old cottage, or whether they should try to reschedule.

"But it looked so perfect," Lila said, her frustration leaking out with the high-pitched wail of her words. "We'll never have it looking so good! Or get such beautiful weather if we reschedule."

Maeve huffed in agreement and muttered something about the rain forecast for the weeks ahead. "Always rains later in June," she said, and nobody dared remind her that last year, June had been blazing.

"They'll understand," Henry said, his voice calm and steady. "These things happen."

Jess didn't bother to say that these things didn't seem to happen anywhere else, and hadn't the judges said as much only a few minutes ago. It wouldn't help. Besides, she was only half paying attention by now. The thoughts churning in her mind were far from the problem of what to do about the judging, but focused firmly on the problem of who had done this to them. Who would benefit from sabotaging their chances at the prize? And who would be callous enough to attack poor Willie while they were at it? She suddenly couldn't wait to get away.

When the four judges emerged from the meeting room, they wore almost-identical looks of sympathetic seriousness on their faces.

"What we have agreed," Lydia said with a small smile, "is that we all noticed how beautiful the pub and shop looked as we drove through this morning."

"In fact," Frances said, "we commented on the cheerfulness of all that orange and said how it looked like sunshine in a basket."

"And how nice it was that the window boxes coordinated so well," said Don. "We slowed down for a good look."

"And we even stopped in at the shop," Patrick said. "Wanted to get some bottles of water, what with the heat and all the walking ahead of us."

"So while Lydia ran in, the rest of us got a great look over the windows," Frances added with a soft smile. "They looked beautiful."

"And I particularly noted that even that old run-down house opposite the school didn't let the side down, with its crown of roses," Lydia said. "We look out for it every year, as it's really the only derelict building in the middle part of Ballyfortnum. It's quite pretty. Every village has its share of derelicts, but they aren't all smothered in roses. You're very lucky; some of the ones we saw last week were a terrible eyesore." Lydia clasped a hand to her mouth a little too late. "Oops, sorry. Forget I said that. We really aren't supposed to pass remarks on the competitors. Sorry." She threw an apologetic look at her colleagues.

"So what we have concluded," Patrick said, stepping forwards, "is that we have seen a perfectly good representation of the standard for the whole village. We'll judge Ballyfortnum on the parts we have seen already, and apply that as the standard for the rest of the village. For example, we'll be able to judge the Best Window category based on our observations this morning combined with the window boxes on show here." He gestured around them although all the village hall's bloom-laden planters were outside, out of sight. "And we'll ignore the vandalism and that old cottage completely. Pretend it's not there at all."

"However," Lydia said, placing a hand on his arm to quieten him. "What we haven't quite agreed on, is whether we should stay and visit the farm this afternoon as planned, and partake of lunch in the parochial house, or whether you would prefer us to leave you to it?"

"And," Patrick added, "we would very much still like to visit the school if possible? We imagine the children will be expecting us and we don't want to disappoint. Not to mention that the sponsors certainly won't want children going off home and crying to their mammies about us not showing up!" There was a feeble ripple of low laughter as the committee acknowledged his attempts to lighten the mood. "You did say the damage and constraints don't affect the school property?"

"I don't think so," Lila said, a hint of doubt lacing her voice as she glanced at Jess. "People seemed to think the school was fine? I mean, there were lots of the mams by the cottage and they never said anything about the school, and Marcus ...?"

"Marcus just went in to ask questions. He'd have said if there were any more problems, I'm sure. Let's call the school, check if it's okay?" Jess turned to Father James, directing the question to him, and he nodded, already pulling his phone from the pocket of his chinos.

"We'll give Matty a call too? Or Anne? About the nature reserve?" Jess suggested to Lila.

"No need," she said, nodding towards the door leading to the entrance lobby as it swung open, admitting Matty, Anne, and Siobhan into the hall.

"Can we come in?" Anne called from the doorway.

"Of course." Henry stood to welcome them, and with a quick shuffling of chairs, the three newcomers took seats around the table.

"We thought it would be easier than phoning," Anne went on, as she helped herself to a biscuit. "Will we call off this afternoon's plans, or do you still want to come on down and take a look?"

"Up to you," Siobhan added. "We'll work around whatever you want."

Father James disconnected the call to the school principal and relayed the conversation. It had been quickly agreed that the judges, accompanied by Maeve and Henry, would go to the school a little earlier than originally scheduled, and stay for longer, to meet the hard-working children and admire their gardening efforts and themed art displays.

After that, the committee and judges, but not Anne, Siobhan, or Matty, would relocate to the parochial house for lunch, then meet the Dochertys afterwards, at the fledging nature reserve, just as they'd originally intended.

Father James had, for once, spoken in a most complimentary way about the usually-aloof and uppity principal, who had risen admirably to the occasion and suggested that the children in the upper classes could share their Green Flag presentation with the judges in practice for their upcoming trip to Dublin. This, the principal had suggested, would fill some of the time previously allocated to walking around the rest of the village.

"What's Green Flag?" Jess whispered to Elizabeth.

"Environmental programme for schools," Elizabeth whispered back.

Jess shrugged, nodded, wondered fleetingly whether her nieces' school did it, and tuned out of the conversation, suddenly mindful that her blouse was spattered with flecks of blood, smears of mud, and had a small tear in the sleeve, presumably caused by a stray briar as she'd tended to Willie. "I think, if it's okay, I should pop home and get changed? You don't need me here now?" She was suddenly desperate for some breathing space to check in with Marcus, and to scribble a quick account of the morning's events into her notebook. She had a niggling feeling she might have seen something important, but couldn't quite remember what. A moment of calm in her own quiet kitchen would give her time to collect her thoughts, process the shock, and sift through the photos she'd taken to see if there was anything she should share with Marcus and his Gardai colleagues. "Besides," she said aloud, "what with Linda here and Marcus caught up in the village, I should let Fletch and Snowflake out. Is that okay?" She directed the question at Henry, deliberately avoiding looking at Maeve and ignoring her huffing sigh of disapproval at yet another change to the plan. Henry, Jess knew, would agree easily.

"Of course."

Without waiting for anyone else to comment or object, she made her apologies, promised to get herself up to the church to join them for lunch, and ducked out into the bright sunshine where she stood for a minute to take a couple of deep breaths before getting into her sun-baked car and driving the short distance home.

Chapter Eleven

I n her sunny yellow kitchen, Jess threw open the French doors, shooed Fletcher and Snowflake outside, and rummaged in the kitchen drawer for her notebook and pencil while she waited for the kettle to boil for her umpteenth cup of tea of the morning.

"Actually," she said to the not-yet-rumbling kettle as she flicked it off again, "I'll have water."

Outside, seated at her small metal patio table, she gulped down a second glass of water and opened her notebook to a fresh page. At the top, in neat capitals, she wrote **SABOTAGE**, then chuckled to herself about how dramatic the word looked now it was written down. "But," she muttered to the page, "it is sabotage, isn't it?" If not sabotage, then what else could it be? She pencilled that thought below the heading—WHAT ELSE?—and added a few spidery arrows branching out.

Coincidence, she wrote, then added another smaller arrow and wrote *Not likely.*

Not having the faintest idea of any other reason for the damage and attack on Willie, she left the other arrows leading from WHAT ELSE? pointing only to empty space.

Okay, she thought. It's not really the *why* that's in question here. It's the *who.*

She drew a thicker, darker arrow leading from the header to midway down the page and wrote <u>WHO?</u> in large letters in the centre. And then she got stuck. "I've absolutely no idea."

She must have spoken the thought louder than she'd realised, as a deep, American voice drifted from the other side of the fence.

"Not like you, Jess. You're usually a fountain of ideas." Gary's bushy face popped up over the wooden fence. "Wanna sounding board?"

She didn't know if she did, to be honest. What she'd really wanted was peace and quiet, but she had to admit it wasn't getting her anywhere. "Sure. Come on over. I'm not stopping long—just getting changed—" She gestured at her still-filthy blouse. "Well, I will, in a minute." She waved a lazy arm around the garden, encompassing the two mooching dogs. "And letting these two out. But then I sat down for a minute and ... well ..."

As she was speaking, Gary loped to the end of the gardens where the fences were lower, to allow a view over the fields and distant mountains. He swung himself over the fence at the end of his garden, into the field, and over Jess's fence into her garden in a smooth, easy sequence that suggested he'd been athletic at school.

Fletcher flung himself on the intruder, thumping his large paws up onto Gary's chest and licking slobber across his face.

"He'll never make a guard dog," Jess said. "Unless he'd lick them into submission and glue them down with drool." She smiled at her neighbour. "I was going to offer you a drink, but ..."

Gary had completed the entire fence-jumping, dog-slobbering manoeuvre with an open can of coke in his hand, and he grinned at her as he sank onto the empty patio chair opposite her. "Can't beat the real thing," he said, quoting an old slogan for the drink with a huge smile splitting his beard.

"It's always coca cola," Jess retorted, returning his smile, and they laughed, some of the tension of the morning broken as the sun beat down on them and the dogs lolloped lazily round the dry garden. For a minute, it was easy to pretend they were just two friendly neighbours enjoying a drink together on a lazy, sun-drenched summer afternoon.

"So," Gary said, "what is it that you have absolutely no idea about, and can I be of any assistance? I'm good at having absolutely no idea about things."

"I just can't understand why anyone would do such an awful thing." She leaned back on her chair and tilted her face to the sun. "Even aside from hurting Willie. Why would anyone be so *petty*?"

They sat in silence, staring at nothing and contemplating Jess's question.

"A joke got out of hand?" Gary suggested after a while, his voice lacking any conviction. "You Irish like to, what d'you call it, have a bit of *craic*?"

"Hmm." Jess squinted at him through half-closed eyes, trying to filter the brightness of the sun as it edged lazily towards noon in the cloudless sky. "But this is just downright nasty. Not *fun*."

"Guess not. You think that old guy'll be okay? Willie, you said? He sure was out cold. I captured a few images on my cell phone, if your policeman would like to see them."

They exchanged phone numbers, and a moment later a series of photos pinged into Jess's WhatsApp. She opened the first, and peered at it, hoping something would stand out. A dropped document with a name and address and a large arrow saying 'Clue', perhaps. A clear footprint amongst the smudges of scuffed earth. A fingerprint on some usefully-placed something-or-other. A smoking gun. No such luck. She scrolled through the rest—just four more—giving each a cursory glance, then forwarded the lot to Marcus with a brief *from Gary* message.

"Did you see anything else?" she asked Gary. "You, know, when you found him?"

Gary took a gulp of coke, wiped his mouth with the back of his hand, and shook his head. "Like what?"

"I don't know." She lifted a shoulder in a half-hearted shrug. "Someone wielding a heavy object, covered in paint, running from the scene? That kind of thing." She smiled weakly at her neighbour. "Willie was already unconscious when you found him?"

Gary nodded. "Out cold."

"You didn't move him?"

"No. Checked his vitals, got a couple of pics—" He gestured at the phone Jess had set down on the table; its screen faded to black and the photos disappeared. "—and came to get help. No time to think about anything else."

Why had he taken the photos before coming for help, Jess wondered. She brushed away the thought; she'd have probably done the same, wouldn't she? Evidence, just in case. And it wasn't as if he'd made a feature-length film of it; just the five quick snaps.

He chuckled; a low, self-deprecating sound. "I didn't even look at them, just snapped a few shots of the scene and came to get some assistance. You, or that Docherty guy, Matt, or whoever. Lucky your policeman was there to take charge."

Jess reached for her phone again. "Look now? You might notice something you didn't register at the time?" She pulled up the first of Gary's photos and lay the phone on the table between them, then shuffled her chair around the table so she was almost beside him. Together, they bent their heads over the phone, blocking out the sun so they could study the image.

In the photo, Willie lay sprawled on his back in the shadow of the tumbledown shed. His upper body, further into the shed, was only partly in shot, blocked by the wall dividing the two sections of the shed, and darkened from the shade. His arms spread slightly out from his body at not-quite-natural angles, one hand fully out of shot.

Jess swiped the screen, replacing the first image with the next one. In this, Gary had focused primarily on Willie's upper body, zooming in towards the back of the shed. From this angle, you'd never tell he was balding at the back; his grey hair was tousled in a look worthy of Einstein, with a few thorny twigs caught through it. His checked shirt was smudged with patches of what she'd presumed to be blood, but the colours of the shirt made it impossible to guess. Could've been anything, really.

She scrolled to the next photo. This one captured the whole body, and Willie looked strangely foreshortened with his legs closest to the camera and his head receding into the dim recess of the shed.

She swiped again, this time bringing up a close headshot. From this angle, the thatch of hair was clearly matted with blood; a few more leaves tangled into his curls, all flecked with dusty earth. "Good camera," Jess said, without looking up from the screen. "It's got great sharp detail." Willie's expression was strangely peaceful; at odds with his crumpled clothing, blood-stained hair, and the streaks of dirt that smeared his clothes and face. Didn't people's faces register pain, when they were knocked out?

She scrolled again. Gary had obviously taken a few steps back for this final picture; more of the shed was included, and it was clearer to see exactly where Willie lay in relation to the space he occupied. She put two fingers to the screen and zoomed in. "There, see?" She pointed to the grass bordering the concrete in front of the shed. "Do you see how it looks like it's been trampled? I wondered if we'd done that, moving him, but looks like it was already squashed down?" She released the screen and the picture immediately resized to fill the screen once more. "I think he'd been moved? Dragged into the shed, out of sight?" She sat back, having suddenly realised something else. "That's why his arms are a little away from his sides; someone pulled him in by grabbing under his arms, pulling him backwards. It's the easiest way to hold someone, to pull them."

Gary opened the photos on his own phone, and skimmed through them again. "Guess you could be right. But I'm not sure it means much? Whoever bashed him wasn't planning to help him, regardless."

"Someone put something under his head. A sweatshirt or something. They did try to help, but I'd guess they got disturbed, and ran off?"

"Nah, shouldn't think so. You'd not move him first, then try to help, then run off. You'd try to help first, and then if you got disturbed, you wouldn't have time to move him, you'd just leg it."

"So why bother? Why not just leave him where he fell and run off straight away?"

Gary took a swig of his coke. "No idea," he said. He looked at Jess, and smirked. "Told you I was good at this; having no ideas."

She laughed. "You and me both. I'd better get on. I promised I'd get up to the vicarage." She gestured to her torn blouse. "I need to go change. Check in with you later? Marcus will know how Willie's doing, so I'll let you know when I hear anything. Thank you so much for coming to help. You didn't even question it!"

"I'm initiated now, into the village, that is. Did I pass?" Gary grinned at her, got up, and loped back down to the end of the garden, where he put one hand on the fence and jumped over it into the field. "Catch you later." He vaulted the fence again to land in his own garden, and Jess gathered up her phone and her empty glass and went inside to have a quick shower and pull on some fresh clothes.

Ten minutes later, she sat on the edge of her bed wrapped in a large towel, half-heartedly and one-handedly rubbing her hair dry with a smaller towel. With her other hand, she opened the photos again, and stared at each for a moment before moving to the next. In the fourth; the one showing the wider shot, something caught her eye and she zoomed in again, this time to the hand that had been out of shot in the first image. A smear of red stained the back of Willie's hand. At first, she thought it was blood, but as she zoomed in, she decided it was brighter and too orange. *Paint.* The same colour paint that had been splashed across the cottage walls and daubed onto the pub and shop windows. It didn't quite say 'clue', but it felt like a step in the right direction. Had Willie been cleaning the paint from the cottage when he'd been hit? She didn't think so, as surely he'd have raised the alarm first; called for help? Come to think of it, where was his phone? Had he in fact called for help? She closed the image and texted Marcus.

Where's Willie's phone? Also how you getting on? Heading up to meet for lunch at Fr J's. You still about? xxx

She shimmied into a clean pair of jeans, pulled on a fresh blouse—two blouses in one day, she thought with a wry smile. Her usual attire was T-shirts in summer and thick jumpers or hooded sweatshirts in winter, all teamed with her favourite live-in staple of blue jeans. As she headed downstairs to call in the dogs and get moving, her phone buzzed in her hand. Marcus.

She agreed to meet him briefly at his cottage on her way to the parochial house. He needed to change, eat, and sleep.

"Not necessarily in that order," he added with a loud yawn, reminding Jess that he had not yet made it home from last night's shift.

"I'll bring you a sandwich. I'll walk up though, so see you in abut twenty minutes," she said, and hung up. Walking would give her time to think.

Marcus had no news from the hospital, and no news about who had attacked Willie or vandalised the village. His eyes were red from tiredness and even though Jess had taken him that clean shirt, he was so rumpled and dirt-smeared that she couldn't be sure if he'd even had time to change. He'd left someone at the cottage, he told her, to keep an eye on things and stop anyone nosing about, but for now, there didn't seem to be very much they could do to make progress. No one seemed to have seen anything until after the perpetrator had left, and no one had any idea who might be responsible.

"I really shouldn't say this," he said, looking at her shrewdly, "but …"

Jess laughed and tucked herself into his outstretched arm. He pulled her in close for a sideways hug, and dropped a kiss on her still-damp hair.

"Don't worry," she said, "I will keep my eyes and ears fully open while you get some beauty sleep. I think the judges will still go up to Dochertys' farm after lunch as planned, unless you say they can't?"

He shook his head. "No. It's okay. There's no reason to stop them. Just don't let anyone trample around the cottage."

She fluttered her lashes and he swatted her gently with his free arm.

"Not even you, Jessica O'Malley. Promise?"

"You'll let me know if you hear anything about Willie? Everyone will want to know?" She deflected his instruction, unwilling to promise to stay away from the cottage. Not that she had any intention of tramping over a crime scene. She'd only look from a *safe* distance, if at all.

After another hug, she reluctantly pulled away. "Much as I'd like to stay, I promised I'd get back to them as soon as I'd got cleaned up and let the dogs out, and you really, really do need to get some sleep."

She let herself out of the cottage, and walked the last few hundred yards to the church car park.

A soft hum of chatter from the graveyard, out of sight behind the church, told her that the judges were back from the school already, and being given a tour of the tidied-for-the-occasion churchyard. She didn't need to join them. Instead, she let herself into the priest's house, called a greeting to announce herself to Mrs Harris, and made her way to the large, sun-streaked kitchen, where the elderly housekeeper was busy arranging platters of sandwiches on the enormous pine table.

Without awaiting instruction, Jess turned to one of the large, over-stocked cupboards and took out a teetering stack of china cups. She set them on the table and went back for saucers, a couple of milk jugs, and enough teaspoons from the cutlery drawer to place one with each cup and saucer. She took a carton of milk from the fridge, filled the milk jugs, returned the milk to the fridge, and only then said, "What else?" to Mrs Harris.

Mrs Harris set an enormous steaming teapot in the centre of the table and pulled an ugly tea cosy—a lopsided knitted rendition of what was supposed to be the church—over the teapot. "That's all. You sit yourself down and pour a cup. Father says you've had quite a shock this morning."

Jess did as she was told, as there really didn't seem to be anything else needing doing. Mrs Harris, despite rumours suggesting she was already almost two-hundred years old, was capable and thorough and had everything else laid out and ready. "You'd never know we hadn't planned it this early. You're a gem, Mrs Harris. Will you have a cup too?" Jess poured tea into a second cup without waiting for an answer, suspecting the older woman would decline if allowed the choice, but would appreciate a moment to take the weight of her feet if it was presented as a *fait accompli*.

Mrs Harris perched on the chair nearest the sink and took the cup from Jess. "Willie's still out cold," she announced, sipping delicately at the tea.

Jess raised an eyebrow, simultaneously surprised and entirely unsurprised that Mrs Harris would know something no one else knew.

"Our Betsy is a nurse in ICU."

Jess didn't ask who Our Betsy might be. Mrs Harris's family was large and widespread and Jess was convinced she knew someone in every corner of Ireland. Why Our Betsy was taking time out from her duties to let Mrs Harris know confidential information about her patients was another mystery best left unsolved. Mrs Harris, Jess had discovered over the last few years, was a mine of useful information and knew at least as much about the goings-on in Ballyfortnum as Mrs Dunne. Jess wouldn't be surprised if it turned out that the two women were spies, working in cahoots to protect Ireland from any conceivable attack.

They hadn't protected Willie Keegan.

Jess shivered, despite the warmth of the kitchen and the sunbeams dancing through the huge sash windows. "Will he be all right?" she asked.

"No telling as yet. Please God he will be." Mrs Harris glanced out of the window at the church and made the sign of the cross over her chest. "They'll be in soon enough," she said, nodding towards the graveyard. "They're not long back from the school and Father suggested they have a quick stroll around, as Willie had it well-kept and the effort was made. Seemed only right to look, so it did."

"Good idea," Jess agreed, following Mrs Harris's gaze. As they watched, the two female judges, flanked by Henry and Father James, rounded the corner of the grey stone building. "You're right. Here they come. Are we ready for them?" She stood, tipped the dregs of her tea into the sink, rinsed her cup, dried it and set it back in place on the table.

"Beating off that hooligan, so he was," Mrs Harris said, getting to her feet and setting her own cup on the draining board. "Never one to let someone do a wrong. You'll see if I'm right." She drained the rest of her tea in one swift mouthful, and had the cup washed and dried just as the sound of footsteps and voices filled the hall beyond the open kitchen door.

"Hooligan?" Jess put emphasis on the singularity of Mrs Harris's statement. "I'd have thought there were at least two of them? You think there was only one?"

"Likely so, for the whole trouble, but as at least one of them ran off, I'd think it was only one of them Willie came up against."

Before Jess had time to question what Mrs Harris had said, the kitchen filled with people, all talking at once, jostling for seats around the table.

"Looks fantastic."

"What a spread."

"Shall I pour tea? Anyone for anything that's not tea?"

"A splash of wine? A snifter of whiskey?" Patrick smiled around the table, bringing a ripple of laughter.

"A cool drink. Water. Orange cordial or suchlike. I'm not sharing the communion wine; not at this early hour. Although if you know anyone who will change the water for you, work away." Father James passed around a large water jug as more laughter filled the room. The upset of the morning seemed to have passed, and the judges and committee members were relaxed and cheerful as they tucked into the sandwiches spread before them.

Jess filed away Mrs Harris's words for later, and helped herself to a couple of cheese and salad sandwiches and a couple of ham and tomato, suddenly ravenous, though it wasn't even one o'clock yet.

Chapter Twelve

Lunch was livelier than Jess had expected. Don, Patrick, and Lydia were clearly quite familiar with Henry, Elizabeth, Maeve, and Father James, and the conversation flitted between sharing news of mutual acquaintances; anecdotes from their time as Tidy Village judges, and cheerful observations about how pleasant the weather had been so far in June, which even Maeve couldn't disagree with.

Now and then the chat would drift towards a specific garden or plant, and here, Jess was able to add something to the conversation. On the whole, she let the conversation wash over her, her mind full of images of Willie Keegan, lying motionless, and the decimated floral displays the village had worked so hard to create. She was also itching to ask Mrs Harris what she'd meant when she'd said one of the culprits had run off. Had Mrs Harris actually seen someone, when the rest of the village seemed to have noticed nothing unusual until after the damage was done? And why *had* Willie got paint on his hands? Had he had something to do with the vandalism and someone had disturbed him? Or had he disturbed the vandals in the act?

"Eh, Jess?"

At the sound of her name, she was jolted from her thoughts. "Sorry," she said to Henry. "Miles away. What did you ask me?"

"Are you still going to walk to the farm as planned? Or shall they go without you? We're about ready, I should think."

The plates were cleared of sandwiches; the tea cups drained, refilled, and drained again. Lunch was over.

Beyond the window, Lila paced up and down on the church driveway, phone tucked under her chin.

Henry followed Jess's gaze. "She's calling Matty; letting him know we're on the way. You sure you're all right to go with them? You don't have to." His kind, steady eyes matched the sympathy in his voice. "They'll manage, if you'd rather go on home."

Jess got to her feet and began to gather the used cups. "No, it's fine. I'll only think about poor Willie if I go home. Let's see what we can salvage from the day; get some expert eyes on the plans? Have they seen them yet?" Her face warmed as she realised she had absolutely no idea whether anyone had discussed the plans for the nature reserve with the judges, as had been on the schedule for 'During Lunch'. "Sorry, I should know. I haven't been paying much attention. Sorry."

"Lila decided they could look at the land first. Then they might make suggestions no one has thought of, if they haven't seen the plans. Said it might be better, and that way we could all just relax properly over lunch, since the day has gone pear-shaped anyway."

Jess flashed Henry a grateful smile. "Good idea. She's coming back in." She pointed towards the window with one of the teacups as Lila pocketed her phone, nodded at Jess through the glass, and headed for the door. "Let's go?"

Obediently, those who were to go to the Dochertys' farm got to their feet

Elizabeth would stay to help Mrs Harris with clearing up and resetting for the much-anticipated afternoon tea of scones and jam. Henry, too, once he'd ascertained that Jess really was happy to go, stifled a yawn and opted to remain in the vicarage with Elizabeth. Father James also bowed out, claiming he was superfluous to requirements and had plenty to get on with while they went on without him, but Jess suspected he might just creep away for an afternoon nap to gear himself up for a plateful of scones. The events of the day were beginning to catch up with everyone.

Maeve, also not part of the nature reserve's planning or development, announced in her usual clipped manner that she would take herself home and write a report of the morning's events for the committee records, no doubt already assessing how badly their chances of winning had been affected by the upset. She would, she told the room, return later to join them for the afternoon tea and see the judges off properly.

As if we can't see them off properly without her, Jess thought, ducking to pretend to tie an already-tied shoelace to hide her smile. Besides, Maeve would hardly have time to walk home and get back again, never mind stop to write the kind of heavily-detailed report she tended to favour. Maeve walked or cycled everywhere; Jess wasn't even sure the woman owned a car or knew how to drive. Admirable, given the state of the climate, but slow, when time mattered. Taking pity on the older woman, Jess straightened her face, got up, and walked to the front door with her. She tugged open the heavy wooden door, and stood aside to let Maeve exit ahead of her.

A magpie flew from the fence opposite them; a startled flash of black-and-white feathers.

Maeve glared at it and crossed herself hastily. She stepped over the threshold. "First the change of judges and then this. Wonder what the third thing will be. I said this is getting to be more trouble than it's worth; didn't I say that to you?"

"Didn't have you pegged as superstitious," Jess said with a small laugh. She stepped through the vicarage door behind

Maeve, and for a moment the two stood on the doorstep blinking in the bright sunshine, the magpie having vanished over the trees and out of sight. "Don't worry. Maybe they'll give us plenty of sympathy votes!"

Maeve cast Jess a condescending look that said she doubted the judges would do anything of the sort, grunted something non-committal, and set off at a brisk pace.

Poor woman, Jess thought, watching Maeve stride away down the driveway. She put so much effort into the Tidy Village preparations, and would be devastated that their chances had been compromised, and even more so if it cost them the prize. Worse still, if they didn't win they would never know whether they had lost due to the vandalism, or lost because some other village had simply outshone them this year. As she waited for the others to join her, Maeve's words reverberated in her mind. *First the judge, then this.*

Could the two things be connected? Jess gave her head the smallest of shakes. *No. Why would they be?*

Lila fell into step between Lydia and Don, leaving Jess to walk with Frances and Patrick. They crossed the road between the church and shop, turning towards the pub and the cottage.

Frances and Jess exchanged pleasantries about how nicely the church grounds were kept.

Patrick said something about what a terrible shame it was that someone had seen fit to vandalise the village centre, and how he hoped it was a one-off.

Everyone murmured noises of agreement; all six heads turning almost in unison as they passed the pub tables, devoid of their flower arrangements and barer even than any ordinary day in Ballyfortnum, where at least an empty glass or discarded beer mat might adorn the rough wooden surfaces.

Up ahead, the Garda car was still parked on the road outside the cottage, now silent and no longer flashing its blue lights. The younger of the two uniformed Gardai leaned against it, looking hot and bored as he scrolled through his phone and paid little attention to the crime scene.

"I wonder how the other one got back to the station," Jess said. "Or perhaps he's still here somewhere."

"Probably." Patrick nodded at the Garda, who didn't look up, and the six reached the junction and turned away from the policeman, the cottage, the village centre, and the mess of the morning.

"How was the school?" Jess asked her two companions. "You probably said, over lunch, but I was a bit zoned out. Sorry."

Frances was quick to reassure her she'd missed nothing. "We didn't actually. Too busy talking about how nice the sandwiches were."

"The children were very sweet," Patrick said.

Frances laughed. "They weren't really. They were excited and full of questions about the vandalism. Wanted to know all the gory details and could barely concentrate on their Green Flag presentations at all."

Lydia, walking ahead with Don and Lila but clearly eavesdropping on those behind her, turned to Jess, walking crab-like along the farm track as she joined the conversation. "One little girl was very cute. She said she'd have made nice new flowers for the baskets and her mum had some lovely blue plastic ones we could look at if we wanted, and she started to give us her address until the teacher stepped in and stopped her. Another pair said they'd catch the—" She broke off. "Well,

I won't tell you the words they used, but the teacher wasn't so quick to stop them, so I think she agreed!"

Patrick, Frances, and Lydia all laughed, leaving Jess to use the full extent of her imagination to fill in the gaps.

"Then they got into some far-fetched stories about what had happened and who might have done it," Frances said.

"Yes, Marcus said as much. He's a Gard. He lives here." Jess waved an arm in the vague direction of the pub. "Not in the pub. Beyond it, in one of the little cottages. He said the children had come up with all kinds of ideas about it. Monsters. Balaclava-wearing robbers."

"Aliens," Don called over his shoulder, also slowing to wait. As they drew level, the six of them fell into a line that stretched across the farm track.

"A baddie in an Audi," Patrick said. "I told him that was our car, and then they thought *we* must be the baddies."

"I was impressed by his observations," Lydia said, her tone serious and admiring. "He knew the make and model, and colour."

"And he said it wasn't a car from around here as he knew all the cars from here."

"I'll bet that was Siobhan's Ryan." Lila swung around, her hair flowing out behind her. "Neighbourhood watch in one mouthy eight-year-old. He's right into his cars. Nothing gets past him."

"But then one of his friends said she'd seen us in the shop," Frances said, "and that we couldn't be the baddies because baddies don't come into the shop to buy water and she didn't see any paint and her mam had said weren't the flowers looking lovely to Mrs Dunne, and then we drove away and all the flowers were still there."

"I felt quite vindicated when she said that," Don said, laughing. "Because before that, I thought they were going to have us all arrested when that boy started his accusations and a couple of them started calling out that we should go off to Kilmainham."

"Then the teacher explained they'd had a class trip to Kilmainham, before Christmas, and they were fascinated by the jail and the stories, so at least that explained that, and we said how at least it showed they'd retained some of what they'd learned there."

They drew level with Lila's house, and the talk turned to gardens once more. Jess was gratified to hear sighs of admiration from Lydia and Frances, and a barrage of compliments from Don. For a moment, Jess thought they didn't know it was Lila's garden and, amused by Lila's nonchalance and lack of admitting ownership, was about to step forward and say so, but when Don turned from admiring the lupins and said, "You've outdone yourself this year, I should say," she realised that of course they'd met Lila in previous years, and would know her garden well.

"I'll get a picture for Jim. He'll be pleased to see it." Patrick fumbled with his phone, took a picture, looked at it, and took another. Thumb was on the first," he said with a sheepish smile. "My Greta says I'll never get up to speed with all this technology and I dare say she's right. She usually is."

"What happened to him?" Jess asked, remembering the thought she'd had after Maeve had inadvertently connected the missing judge with the vandalism, and trying to sound casual. "I hope he isn't very sick? Jim, I mean. Did he know Dad too?" She hoped it would be enough to lead the conversation around to what, exactly, had caused Jim to withdraw from this year's judging at such notice, just in case Maeve was right and it *was* somehow important.

He'd been taken ill, at their weekly pre-judging dinner over the weekend, Patrick said, which Jess had already gathered, when they'd first arrived at the village hall and made the introductions.

"Usually robust as anything," Patrick went on. "So quite the shock altogether when he keeled over clutching his midriff in between courses. Before dessert," he said, in a somewhat wistful tone. "Seems something hadn't agreed with him, but some of us had the same, so ..." He shrugged. "One of those things. We were just about to order puddings ..."

"Hadn't even got to the schedule, had we?" Lydia gave them a wry smile. "And yes, I had the same starter. It was delicious. And you had the same main, I think?" She turned away to look where she was going instead of continuing the sideways shuffle of trying to walk forwards while speaking to people behind her.

"Aye." Patrick nodded at Lydia's back. "She's right enough. We were right shook up after Jim got carted off in an ambulance. Took a couple of drinks in the bar instead of the usual coffee and planning. Surprised we've managed to get the week straight, after that. Miracle we got here on the right day." He chuckled. "Due in Abbeydare tomorrow, so we are." He cast a quick glance at Frances, who inclined her head a fraction, acknowledging his words. "Carrigallan on Thursday. Then Mullraney and Dunkettle on Friday. Good thing Frances was available to step in and get us back on track. She's great organisational skills, so she has." He cast an appreciative glance at his colleague.

Frances accepted the compliment with a small smile. "Glad I could help."

"Abbeydare?" Jess's ears pricked up at the name of the village a mile or two the far side of Ballymaglen. "That's where you said you're from, isn't it? Does it cause any problems for you to judge your own village?" She turned to Frances, then back to Patrick, who answered for his last-minute co-judge.

"Not a bit of it," he said, with a breezy smile. "We trust her to be fair." Having dismissed the notion without seeming to even consider it a possibility, he turned back to Lila's garden and took one more photo, before starting onwards along the lane towards the farmland.

Was he too complacent? Jess wondered, looking from Frances to Patrick and back to Frances. Did she look a bit shifty? Guilty? As if she'd scupper the current leader's chances at the prize to advance her own home-village? Jess couldn't tell.

"I'm quite enjoying myself, to be honest. Aside from the ..." Frances flapped a hand back the way they'd come, towards the cottage, without finishing the sentence. "And the circumstances. Of course, it's just awful about poor Jim. Still, I'm sure he's on the mend, eh Pat?" Patrick stopped walking and turned back to face her.

"Please God," he said. "He's been one of the judges every year since we began. Longer at it than anyone. Not the same without him. "Wonder if there's any update." He peered at his phone, shook his head, and sped up a little to catch Lila, Don, and Lydia, who'd already passed the next house—a neat bungalow belonging to the Shaughnessys, who Jess had never met and knew little about—and reached the third of the bungalows along the farm lane.

The house was currently rented to a lovely Canadian couple, and the garden was neat, but bare, with a brick-weave drive, a few pots of flowers, and one enormous tabby cat cleaning its bottom on the doorstep and another sleeping in the sun on one of the windowsills.

"Fweddie and Teddie," Jess said, pointing to the cats. "They're from Canada. Can't imagine how that works. Must have been quarantined for ages."

"Not sure I'd bother," Frances said, watching as the one on the doorstep yawned, turned over, and began to lick its hind leg.

Jess and Frances cast one last glance at the Canadian cats and quickened their pace to join the rest of the group as they approached the farm driveways; Billy White's on the left of the track and the Dochertys' on the right.

"Anyone heard any update on Jim?" Patrick said, just as Jess and Frances caught them up.

"That's Willie Keegan's house," Lila said, pointing as they passed, but not slowing.

Lydia nodded acknowledgement to Lila. "Not me," she said to Patrick, and turned back to Lila to say something about aphids, and organic alternatives to pesticides—a conversation Jess may have joined in with if her mind wasn't churning with thoughts about Willie's attacker; the vandalism of the village, and the sudden illness of the missing judge. She glanced back at Willie's bungalow, where a rusting car was propped up on bricks, its wheels nowhere to be seen, on a wide driveway beside the house. "I do hope he's going to be okay," she said. "Both of them, that is. Willie and your friend Jim."

Don pulled his phone from his pocket and stepped to the edge of the track to stand under the shade of a tree in front Billy White's farm. "I've not heard anything either," he said to Patrick. "Oh! Hang on." He poked at his phone screen; his brow crumpled in concentration, then lifted the phone to his ear. He held up his hand to indicate he'd be a minute, and turned away to listen, the conversation inaudible to Jess as she guided the group towards the Docherty farm's driveway.

"As you know," she told Lydia, Patrick, and Frances, "this one has been over-farmed and sterilised to within an inch of its life by the previous farmer, but now Matty has taken it over and is planning to rewild a huge part of it." She stopped and turned to Frances. "*Do* you know? I just realised that perhaps you don't as you only just stepped in?"

They'd talked about it briefly in the car, apparently, on the drive to Ballyfortnum that morning, and Jess was relived not to have to go through a long explanation of the hows and whys. "Anyway, if you do have questions, you may as well hold onto them until we get up there. Matty and Anne and Siobhan will be far better able to answer. Matty and Anne are brother and sister. It's their family farm. Siobhan's a cousin. Do you know if Peggy got there?" She directed the last question at Lila, who shrugged.

"Don't know. Anne was still expecting her, I think."

Peggy worked for the Parks and Wildlife Service and had been only too delighted to be asked on board. Like so many of her new friends in the village, Jess had only met Peggy a few weeks ago, after she'd reported finding a dead buzzard not too far from the Docherty farm. She and Peggy had become fast, easy friends, and had already shared a few Friday evening takeaways, and joined the Dochertys at the pub a couple of times, for evenings filled with laughter, friendship, and sometimes a bit of trad music.

They hadn't got far along the Dochertys' long, sweeping driveway before Don caught them up. "Pat? Lydia? Fran?" he said quietly as he joined the group; his eyes narrowed and his mouth set in a thin line.

Lydia's forehead crumpled into a frown as she stopped mid-conversation and turned to her colleague. "Everything all right, Don?"

He shook his head. "I had a voice message. I'd missed it. I just stopped to call Helena but it went to her voicemail. The message was a bit broken up so I only got some of it but I *think* what she is saying is that Jim's taken a turn for the worse. I only got snippets but she definitely said *intensive* and getting worse and I don't want to jump to conclusions without getting hold of Helena. Her voice was so broken up, I really couldn't tell *what* she was trying to say. Listen?"

Don was right; the message was very distorted. "Sorry ... on ... way ... Jim ... he's not there ... sorry ... intensive ...this afternoon hope ... can hear me ... dying ... why I'm calling ... luck ... sorry ... getting worse ..."

There was a silence as his colleagues digested the information.

"The other judge?" Jess whispered to Lila, who nodded, wide-eyed. "Shite. Dying?" Jess mouthed soundlessly and Lila nodded again. The two of them stepped a little away from the judges, and Jess whispered frantically in Lila's ear. "What are we going to do now? I guess they'll want to go back to the vicarage?"

"You mean the parochial house," Lila almost smiled, but checked herself. "Sorry. It always makes me smile when you call it that. Can tell you lived in England for ages." Her face became serious again. "Guess so. This day has turned to absolute shite. I'll ask them." She started towards the wan-faced judges, all looking equally blindsided by this latest piece of bad news.

Jess grabbed her arm, pulling her back. "Do you think ..." She was almost afraid to voice the thought that had already begun to niggle, even before this latest bombshell. "Do you think it's somehow connected?"

Lila looked blank. "What is?"

"You know," Jess whispered, gesturing towards the village. "Willie. The mess in the village. A sick judge. Do you think ...?"

Lila threw her an incredulous look; her mouth hanging open as she stared at her friend. "Don't be an eejit. How could it be?" But even as she said it, a hint of doubt shadowed her face and trickled into her words. "It couldn't, could it?" She shook her head as if to dismiss the very idea of it, pushed her hair off her face, and turned to the four judges. "Why don't we call it a day? No one is really in the mood for this anymore, are they? Shall we head back? I can't imagine for a minute that you really want to see an empty field marked out with string and fence posts today. Come on." Her voice was gentle, and she slipped an arm through Patrick's as she guided the sombre party away from the Docherty farm and back towards the church.

Chapter Thirteen

It was a quiet, reflective party that traipsed back towards the parish house and its bright, welcoming kitchen. Where better to absorb yet more bad news? Jess thought, as they walked along in silence.

Lila walked alongside Patrick; her arm tucked through his as if to hold him up. His slow gait and quiet melancholy made him seem somehow older than when Jess had first met him that morning. A flutter of fear tickled in her chest as she hoped he wasn't going to have a heart attack or anything. Good thing Lila was hanging on to him, just in case. One sick judge far away in Dublin was one thing; a sick one in front of her was another thing entirely, especially after Willie Keegan. A shiver chilled her neck, despite the blazing sun. Meanwhile, Don and Lydia, also quiet, walked side-by-side along the farm track, talking softly to each other.

Frances, perhaps feeling as much an outsider from the group as Jess, ambled along by herself, her gaze flitting here and there as they walked along; her head turning to the two tabby cats, both now lying on the driveway, sprawled out in the afternoon sun, then towards Lila's beautiful garden as they passed it.

Jess, avoiding conversation with any of them, walked slowly at the back of the group. She pulled out her phone and called Anne, bringing her up to date with the latest spanner in the day's works, and explaining why they hadn't arrived. "We got so close," she said. "We were halfway up the drive when Don got the news to say the other one had been moved to intensive care—we think. Not really sure; we couldn't get any details. It was a really garbled message." Jess moseyed along, making mindless chat with Anne as the rest of the group drew further ahead, dragging out the excuse not to make smalltalk with Frances. She threw her the odd apologetic glance, any time the woman turned to see if Jess was still with them, feigning the ongoing importance of the phone call. Frances was perfectly pleasant; it was just that Jess had run out of things to say, having already broached the mutual "I'm new to this"; "Do you garden?", and banal chitchat about the weather through the earlier parts of the day.

She'd got the impression that Frances didn't know Jim as well as the other three judges, or indeed that Frances even knew the other three as well as they knew each other. It must be hard for her, to be standing in at the last minute for such a momentous task as judging a national competition. Jess felt a sudden pang of sympathy for the woman, still walking a little apart from her colleagues, and now peering curiously towards the overgrown derelict cottage as she waited on the edge to the pavement for a couple of cars to pass. Jess broke off the chat with Anne to check the time on her phone. Almost three o'clock. School pick-up time. They ended the call and Jess caught up with the others, stopping on the pavement beside Frances as a few more cars trundled past.

"Sorry state of affairs," Frances said, nodding at the house, where the lone Garda still lounged against his car. This time, he acknowledged the group with a nod of his head, but he didn't straighten up or try to look any less bored.

"It did look pretty, with all the roses tumbling over it," Jess said, and the other woman nodded. "I can't believe anyone would do anything like this, just for the sake of a competition."

Frances shifted her gaze from the cottage and looked at Jess with narrowed eyes. "You think it was about the contest?"

Jess shrugged. "I don't see what else it could have been, to be honest. Oh! You said you're from Abbeydare, didn't you?" she added innocently, grateful for the opening.

"My family home is there," she said. "I live in Dublin now."

"But ... Well, what I mean is ... Has anything similar happened there? Has there been anything like this in Abbeydare this week?"

Frances stared at Jess, open-mouthed.

The rest of the group crossed the road, heading towards the parochial house and yet more cups of tea. *We should have told them to expect us,* Jess realised, a little too late. *Never mind.* Jess and Frances remained poised on the edge of the pavement on the pub-side of the road, as Jess's question sank in.

Wordlessly, Frances took out her phone and squinted at the screen, searching for the correct buttons to tap under the glare of the sun. "There's no message to say so. I'll call Da." She jabbed at the screen, held it to her ear, and waited, making no move to cross the road.

Jess waited beside her.

"Da? Me, Fran. I'm here in Ballyfortnum. Has there been any—" She broke off and cast a glance at Jess, who nodded encouragingly. *Go on.* "—well, anything unusual? Any trouble in the village there?"

As far as Jess could tell from the one-sided conversation, all was well in Abbeydare; still a perfectly Tidy Village; still expecting judges the next day, and completely untroubled by any vandalism or upset. Frances fell quiet as her father seemed to be asking a string of questions about why Frances wanted to know.

"Tell them to be vigilant," Jess said. "Especially tomorrow morning. It was all fine here until after you'd driven past on your way to meet us."

Frances relayed the message and, although her father was still speaking, cut the call short. "I'll take a couple of pictures; send them to him," she told Jess, as she angled her phone at the cottage, the pub, and back to the cottage. "That'll get him to pay attention."

"Are you allowed to judge your own village? Or is someone else going in your place?" Jess was quite sure Frances had already said, earlier in the day, that she would be going to Abbeydare with the other three judges, but Jess wanted to know how she felt about judging the place where she'd grown up, and where most of her family still lived, and where so many people knew her.

"Yes, it's always the same group of judges, to keep it consistent and fair. Aside from emergencies, of course, like Jim." She looked suitably sombre for a moment, pausing to cross the road before carrying on. "I do hope he'll make a quick recovery; that it's nothing too serious. But as I was already set to cover him for the whole week, nothing's changed, as far as I know." A cloud crossed her face and she wrinkled her brow into a frown. "I suppose I should be prepared to cover the next few weeks too." She shrugged. "I guess we'll have to wait and see what happens. "But—" Frances gave a weak laugh, lightening the moment. "To answer your question about whether I'm allowed to ... I'm quite good at being impartial. I have to be—I've eight siblings. That's enough to teach anyone how not to take sides! Look." She held her phone towards Jess, showing a screensaver of a laughing group of about a dozen people, all pulling daft faces at the camera. "We don't often all get together, these days, but this is the lot of us. Six boys; three girls. Callum's the youngest. He's eighteen. I'm the second one down." She didn't volunteer her age, but Jess would guess her to be about forty; maybe five or six years older than Jess. "It's a madhouse. Two lots of twins, too. Luckily my sisters are both teachers. That helps keep us in order." She smiled at Jess, then back at the photo. "Glad I didn't get the red hair most of the boys got! Only Chris and Callum missed it, and us girls."

Jess laughed too, thinking of Eric's Irish-orange curls, and of how often she and Eric had teamed up as a tight-knit twosome, and wondering if things would have been different if there had been more of them than just her, Eric, and older, aloof Alice. "I can't imagine having eight," she said. "I only have two, and taking sides got us all into trouble at times! Alice—that's my sister—hated me and Eric leaving her out, but she didn't want to join in with us either!" She wrinkled her nose in a flash of wistful sadness. How difficult Alice had been, back then.

Silence descending between them once more, the two women made their way up the church's driveway. Despite Frances's reassurance, Jess couldn't help but wonder whether it *would* be possible to remain impartial if your family and friends' village was entered for the contest you were judging.

And whether substituting one of the original judges with one who was local to one of the running favourites in the contest was entirely coincidental.

And whether Frances knew more about the vandalism than she was admitting.

She shook the thoughts aside. There was no way that Frances could have destroyed the planters or attacked Willie. She'd been in the car with the rest of them, on her way to the village hall, hadn't she? And then in the hall with the whole committee there. The damage hadn't been done until after the judges had passed through the village. It was simply not possible. Frances couldn't have been involved.

Whoever it was, they must have known who to watch for, though, and exactly when the window of opportunity was open.

Unless that, too, was just coincidental.

Big coincidence.

Far too many coincidences.

Jess watched enough of those TV mystery shows to know coincidences were *never* just coincidences.

"Actually," she said, as they stepped up to the open door of the parochial house, where the others were standing around talking, not yet gone inside to break the news of Jim's unexpected deterioration to Henry, Elizabeth, and Father James. "I should go and sort things out with everyone up at the farm, and see how Mrs Dunne is after the shock of the morning, and ..." She tailed off, letting the judges assume she had plenty of busy and important things to get on with. "I'm not really needed here, am I?" She looked hopefully at Lila, hoping her friend would realise that what Jess really wanted to do was to go and investigate.

Chapter Fourteen

J ess was almost at the shop when a large van passed her, screeched to a stop, reversed a little, and drew level.

"Jess? Why aren't you at the farm?" A tousled head of unruly curls bounced up and down in the driver's-side window, framing the petite, freckled face of Peggy McCaffrey from Parks and Wildlife.

Jess filled her in as economically as she could, although as Peggy was quite the talker, this still took longer than it needed to. "If you give me a few minutes to check in on Mrs Dunne, I'll come with you. And then you can drop me home after. I'm too knackered to walk. Was going to get Marcus up, but as he's still not called, I guess he's still dead to the world."

"Bad choice of words, knowing you," Peggy giggled. "But sure, you run on in and I'll wait here and—"

"Hang on." Jess cut Peggy off, holding up her hand. "I'll just be a minute." With that, she ducked into the shop; the little bell over the door announcing her arrival with a tinkle far more cheerful than Jess's mood.

Mrs Dunne, reinstated in her usual stance behind the shop counter with a romance novel propped open in front of her on top of the no-longer-tidy stack of weekly papers, seemed to have recovered well enough. She wasn't reading the book, but was deep in conversation with the only other customer in the shop: Colm Docherty.

Jess went straight to the counter to join them. "I came to check you're okay?" She turned her question from Mrs Dunne to Colm. "You too? I saw that most of the mess got cleaned up in the end. No traces of paint on the pub or here, anyway. Well done." She pointed to the shop windows, freshly-washed and gleaming in the sunshine. "We should replant the baskets; show them we won't be beaten. Whoever *them* might be. Any ideas, Mrs Dunne? You must have some ideas?"

Mrs Dunne rarely missed anything, but before the shopkeeper could answer, Jess swore and put her hand to her mouth. "Sorry. Just remembered I think Mrs Harris saw something and I forgot to ask her again. Sorry. Go on."

"Honestly, love, first I knew of it was when the feckers tossed paint on the glass. Didn't know what it was, I didn't. Thought a wee bird had flown at it or something. Went kind of darkish, and there was a bit of a noise. Nothing much, like, just as if something had tapped on the glass. But it stayed darker, not like if something just went by, you know? I was busy at the fridge, putting in the milk, round the other side." She gestured at the refrigerated unit, at the far end of the shop, opposite the window. A row of five-foot-high shelving piled with an assortment of everyday necessities from washing-up liquid to teabags to biscuits and cans of baked beans divided the wall with the fridge from the front of the shop, blocking the view of the window.

"And by the time I'd got around the shelves, there was all this red dripping down the glass but when I went to the door, there was no one in sight. Took me a fair minute to realise it was paint, that shocked I was. Couldn't think what it might be, not at first."

"Was it all over the window, or just a splash? Don't suppose you took a picture?"

Mrs Dunne shook her head. "Well now, love, while I stood there on the pavement, I saw the muck all over the ground, too, and I looked about to see what it'd come from, and weren't our beautiful window boxes and baskets all pulled apart and the flowers strewn all about the place and I was all of a fluster and I'd say I just stood there for a bit, not believing what I was looking at."

Jess nodded sympathetically. "I can imagine."

"I ran back in fast as you like, and picked up the phone, but I couldn't think who to call first. What with knowing what day it was, and the judges in the village already, and was it something to bother the Gards with or just a bit of *craic*, and I was all of a dither, I can tell you. Then a couple of the mammies from the school came in like they do most days after drop off, and said whatever was going on and the pub was just the same and they took whatever it was they'd come in for and I went out after them to see about the pub, and it weren't too long after that that word must have got about, and Billy White turned up to see was I all right, so he did."

Billy, according to Mrs Dunne, had been the one who'd taken charge of things. He'd sized up the damage and allocated jobs. Mick, who Jess had found on the chair when she'd called at the shop that morning, had been given the task of washing the paint from the shop windows, and another of Billy's farm labourers had been given the same job at the pub. Billy had set other villagers to gathering up the plants, and others to sweeping up the soil that the plants had left all over the pavement from the shop to the pub.

"Well done, Billy," Jess said.

"Aye."

"He's a good fella, is Billy White," Colm agreed. "Any news on how Willie's doing?"

Jess, surprised that Mrs Dunne's grapevine had no new update, was able only to share Mrs Harris's earlier report. "Stable but still out of it. But," she said, glancing towards the window, mindful of Peggy waiting outside on the road, "the judge who didn't come? Well he's got worse this afternoon. Also been moved to ICU. What are the chances, huh? There's a good few coincidences about what's gone on today, if you ask me. You must've heard *something*?" She directed this last question to Mrs Dunne. "You *always* know what's going on."

Mrs Dunne shrugged; her ample bosom jiggling up and down and rustling the papers on the counter. "Not a dicky bird. But I'd say if you come down for a carton of milk in the morning, there might be more news, eh love?"

Jess was halfway across the shop floor, heading for the door, when she spun on her foot. "You said you knew the judges were here already? I heard they'd come in? On their way to meet the committee?" She stood poised in her half-turn, waiting while Mrs Dunne sifted through the day's memories.

"Aye, love, they did that all right. Came in for some water, what with it being so hot. Only one of them came on in—Lydia what's-her-name, she's been here the last few years for it. Didn't see the others. Running a little late, she said, after collecting the new one at the junction." She gestured with her head towards the Dublin road. "Hadn't seen the point in her getting herself all the way into Dublin only to turn around and come back out again. Wonder why they didn't just have her drive herself all the way here, like?"

Jess didn't have an answer, but decided it may be worth finding out. If Frances hadn't travelled all the way from Dubin with the others, what had she been doing early that morning? Had she stayed the night in Abbeydare? And if so why? And why hadn't she mentioned it when Jess was asking her about Abbeydare that afternoon? There'd been countless times could have said she'd taken the opportunity to visit her family, since she had to be in the area anyway. It would've sounded perfectly reasonable. But *not* saying it? *That* was suspicious.

"Anyone else unusual come in today? Early on, I mean, before it all kicked off."

"No one who's not been in before, shouldn't think. The schoolchildren and their mams, or the mams without the children or just with the wee ones. A few passers, like always. Lads from the farms. People heading to work."

The bell over the door gave another cheerful tinkle as Jess stepped out into the sun, blinking in the brightness.

Peggy, ever-impatient, had already released the handbrake and had the van already rolling slowly forwards as Jess opened the passenger door and clambered in. "Come on! Sounds like we have a mystery to solve! Tell me everything you know!"

Chapter Fifteen

At the Dochertys' farm, Jess, Peggy, Anne and Matty sat in what they called the Docherty family called the Conservatory. Anne and Matty's parents lived in the adjoining white farmhouse, but over the years, some of the outbuildings had been converted to living space, and some wannabe architect in the family—no one seemed willing to admit to who exactly had been responsible for the monstrosity—had decided it would be a good idea to connect the spaces by building a large, glass-walled room between them. It was one of the ugliest extensions Jess had ever seen, but it was filled with enormous squishy sofas and rugs, and, from the inside, it was lovely. Anne lived in one of the converted outbuildings but Matty lived in a renovated cottage somewhere over the fields. As far from the rest of them as possible without leaving the farm, he'd once told Jess.

Peggy sat primly upright on the edge of one of the sofas.

Jess, with no such niceties, had kicked off her shoes and tucked her feet up beneath her at one end of a large Chesterfield, mirroring Anne's position at the opposite end.

Siobhan, according to Matty, had gone off to collect the reprobates. Jess looked at him blankly. "The what?"

"Her kids." Anne's nose wrinkled but her eyes were smiling. "She's bringing them back here. Be prepared."

Anne and Matty talked fast, to ensure Peggy was brought up to speed with the day's events before the children arrived, or, Jess thought with an inward smile, perhaps to stop Peggy talking so much they couldn't actually tell her anything. Peggy tended to talk in exclamation marks and questions and was whirlwind enough without adding three boisterous children to the mix.

As they talked, Jess, too, learned more about the state of the village that morning, and how the events had unfolded.

"Shuv will tell you this again, no doubt, but she was dropping the kids at school and someone—"

Peggy leaned forward. "Who was—"

"No—" Anne pre-empted Peggy's question and carried on. "I don't know who. I don't know many of the school mams. Someone told Shuv about the mess. So then she shoved her kids in at the gate and went straight over to find out what was happening, and—"

Outside, the dogs barked.

A minute or two later, there was the sound of a car on the gravel courtyard; the banging of car doors; louder barking; children's high-pitched chatter, and above all that, Siobhan's voice: "Shut up, you brats. Shut up."

The dogs quietened, but not the children, so Jess guessed Siobhan's yell had not been directed at her noisy offspring.

"You lot go off and play. Homework can wait."

The children stopped chattering for approximately half a second, then started again in a roar of mutual protest about something else.

"Well then go in and see if Auntie Mags will give you something. Ask her nicely, mind. You can do your homework at the kitchen table while you're at it. She won't mind. She was expecting you, anyway. Go on, the lot of you."

The door to the conservatory crashed open and Siobhan plonked herself heavily onto the sofa between Jess and Anne. "Fecksake," she said with a loud sigh. "I'm done in. Jess. Peggy." She nodded a greeting, kicked off her shoes, and swung her feet up onto the coffee table. "Anyone got the kettle on?"

Since everyone else in the room was holding a mismatched mug, the question needed no answer.

"Help yourself," Anne said, inclining her head to her own front door, behind the sofa Peggy and Matty shared.

"Oh go on," Siobhan wheedled, her voice not unlike that of her children as she turned puppy-dog eyes on Anne. "Grab one for me, won't you."

Anne sighed, swung her feet from the sofa and went off to do her cousin's bidding, muttering loudly about "just this once, if it shuts you up, but don't be expecting waitress service again you cheeky cow" as she left the room.

Siobhan, as Anne had predicted, immediately began to tell Jess and Peggy what had happened that morning, and while she repeated some of what Anne had just told them, Jess was happy to hear it again. Siobhan, she thought, was actually there. She'd have noticed things the others wouldn't. Or something that happened before the others got there.

"I was chinwagging with Joanna—Joanna Heron, that is—and Ger Brady came flying up to us at the gates talking nineteen-to-the-dozen and saying someone had trashed the place and the shop and pub were covered, just covered, in paint and it would never come off, and it was all over the road too—" She broke off and grinned at Jess. "Of course, it wasn't anywhere like that bad, but you know how it is. Everyone likes to be the bearer of bad news."

Jess laughed. Siobhan had exaggerated too, if Anne's message to Lila that morning was anything to go by. Although, to be fair, perhaps Siobhan was relaying the information she'd been given, and hadn't known the full details at that point.

"So I shoved the reprobates through the gate quick as, and went straight over to see for myself."

Jess smiled again as Siobhan used the same disparaging term for her children as Matty had. Judging by the noise the three children had made when they'd arrived, it might be well-deserved.

"And of course I saw the cottage first, with it being right there opposite, and with the flowers all pulled down from the front and all covered with paint like someone'd just tossed a can at it, and there were some of the mams standing around yapping, and none of them doing anything about it, just standing there gawking and gossiping like, but then someone said, 'Have you seen the pub?' so I left them to it and ran down there, and that's when I called you—" She waved a hand towards Anne, who'd just come out of her converted-stable apartment with a poppy-patterned mug in her hand, which she sat down in front of Siobhan.

"Here you are, your highness. You'll be making the next one."

Siobhan shot her cousin a look that was somewhere between thanks and a glare, and kept talking. "And I was talking to Anne and trying to suss what was going on, and people were beginning to get wind, cause Paddy was out in his boxers, God love him, and Mrs Dunne was out on the pavement looking at the state of her windows and I don't think she'd even clocked that the flowers were trashed, but she was speechless. Just standing there, speechless." Siobhan took a deep breath, picked up her tea, and looked first at Jess, then Peggy, to check they understood the importance of this. Mrs Dunne was *never* speechless.

"What did you do after you'd called Anne?" Jess asked, now Siobhan was sipping at her scalding tea and had stopped talking for a moment. "What I really want to know, is if anyone saw anyone—anyone actually *doing* it, or anyone acting oddly, or anything like that. Any cars no one recognised; any people no one recognised, that kind of thing?" She took another mouthful of her tea and looked at Siobhan. "You go first, because you were there first."

Siobhan, her initial excitement waned slightly, leaned back against the sofa, wriggled her toes on the coffee table, took another sip of her tea, and seemed to be deep in thought, replaying the morning in her head before she spoke again. "Okay," she said, after the pause. "So Mrs Dunne said the judges had been past already, because they'd stopped in for bottles of water. She didn't mention anyone else, so probably no one unusual, or she'd have said."

Anne and Jess nodded their agreement. Mrs Dunne *would* have said. Gossip was what she lived for.

"One of the mams out on the pavement said—just now, that is, when we were picking up the kids—a couple of cars had gone by as they were standing at the cottage. Everyone was talking about it. But she said they'd only slowed for a bit of a gawk, then gone on. The cars, I mean. One of the feckers had beeped and given them a bit of a wave, but that was all."

"What time does school start?" Jess asked.

"Nine," Siobhan and Anne answered together.

"But we'd be dropping them off anytime from, say quarter to, give or take," Siobhan added. "'til about five past, if you count the Hegartys. Everyone else would be there by nine. Doors open at five-to. Then there's sometimes a bit of chat at the gate, you know. Could stand around gassing till half past, on a good day. Others just drop 'em and run." She laughed, and nudged Anne with her elbow. "Got any biscuits?"

Anne glared at her and didn't answer.

Matty got up and went through the door to the main farmhouse, reappearing a minute later with a biscuit tin and a small boy. "Buns," he said, dumping the tin on the table. "And Ryan. While yous were all talking, some of us were thinking. If you want to know about cars, Ryan's your man."

Oh, yes, someone had said that earlier, Jess remembered with a flash. She studied the small boy in the scruffy school uniform, his red sweatshirt streaked with what might be mud, or ink, or grass stains, or heaven knows what. He had slightly crooked glasses, a smattering of freckles, ruffled brown hair, and dirt on his cheek.

"Can you tell us what cars went past the school this morning?" Matty asked. "In any direction, on either road, at any time from when you went outside until you went into your classroom."

Jess, impressed at how specific Matty was with his instructions, held up a hand. "Hang on a minute. Does anyone have pen and paper? We should write it down." She addressed the little boy directly. "Do you mind waiting just a minute while someone finds paper? Is it okay if I write down what you say?"

The boy looked back at her with a steady gaze. "Who are you?"

Jess introduced herself, and then, realising he probably didn't know Peggy either, introduced her too, as Matty went off into the farmhouse again, to hunt for pen and paper.

"I know you," Ryan said. "You have a red Toyota Corolla. Hatchback. It's a 2012. Why is your car so old?"

"I'm impressed," she said, acknowledging he was correct but choosing to ignore the question. Was her car old? She hadn't really thought so, but she supposed it was well past ten years now … "Do you know what car Peggy has?"

He stared at her as if *she* had just failed a test. "Easy. That big van with the Parks logo on the side. It's outside in the yard. If you don't know that you can't be very smart."

Jess's face warmed. Fair enough. Luckily she was saved by Matty returning with a sheet of paper and a pen. "Took it from Anna's copy," he told Siobhan. "She tore it from the back of the book. Hope that's okay."

"Bit late if it's not," his cousin retorted, pulling a face that reminded Jess of her own siblings. She must call them later. They'd love to be involved in this newest mystery.

Matty passed the sheet of stolen paper to Jess, and she plucked a tattered paperback with a creased-up cover from the coffee table to lean on.

"What time did you leave your house?" She asked Siobhan.

"'bout five-to, I should think. We were almost ready before that but then Anna remembered it was PE and Patrick had forgotten his snack." Siobhan looked hopefully at her son as she answered.

Her son gazed back at her, his eyes wide and owlish behind his glasses. "I was outside at ten-to. Only you were late because you had to keep running back in. You always do."

Siobhan sighed and prized open the lid of the biscuit tin. "He's right, of course. He's always ready and at the gate at ten-to, but there's always something someone hasn't got—"

"Not me."

"Not you." She threw him an indulgent smile. "Ryan," she said to Jess and Peggy, "is *never* late. And never forgets anything."

Jess cast an appraising look at the child. If any strange car or person had been anywhere near the school between about eight-fifty and nine o'clock that morning, she was confident this boy would know it. "Can you see that old cottage from your house?" she asked.

"You can't see it from the house, because it's blocked out by the fence," he told her, his voice solemn and serious.

"But you can see it from the gate." Siobhan said.

"You can see it from the gate," Ryan agreed.

"So while you were waiting for you mum, you could see the cottage?" Jess asked.

"Why do you say mum and not mam? Are you from England?"

Jess explained that she had lived in England when she was little, trying to keep her patience with him, even though she was desperate to hurry him along. "Can you tell me exactly what you could see from the gate this morning?"

"You're not a Garda. Why do you want to know? Is it about the vandalism? And the murder? Can I have one of those buns, Mam?" He pointed into the open tin, crammed with plain, un-iced cupcakes in paper cases.

"Yes, but just one. In a minute. And it isn't a murder. Willie's not dead—"

"He might die, though, like Uncle Thomas and Granda." He was matter-of-fact, not asking.

Siobhan ignored his comment, carrying on as if he hadn't interrupted. "And no, Jess isn't a Gard, but Mr Woo is her boyfriend."

Jess felt the blush spread over her face once more. She still wasn't used to thinking of Marcus as her boyfriend, although they'd been seeing each other for a while now. Besides, the term sounded so childish. Nonetheless, it seemed to appease the boy, and he turned to her with new interest.

He could, he said, see nearly all of the front of that old cottage, its big gates, and most of the front garden but not as far as its other gate. He said he'd once seen a fox jump over the wall even though it was already morning, and did she know that foxes are not really nocturnal as they are often out in the day. She said yes, and she sometimes saw foxes when she was out walking Fletcher, usually either early in the morning or when it was dusk, but then she worried they were getting sidetracked, and tried to steer him back to telling her what else he could see. "Can you see the pub, too?"

He could, but not so clearly as the cottage because of it being further away and because of looking at it through the school gates and the chainlink fence along the playground. He couldn't see the shop properly, as the trees from the church driveway got in the way. Overall, Jess deduced, while Ryan waited impatiently at his gate for his mum and siblings each morning, he had a reasonably good view of the stretch of road between the pub and the derelict cottage, including the start of the farm track that went down past Lila's and on towards the farm, and a blurred-by-trees-and-distance view to the shop. He could also see the entire frontage of the school grounds, which faced Siobhan's house, including its car park and much of its playground and playing fields.

"Except the bit behind the school," he added, unnecessarily.

"Of course," Jess agreed, matching his solemn tone.

And while Ryan waited at the gate each morning, he liked to watch cars.

He noticed cars more than people, Jess thought, as the boy kept talking. He was able to tell her exactly which of the teachers had already been in school before he left his house, and which only arrived with minutes to spare. He could tell which children had arrived early, and who had been dropped off by their dad instead of their mum—Harry and Aaron, apparently, and Fiona McGinty, not that Jess had any clue who Harry and Aaron or Fiona McGinty were.

"Do most children come by car?" she asked Siobhan.

"Half and half, I'd say. More when it's raining, 'cause they're lazy feckers who complain if they get wet. But the catchment area's quite big, so some are too far to walk."

"What we really need to know," Jess said, "is whether there were any *different* cars on that part of the road this morning."

Ryan, as she already knew from Lydia's earlier comment about the schoolchildren, had noticed the car the judges had arrived in. And what she really hoped was that he might have noticed another. Another car stopping in the village, and not just passing through.

"Do want me to tell you about all the vehicles, or just the cars?" he asked.

"All the vehicles, please."

As Ryan talked, she scribbled frantically on the scrap of paper, trying to keep up with him. He'd seen a total of fourteen vehicles that morning if you didn't count the ones already parked in the school carpark when he came outside, which belonged to the school staff, or the cars parked in his neighbours' driveways, which, Siobhan reminded him, all belonged to the people who lived there and weren't unusual or unexpected.

Of those fourteen, eleven were either bringing children to school or belonged to people who drove through the village most weekday mornings at around that time. Only three of the cars, he said, were different. One was the judges' Audi. Another was a silver Vauxhall Astra estate, and the last was a Massey Ferguson tractor belonging to Mr Geraghty but not driven by Mr Geraghty. This last, Ryan said, was different because he only saw it sometimes.

"How often is sometimes?"

Ryan was silent for a moment. "The last time I saw it was last Wednesday," he said, after thinking about it for a little while.

Jess put a circle around *silver Astra estate* and the Audi they knew belonged to Don. None of other vehicles seemed out of place.

Ryan put his hand into the biscuit tin and took out a cake, looking at his mother for her approval as he did so. She nodded at him.

"So," said Jess, "that's it. Just those two that were out of place."

"Did the Astra stop too, or just the Audi?"

"I didn't see the Astra stop. It didn't make the noise like it was slowing down, so it probably just kept going. And the two bikes might've stopped by the shop but I couldn't see past the trees so I don't know if they stopped or if they didn't," Ryan said, as he pulled the paper case from the cupcake and bit into it.

Chapter Sixteen

"Bikes?" Anne said, voicing everyone's question.

Bikes, thought Jess. Bikes would be quiet, and quicker than walking, and could be hidden behind walls or trees or fences. Bikes.

"Two bikes. After the car that was last—Emma's mam's blue Focus. And then Miss opened the doors and we went in, so I didn't see any more after that."

"You mean bicycles?" she asked, for clarification. "Not motorbikes?"

He nodded, spilling cake crumbs down the front of his sweatshirt.

"Do the doors get opened at nine?" She looked to Siobhan for confirmation.

"Pretty much bang on five to nine, actually," she said. "A minute either side, no more. Stickler for time-keeping, that one."

Jess wasn't sure who 'that one' was, but suspected it could be the principal of the school, Mrs Byrne. Rumour had it she only held the position of principal because her father had been the principal previously, and not because she deserved it or worked for it. "So at some time between ten to nine and nine o'clock, you saw two bicycles?" she asked Ryan. "Where were they, exactly?"

The bikes had come from the direction of the Dublin road, Ryan said, but he did wonder why they were on the wrong side of the road when he saw them. He wasn't so confident about the accuracy of this as they'd been going in by then, and everyone was bundling through the door at once even though Miss always said to them to line up and walk in properly but no one ever did except him.

He huffed as if he were a much older man, tired of being the only rule-follower, and weary of the chaos of the world.

Jess felt a sudden pang of sympathy for this serious, observant child who seemed as if he might be a little out of place among his classmates. She knew how that felt, having suffered years trying to fit in after her parents had uprooted the O'Malley siblings from their schools in England to drop them into secondary school in a new town in new country. Despite having been born in Ireland, Jess's English childhood had left her sounding different from her Irish-Irish classmates, and not part of any pre-formed cliques. School was tough enough, and even worse if you didn't fit in.

"Thank you," she told the boy, smiling at him. "You're really observant. I'll tell Marcus! He might even want you to tell him, too."

Ryan flashed her a quick smile. "Can I go now?"

"Do you want another one?" His mum lifted the tin and offered him a second cupcake.

"Really?"

"Really. As a reward for helping. Take one for your brother and sister, too."

Hands full of cupcakes, Ryan disappeared back into the farmhouse, presumably to finish his homework under the supervision of his great aunt Mags.

"He's not always a reprobate." Siobhan sounded wistful as she watched the door her son had just gone through, as if she could still see him. "He must've been inside the school at about five-to. They were opening the doors just as we crossed the road, so he wasn't late at all. He always goes straight in. He's never *actually* late." She said this with a glare towards the closed farmhouse door, as if Ryan had unfairly accused her of something, but a giveaway twitch of her mouth took any real crossness out of the look.

Jess remembered something else he'd said. "What was that about the little gate?" she asked, looking from Siobhan to Anne to Matty. "He said he can see the big gates but not the little gate?"

"And," said Peggy, who'd been uncharacteristically quiet as the others had been talking, "something else isn't adding up."

Forgetting her own question for the minute, Jess turned to Peggy, who was no longer sitting demurely upright but was jiffling impatiently on the edge of the sofa as if she'd been bursting to speak. She probably had, Jess thought, biting back a smile at thought of chatterbox Peggy not managing to get a word in. Perhaps she'd only been quiet because she didn't know the Dochertys very well. Although that didn't usually stop her. "Go on, you go first. I can't believe you've been quiet for this long. You must be busting to talk!"

Peggy turned to face Siobhan. "Well, if your son saw the judges go by at about ten to nine, but someone came and told you about the mess before nine, that only leaves less than ten minutes for someone to have done all that, conked that poor fellow over the head, disappeared off out of sight, all while the village was at its busiest, with all the schoolchildren arriving and all the mams out gossiping at the school gates in full view of the pub and that cottage? Doesn't seem likely to me. You wouldn't, would you? Do all that while so many people were around? Oops." Peggy, who tended to wave her hands about as she talked, almost sent her mug flying from the edge of the sofa. She caught it, drank whatever was left, and continued, arms still flapping like a butterfly's wings against a window. "Even if there was the time, which I'm not sure about either. Could you pull up all those flowers, throw paint on three different buildings, and pull all that ivy and stuff off the cottage all in ten minutes? How long would it take to walk from the shop to the cottage? And how many of the school mams would've still been walking along there at that time?"

Jess held her hand up again. "Blimey. But slow down. Let's go through those one at a time." She looked around at the others. "How long from shop to cottage? Walking? About five minutes, not even?"

Siobhan nodded. "It's only five minutes to the shop from mine. Close enough. Two, three mins, I should think."

"If you're just walking normally," Anne agreed.

Jess tried to walk it in her mind, imagining Fletcher stopping to sniff at every opportunity, or pee up a wall or lamppost. "A bit longer if you're meandering. Walking a dog; chatting? But still no more than five, I shouldn't think."

"But pulling up flowers and throwing paint?" Matty said. "And it was aimed, wasn't it, not just thrown roughly at the buildings as someone ran by."

It was true. The paint on the shop and pub had been mostly over the windows, with only a small amount of splatter hitting the walls.

"Was the paint poured onto the road or just splashes?" Jess asked. By the time she'd got there, the paint on the roads had been mostly washed away. Someone, or several someones, had thrown buckets of water over it, and brushed the whole mess into faint pinkish streaks, a few soapy bubbles, and puddles of pink water drying rapidly as the sun rose higher in the sky.

"Splashes, I'd say." Matty looked at his sister and cousin for confirmation.

Both nodded slowly.

"Yeah, splashes," Siobhan said. "Like if you threw something at something and most of it got where you wanted it to—"

"Like on the windows," Matty said.

Siobhan nodded. "—and then just a bit of it dribbled around as you threw it."

"So like someone's taken the time to be kind of careful about where they are throwing it." Jess nodded slowly, scribbling hurried notes on the other side of the paper. "Okay, what were the other things you just said?" She waved the pen towards Peggy, hoping she'd be succinct and not go through the whole convoluted spiel again.

"Well, the timing is off. For two reasons. Like we just said, to do all that in just ten minutes is pushing it, I'd think, but then there's all the people. How many at the school?" She threw the question towards Siobhan.

"Seventy-two children. Three teachers. Two SNA. One part time secretary."

Jess stared at her, impressed. "You just reeled that off without even thinking about it. What's SNA?"

Siobhan shrugged. "I'm on the Parents' Group, and special needs assistant. Two of them."

"Committee," Anne said, catching Jess's fresh confusion as Siobhan said 'Parents' Group'.

"Oh. Okay. I think Bel's on that, actually, for Bry and Clara. My sister-in-law, and nieces," she added, as it was Siobhan's turn to look confused. "And you said about half of them walk? So there'd be about ..." She tried to do the maths. "Thirty-six walking and thirty-six in cars. Ish. Thirty-something cars and sixty-something people walking about? Blimey! I wouldn't have thought Ballyfortnum was that busy in the mornings. What?" She looked up as Matty let out a loud laugh.

Siobhan, Peggy, and Anne seemed to share his amusement, all laughing at her as she stared at them in bewilderment.

"Is my maths that bad? Half seventy-two is thirty-six, isn't it?"

"Jess," Siobhan spoke to her as if she might speak to a toddler. "Most of the families round here don't just have *one* child. There are four of the Gallaghers, for instance. One mam walking them along, from further on down past my house, not four mammies. I have three. Children, I mean, not mammies. One mam for my three, though God knows I'd give them away to another one, most days."

"Oh. Yeah." Jess laughed too, and tried to recalculate, giving up and shaking her head. "Okay, how many families, roughly?"

This time, Siobhan did need time to think about it. She began to use her fingers, counting soundlessly but mouthing the names as she went through each family in the school. "About thirty-three, maybe. Something like that."

"So half that," Anne said. "Say about fifteen parents walking; fifteen in cars."

"And they don't all go through the village. Most do, though. Think there's only me, Gallaghers, O'Sullivans—Charles and Isobel, that is, not the other ones ... the other O'Sullivans would come through the village all right ... erm ... Herons ... think that might be it, who come up my road."

"Johnsons?" Matt said.

"Oh, yeah, and them. Can't think of any more, can you?" She looked at her cousins, but both looked blank, shaking their heads in slow unison.

"Even so," Peggy said, "That's still around thirty parents in the right place at the right time to have seen someone throwing paint around or trashing the plants, or thirty parents *and* all seventy-two kids if it happened before school started." She held out her hands, palms upwards, as if to say, 'Here you are, here's your problem'. "And it's not likely *no one* would see a thing, even if everyone was rushing or chatting or looking at their phones, I wouldn't think, would you? So we're what? Looking for an invisible man?"

Everyone laughed, but the laughter was muted and died away as quickly as it had started, as they fell silent to consider Peggy's words. She was right. It didn't add up.

Jess turned to Siobhan. "Might Ryan have got the times wrong?"

"That wouldn't change things," Peggy said, flapping her hand again. "I don't think it's him can be wrong. You also said the judges arrived at the hall at nine, as expected, right?"

Jess nodded. Maeve had announced the time at five-to, and said they were late, and Father James had said hardly, and they'd arrived not very long after that. "It must've been almost bang on. Definitely no later, anyway, so all that fits with what Ryan said."

Matty peered over the edge of his mug at his cousin. "Ryan doesn't get things wrong. Sounds to me like Shuv's got it wrong. Wouldn't be the first time, eh Shuv." He smirked at his cousin, set his mug on the coffee table, and got up. "I suppose I'd better go do some farming. Someone round here has to do something. Da's out in the barn looking at that cow," he said to no one in particular, and left the room by the door that led outside into the courtyard.

"Come to think of it, I probably did get it wrong." Siobhan, once again, was counting on her fingers. "I guess it was a bit after the kids'd gone in that Ger came running over and said about it all. Come to think of it, I'd say me and Joanna had moved over and were talking outside my gate, not at the school, because she said she'd give me hand with shoving the kids' toys round the back out of sight. God only knows how they got so many out when I only put them away last night." She closed her eyes, thinking for a moment. "So, yeah, I'd shoved the kids through the gates in a rush all right, but that's because I wanted to get back and check the garden was straight, before the judges came around, and then I got chatting with Jo, and she followed me back, and ..." She tailed off as she worked it out silently in her head. "So we were at mine when Ger came over all in a flap. And Jo came with me, when I went to look. Probably more like ten past, so. Everyone else was gone, by then. If they don't stop to chat, they dump and run, 'specially the ones who come in cars. Most don't even get out."

Anne raised her eyebrows at Siobhan and stared at her pointedly. "You and Jo? Only chatting for ten minutes?"

Siobhan ducked her head. "Hmm. S'pose you're right. Let's say quarter past, then, max."

Anne snorted into her tea. "What time did you call Lila? What time did you call *me*?" She picked her phone from the table and scrolled for a few seconds. Nine twenty-four. You called me at nine-twenty-four. So, let's say four minutes for you to run over the road with Ger Brady, take in what had happened, and call me. That widens the window until about nine-twenty, starting from when the judges went through the village at round about ten to nine. They can't have been sooner than that, or Ry wouldn't've seen them, and not much later, if he'd gone in by five-to."

"And they got to the village hall by nine anyway," Jess reminded them.

"So," said Peggy, almost bouncing on the edge of her seat. "That gives more like thirty minutes, but we should still knock off the first ten, while parents were still throwing their kids in at the school. Still a very tight window, to do all that damage.

Wonder how long yer man'd been lying there, before you found him? You think he was hit first, or after?"

Jess shrugged. "Dunno. And we also need to consider that maybe *he* did it, and then someone clobbered him because they caught him, so we could be looking at two different crimes—two different people?"

The room fell silent, then Anne and Siobhan both spoke at once:

"Don't be daft."

"He wouldn't."

Jess shrugged again. "Seems unlikely, I know, but it's not impossible, is it?" The two Dochertys stared at her in much the same way Ryan had stared at her when she'd asked him about Peggy's van. Her face burned. "All right, all right." She suddenly remembered that no one had answered her other question. "The gate? Tell me about the gate." A fuzzy image was forming in her mind. Many of these bungalows with wide gardens had a double gate for vehicle access, and a separate, smaller, pedestrian gate, often lined up with the front door of the house. Had she somehow missed an entire gate when she'd looked around the property. "I only really looked at the back," she said aloud, to identical confused looks from Peggy, Anne, and Siobhan.

"I took photos. Of the bit behind the cottage," she explained. "While I was waiting for the ambulance to get there. Willie was out cold, so I couldn't do a lot for him, once he was in the recovery position. But I stayed round the back with him. I didn't really look at anything at the front. Marcus was talking to people there, I think?"

"Yeah, there were a few of us on the pavement all right," Siobhan said. "We'd been talking in the garden, at first, but he made us get out onto the pavement. In case we were trampling over anything important, I suppose. And yes, there is another gate. You wouldn't notice it, these days. It used to lead to a nice little orchard, back in the day. It's all overgrown with ivy and the like—oh!" She put her fingers to her lips. "I'll bet that's where a lot of the roses and ivy lying in the road and on the pavement had come from, come to think, because when we were stood there yacking, the gate *was* visible. Or least, the gate post was, because I leaned against it when we were talking. It's further along, in front of the old orchard. I bet if we went and looked, it would be all uncovered."

"You don't know if it was open?" Jess asked.

Siobhan shook her head. "Can't say, for sure. I'd be guessing. I'll look on the way home, if you like."

Jess scribbled a note on the edge of the page: *Check gate*. She considered texting Marcus about it, but decided he'd already know—his team must've searched the whole property by now. Probably trampled every inch of it. She wondered what he was up to. Had he managed to get some sleep, or was he still caught up with the investigation? She yawned, trying at first to hold it, but with little success. Suddenly exhausted and with tears threatening in that way they sometimes did ever since her dad had died, she just wanted to get home, curl up on the sofa, and have a nap. Preferably with Marcus there to lean on. She yawned again.

"I think I need to get home. Will you give me that lift?" she asked Peggy. "If any of you still want the tea-and-scones part, there'll be plenty of it on offer. I expect the judges have gone by now; I doubt they had any, in the end. Unless they just sat about eating scones all afternoon, which I suppose is as good as anything to do on a day like this."

Chapter Seventeen

Peggy chattered away in the driver's seat as she drove like a bat out of hell towards Orchard Close. Peggy's driving, like the way she talked, was filled with rapid movements and exclamations.

Jess only half-listened. Peggy never seemed to leave space for anyone to answer, anyway. Jess wiggled to get her phone from the back pocket of her jeans and texted Marcus: *Where are you now? I'm headed home. You ok? Xx* She watched the screen for a bit, hoping he'd reply, but instead, it faded to black. She brought it back to life. *I miss you,* she told him in a second text.

"Sorry your day got messed up," she said to Peggy as they pulled into Orchard Close. "I'd say come in, but honestly, I think I'm about to fall asleep. Marcus is back at work on Friday, so let's have a takeaway night? I'm going to see if Alice wants to come down for the weekend, but she'll be happy to see you, so that won't matter."

"Friday's good and it'll be grand to see Alice ..."

Jess pushed open the passenger door and jumped to the ground, shutting the door with Peggy still talking. "See you Friday!" Jess called, as Peggy pulled away from the curb and manoeuvred the large NPWS van through a swift three-point turn where the end of the close widened out, in front of Sean's and Gary's house, swerved around Marcus's car, parked on the side of the road, beeped and waved, and drove away.

Oh good, he's here. Tears prickled Jess's eyes as the emotion of the day caught up with her. She wiped them away with the back of hand and let herself in. She kicked of her shoes as she fended off the full-on force of Fletcher's greeting, bent to give Snowflake a rub, and sent them ahead of her into the living room, where she found Marcus dozing on the sofa. "You can't have been asleep," she said, "not with Fletch making all that noise." She bent to hug him and he pulled her down for a kiss. "Also, how come you're here?"

"I woke up. Thought you might be caught up with things still, and the dogs might need to get out. I guess I fell asleep again." He rubbed his eyes, yawned, and stretched, giving Jess her second glimpse of his midriff that day as his crumpled T-shirt rose an inch or so. Not the same blood-stained shirt he'd had on earlier, or the replacement she'd given him through the Mini window either. "I really need to wake up; check how they're getting on. I guess Kev and John were still there, in the village? And don't bother to pretend you don't know; I know you'd have looked."

As he yawned again, so did she, and she sank down onto the sofa beside him to rest her head on his shoulder and close her eyes. "You might need to wake up, but I need a nap. And actually, no, I came back with Peggy. I didn't look that way ... she was—"

"Talking?" He laughed and pulled her in for another long hug. "I'll make you a cup of tea. You mightn't have seen John or Kev but I presume you have been snooping about. Have you discovered who did it?"

She pulled a face at him. "Have you?"

They grinned at each other like soppy teenagers, and burst into laughter.

"No," he said reluctantly, as she stared him out.

"Me neither. Make that tea? We'll talk after. If I haven't fallen asleep by then." She lifted her feet onto the empty space he'd left on the sofa, rested her head on the arm, and closed her eyes again, half-listening to the sounds of him clattering about in the kitchen, telling the dogs to go away, stop getting under his feet, shutting the French door—presumably with the dogs on the outside of it—getting cups from the cupboard, opening the fridge, closing the fridge...

When Marcus shook her gently awake, the first cup of tea had gone cold, and the house smelled deliciously of turmeric and fried onions. He set a fresh cup of tea in front of her, and said, somewhat redundantly, that he was making curry, would that do?

"Of course. Thank you. What time is it?" She groped on the floor for her phone. "Oh!" She'd been asleep for almost an hour. "Shite. Sorry." She sat up, swung her legs to the floor, and opened the first of several text messages she'd missed. "Father James says Mrs Harris says no update on Willie still?"

"No, I've had nothing new either. They've promised to let us know as soon as he wakes."

"If," Jess said, holding Marcus's gaze for a moment.

"If," he agreed. "The longer he stays unconscious ..." He let the thought tail off, but she knew the longer Willie took to come round, the worse his chances of recovery.

"You do think he'll be all right?" she said, an edge of desperation in her voice as she gazed into Marcus's deep, brown eyes, hunting for reassurance she knew he couldn't give.

He stroked her hair back from her forehead. "Let's hope so."

"Have you tried to see him? Have you been back into town?" She shook her head, answering her own question. "Of course not. You wouldn't have had time."

"In Dublin? Even if he was conscious—"

Jess let out a gasp of surprise. She hadn't realised they'd moved him to Dublin. That was never a good sign. "When did they move him?"

"Soon enough. I think he was only in Lambskillen for an hour or so. Since he didn't show any sign of coming round, they took him off to St James's almost straight away. Someone will go in to him as soon as he wakes up."

If he does, Jess thought again, but didn't say it. "Mrs Harris knows someone who was looking after him. I wonder if that was in Dublin or Lambskillen. 'Our Betsy works in ICU', she said."

"Dublin, then," Marcus said. "He never got past A and E in Lambskillen. Not even sure they took him off the ambulance."

"Funny, that's where the judge is, too. The one who got sick and couldn't come. He just got moved into the ICU this afternoon. Bit of a coincidence."

"Mm. Bit."

"Marcus," Jess said, in the tone she used when she wanted something from him. "Have you found any clues?"

"You sound like Bryony!"

Jess's oldest niece was eight, and, in large part due to encouragement from Jess and Eric, loved mysteries almost as much as her aunt and father. Once, when Eric and his family had come to visit, Bryony had been so disappointed to find that nothing exciting had happened that Jess had thought up a daft mystery story involving Fletcher, Snowflake, and a missing Dalmatian. Then they'd ended up having to go off for a walk along the road towards the river, just to check if the Dalmatian that lived on that road was safe in his garden, after

Jess's younger niece, Clara, had burst into tears imagining the worst.

Luckily, the Dalmatian had been bouncing around his garden, very much alive and not made into a fur coat, and all was well in the end. "Another mystery solved," Eric had said, as Bryony had explained, quite seriously, over the garden wall to the Dalmatian's stunned owner that they thought the dog had been victim of Cruella de Vil's sewing machine and were very pleased he hadn't been.

"Can I pat him?" she'd asked. "Just to make sure."

Jess smiled at the memory, and stuck her tongue out at Marcus. "I do not. Actually, you reminded me, I must text Eric. But have you? Found anything useful, I mean?"

Marcus turned away, heading back to the delicious smells wafting from the kitchen. "You know I wouldn't be able to tell you if I had."

She frowned at his receding back and turned her attention back to her phone. Instead of texting Eric, she texted Siobhan. *Hi. Can you ask Ryan if he saw Willie Keegan at all this morn? Jess x*

As soon as she'd sent it, she remembered the other thing she'd wanted to ask. *Also, did you get a chance to look at that gate?*

Siobhan's reply was instant and included both a message and a photo. *Will ask him.*

As Jess opened the photo, a second one arrived. The first photo was of a small, rusted gate, made of twisted metal that seemed to have once been painted white. The second was a wider shot of the front of the cottage, which Siobhan had annotated with a large orange arrow pointing to the same small metal gate. The wider shot placed the little gate at the righthand side of the image, to the side of the cottage with the copse of straggly old fruit trees behind it. The gate wasn't fully open, but also not closed; maybe a space of about six inches, as if someone had pulled it shut, but not made sure it was properly closed or taken the time to fasten the catch. Some strands of greenery were caught in the bars of the gate, but, as Siobhan had suggested, the gate post nearer the house had been cleared of the foliage that covered its twin. Jess was almost certain she'd never noticed this second gate before, despite having given that house a lot of attention in the past few weeks in the lead up to the Tidy Towns contest as it had been a bone of contention amongst the committee members.

Well, she corrected the thought, *Maeve. It was a bone of contention to Maeve. The rest of us thought it was okay.* Lila had told her they had the same conversation every year, and she didn't know why Maeve got so worked up by it. "No one's going to lose points over one derelict cottage in a village this pretty," she'd said. "Find me a village in Ireland that hasn't got a derelict or two. You won't. I'd put Dom's Harley on it."

Lila's husband didn't have a Harley. He may have looked the part of a serious heavy-metal band member crossed with the most stereotypical of Hell's Angels, but the Harley was nothing more than a longed-for wish. It was, however, true that any village in Ireland had a good few abandoned houses. People built new houses on the same land, and didn't bother to knock down the old ones. Jess never had worked out why you'd go to the trouble of building a lovely new house on your land, and then look out over an abandoned, falling-down eyesore you could have easily knocked down when the building work was going on, but it would never be a problem she'd have. The neat semi-detached houses in Orchard Close hardly had room for a dog kennel in their front garden, never mind a whole derelict cottage.

Jess brought up the first photo again, zooming in to make the gate bigger, then working her way around the image, enlarging different areas. Where the gate had been forced open, the grass was shorter, but perhaps whoever had cut the grass in the front garden had continued on behind the gate, so she couldn't tell if the grass was flattened from the gate being pushed open, or just short from being cut.

"Marcus," she called through to the kitchen, "did you or anyone look all round that cottage? Like at the far side, away from the gate we went through to get to the sheds? Like around the bit where the fruit trees are."

"Should think so," he called back, his voice muffled by the sizzling and burbling from the kitchen. "Not me, but Kev or John should've. Why?"

"Bikes. Did they see any sign of bikes?"

There was a clatter and a splash and the sound of the tap running then stopping. Marcus appeared in the kitchen doorway. "Bikes? Why? Oh, hang on!" He turned abruptly and disappeared back into the kitchen.

She sighed and tore herself off the sofa, picked up her tea, padded into the kitchen, and sat on one of the kitchen chairs.

Marcus tore a couple of sheets of kitchen paper off the roll and dabbed at the spill of water on the hob where the rice pan had boiled over.

"Sorry, I shouldn't've distracted you. I had a thought. I'll tell you when you've done that." She yawned, and finished her tea in silence while Marcus stirred things and added things to the other pan, and stirred things some more, then came to stand behind her chair and wrap his arms around her.

He rested his chin on her head. "Okay, Sherlock, what have you got for me this time?"

"Siobhan's son—he's eight and has a thing about cars—he said he saw two bikes near the cottage at about ten to nine. And, well, I wonder if they went through that gate. The little one, I mean, that I just asked you about. And whether the reason no one saw any strange cars—actually he did see a strange car too, but it didn't stop anywhere, not where he could see, at least—is that whoever did this came on bikes?"

Marcus tightened his arms as he held her, and the weight of his chin pressed into her head. He said nothing, which was a sure sign he was thinking it through. Taking her suggestion seriously. Sure enough, a moment later he relaxed the hug, dropped a kiss where his chin had rested, and stepped out onto the patio, his phone in his hand.

Any second now, he'll start pacing. He always paced when he called the station.

With the French doors still open, Marcus's side of the conversation drifted into the kitchen, fading in and out as he walked first towards her, then away again, but the gist of it was that someone, whoever that might be, should check for signs of bikes beside the cottage. "Maybe not actual bikes, but tyre marks in the ground, a bike-wheel-width trail through the grass, that kind of thing," he said, turning away and striding towards Sean's fence again.

Jess sat up straighter. A bike trail? Not narrow tyre tracks in muddy ground—the ground was far too dry for that, but perhaps a narrow path of flattened grass. A narrow path of flattened grass like the narrow path she'd thought was from a fox?

"And Kev," Marcus said into his phone as he came towards the door again, "Can you pop round to Siobhan Docherty and ask if you can talk to her son?" He directed Kev to Siobhan's house and told him to ask Ryan about the cars and bikes he'd seen. "See if you can get a description of the cyclists." He stopped outside the open French doors, and disconnected the call.

"Kev's the one who's been up at the cottage all day?" Jess asked. "Lounging against the car looking bored? Playing

Candy Crush or something, poor bloke." She knew it wasn't John—she'd met John before, and he was older than the Garda she'd seen outside the cottage earlier.

Marcus laughed. "Sounds about right. He'll be delighted to get away and talk to someone. He'll be heading off soon anyway. No point him standing there all night."

"Is John up there too? I didn't see him."

John, Marcus said, had been the unlucky one who'd got to wander around the village asking questions all day while Kev lounged against the car and Marcus had a nap. He glanced at the clock on the kitchen wall. "They'll go on home after this. Shifts end at five so they'll already be on overtime by the time they get back to the station and clock off."

"They'll let you know if they find anything, though?"

He smiled at her indulgently and shook his head slowly, like a parent might look at a child asking what their Christmas present is. "They might, if they find something important, but that doesn't mean I'll tell you."

All right, Detective Woo, she thought, as he went back to the stove, *I'll do my own find-outing.* "Did you take the dogs out?"

He hadn't. He'd let them out, then fallen asleep, then started on dinner while she'd fallen asleep.

"Shall I, while you're cooking?" Listen to me sounding like the epitome of domestic bliss, she thought, but the idea of domestic bliss with Marcus made her stomach flip. In a good way. They were good together. Everyone said it. Alice and Eric and Belinda and Bryony and Clara all adored him, and so did she.

Five minutes later, Jess and Snowflake walked leisurely towards Maeve's house.

Fletcher, incapable of doing anything sensibly, did his best to trip her up until she gave in to his idiocy and unclipped his lead as soon as they'd turned the corner onto Maeve's road, which was quieter than the main road through Ballyfortnum and had wide grassy verges.

"All right! But stay close and come back if I call you."

Fletcher lolloped up onto a grassy bank in front of one of the houses and found something to sniff at.

"Fletch! Don't go in the gates or I'll have to put your lead back on."

Snowflake trotted daintily beside Jess as if he hadn't even noticed she'd taken off his lead.

At Maeve's she clipped the leads on again and tied the two dogs to the gate, just as she'd done twenty-four hours earlier. "Feels like that was weeks ago," she told the dogs. "You sit there quietly and wait. Won't be long."

Maeve was wielding a trowel at a flower border as if the garden might explode into jungle-like anarchy if she neglected to watch it for even a second. She frowned as she saw Jess, then smiled, although sometimes with Maeve it was hard to tell the difference. She set the trowel down and got to her feet.

"I needed to walk the dogs anyway, so I thought I'd check that you're okay after all that earlier," Jess said.

"Of course I am. Why wouldn't I be?"

"It was all a bit ... well, a bit *unplanned*."

Maeve put her gardening gloves down on the porch wall. "Yes," she said, with a frown, "I suppose it was, wasn't it. I do so hate it when things don't go to plan."

Jess hid a smile behind her hand. "I wondered if you'd heard any more about Jim? Do you know what it was? You know, what ..."

"No, no one managed to get hold of Helena. You'd think with all this technology, these smartphone yokes, you'd think ... He took ill at the weekend. Some kind of reaction to something he ate, Helena told Patrick. After the meal. Bad case of vomiting and diarrhoea." Maeve huffed as if it was entirely his own fault he'd eaten something that had caused an upset. "Sent him in for rehydration, as it was so bad, but he was on the mend, we thought. He'd asthma, too, but he had all that under control, I believe. Didn't rush about or do the kind of exercise that would trigger an attack; that sort of thing. And he always carried one of those what do you call thems?" She huffed again.

"An inhaler," Jess said, trying not to smile at Maeve's indignant attitude to someone having any kind of illness. She bet Maeve was never sick.

"Yes, one of those. And he was perfectly all right. It didn't stop him doing what he wanted. He was a very good judge. Anyway, we really can't speculate. You know how these rumours get out of control, once people start speculating." She huffed again, then gathered herself. "He's a lovely man." She sniffed, and Jess was startled to realise Maeve's eyes were damp and glistening. "A lovely man." She turned away suddenly and dabbed her eyes on the short sleeve of her blouse. It was the same blouse she'd been wearing that morning, yet it was still as crisp and unlined as if she'd just plucked it from an ironing board.

However does she do it? "It has all been such a terrible shock," she said, and this time, when she reached out her hand to gently pat Maeve's shoulder, the woman let her.

After a moment, she took a deep breath, turned back to face Jess, and said, "And he should have recovered easily, on the IV whatsit." Her tone trembled just a fraction, and Jess sensed anger as much as sadness in Meave's words. "We thought he was going home."

"Well, as you say, it may not be as bad as they think."

"Let's hope so, Jessica. Let's hope so."

As Jess turned to go, another thought hit her. "Is he in St James's?"

"Yes. Why do you ask?"

"Oh, no reason, really. Just Marcus just said that's where they've taken Willie Keegan."

Maeve harrumphed and nodded sharply. "Tough as boots is Willie. He'll be all right, he will." And with that, she picked up her gardening gloves and snapped them on. "I'd best get on. We'll talk it through at the committee meeting. See you tomorrow."

Jess had forgotten. "See you tomorrow, Maeve. I just wanted to check you were okay."

Maeve smiled again, raised a hand to wave goodbye, and went back to her trowel and kneeling pad, and Jess headed for home with two conflicting thoughts arguing in her mind:

Maeve seemed genuinely concerned about Jim and Willie and upset and angry about the attack on the village.

Maeve had said several times she was fed up with the contest and it was time to think about stopping it.

"Don't be daft, Jess," she said aloud as they neared the corner of the road. "Maeve was there in the hall with us when the damage was done, so it can't possibly have been her."

Chapter Eighteen

J ess and Marcus spent the rest of Tuesday evening lazily curled up together on the sofa watching McDonald and Dodds, a favourite of Jess's, and tolerated by Marcus, who only occasionally muttered something along the lines of "They'd never do it like that, not in real life."

"I'm going to invite Alice for the weekend," Jess said, as a dark-haired character called Alice sauntered onto the screen. "That's reminded me." She fired off a text while DC Dodds made his usual seemingly clumsy attempts at interrogating the girl. "He's onto something," she said to Marcus, nodding at the television. "He always is. He's not as bumbling as he pretends."

Marcus grunted non-committedly.

"You'll see." Jess typed out a second text—*How're you? Wathcing McD+Dodds and thought of you. Seems like there's another mystey brwing here, but at least this tiem no one's dead. At elast not yet. Love to girls xx*—and sent it to her brother, only noticing the typos as she hit the SEND button. "Ah well," she said to Marcus, "he'll work it out. If he can't, he's no place in the Lollipop Club."

Marcus ruffled her hair. "Jess. Leave it to the Gards."

She nudged her elbow into his side, ignored his advice, and texted Siobhan, deciding against asking Marcus first whether eight-year-old Ryan had been able to give a description to Kev. If she didn't ask, he couldn't tell her not to ask.

Siobhan's answer pinged in almost immediately. *Feck all use – R's good with cars but shite at people - Men. Hats. Bikes. Tell Marcus good luck with making THAT identikit!!!*

Not even what kind of hats? Jess texted back.

Not even xx

Jess rolled her eyes at the phone, put it down, snuggled against Marcus, and got stuck into McDonald and Dodds and their onscreen mystery, which was looking like it would be far easier to solve than the mystery of who vandalised Ballyfortnum and put Willie Keegan in hospital earlier that morning.

Wednesday was a college day for Jess, but that wasn't the only reason she was up so early. She let the dogs out with a promise that Marcus would walk them properly later, and took him a cup of tea in bed.

"You're bright and organised this morning? What's wrong?" he said, shuffling up the bed to sit against the headboard and take the mug from her.

"Nothing, just woke early," she lied, a blush warming her neck. She never willingly got up early if there was even half a chance Marcus would go down and make the tea first.

"You're up to something."

"Gotta go, see you this eve. You'll take the dogs out, yeah?" She stooped to kiss him, taking the tea from his hands and setting it on the bedside table so she could give him a proper cuddle, almost tempted to abandon her plan and snuggle back in for another half hour. Almost.

She dropped one last kiss on his forehead, grabbed a thick hoodie from the chair even though the day already promised to be another hot one, and left the house.

She needed to be in Kildare by nine-thirty for the start of her college day, so usually aimed, badly, to leave Orchard Close by eight.

She was almost always late, so Marcus was well within his rights to be suspicious.

By seven-thirty that morning, however, Jess had pulled up in front of the shop—in case anyone saw her car at this ungodly hour and wondered what she was up to—pulled on the hoodie, stuffed a couple of things in its pockets, and walked to the old cottage, fast and furtive. She checked the time on her phone. One minute and fifty-two seconds. Less than two minutes to get from Mrs Dunne's shop to the cottage, but she'd walked fast, so at a more normal pace, it would probably take three minutes or so. As they'd guessed.

She ignored the rusty double gates she'd gone through yesterday, and continued along the pavement in front of the cottage. There, as Siobhan's picture had shown, was a small pedestrian gate she was sure she hadn't noticed before. The wall between the double gate and this smaller gate had been previously hidden under a thick thatch of ivy, but most of it had been pulled off in yesterday's attack. Beyond the smaller gate, where the front wall continued until it joined the neighbouring property, ivy still smothered the crumbling rendered brick.

At the corner of the property, more roses spilled across the ivy-clad wall and the dividing fence between the cottage and the next garden. Unlike the pale-pink wild roses in the back, these were a vibrant yellow; sprung from a cultivated climbing rose, and they smelled delicious. She inhaled deeply, breathing in the scent until a passing car reminded her to hurry. She didn't want to be seen; didn't want to answer any awkward questions about what she was doing, or why she was nosing around a crime scene.

She returned her attention to the gate. In Siobhan's photo, it had been partly open. Now it was latched shut. She pulled up the picture on her phone to be sure. It had definitely been pushed ajar when Siobhan had taken the shot. Good. Hopefully that meant Marcus's team had done their job, and now if she walked through it, she wouldn't be compromising any evidence. If they hadn't finished, they'd have left it as it was. Now she thought about it, she realised the police tape was gone, too. They must have got all they needed from the cottage.

And, she told herself firmly, if there's no tape, I can go in.

She nudged the gate, which opened easier than she'd expected. She stepped through and closed it behind her, her eyes focused on the ground. The grass had been cut in front of the house, but whoever had done it had stopped in line with the gatepost and not bothered to go any further around this side. In front of the old orchard, the grass and weeds had been trampled down. In places, the weeds had already sprung back up; a little bent, a little crumpled, but rallying. In other patches, they were wilted and flattened.

Why had they cleared the other side but not this side? The scent of the yellow rose wafted into her nose. *Probably because the committee had agreed that the fruit trees and the ivy and the pretty yellow roses made a picturesque image.* Lila would've argued the case with Maeve, sometime before Jess had been cajoled into joining the committee. Jess would've been on Lila's side, for sure.

She picked her way carefully between the apple trees and the side of the house; treading down the longer grass, nettles, and dock besides the path she'd assumed to be an animal track. From this direction, it looked wider; caused by something far larger than a fox or badger. She was sure it hadn't been this trampled yesterday. *Dammit.* She'd no chance of finding any track marks now. Kev, she supposed, with a flash of annoyance that he'd trodden it down so badly. She really should've looked more carefully at this side yesterday.

A tiny patch of colour caught her attention and she bent to look. *Paint.* That was very definitely paint. A splash of red-orange paint. She mightn't even have noticed it if the grass hadn't been so flattened. She silently revoked her annoyance that Kev, or John, or whoever, had trampled the grass, and whispered a silent thanks as she took a few photos.

She ventured further into the garden, coming out past the house beside the patch of concrete in front of the sheds. The splash of paint was useful, for sure, but she had something else to find, too. Something that had caused the shine she'd seen through her phone's camera. The shine that had lured back into the garden at this unearthly crack-of-dawn hour when she could have had an extra half-hour in bed. The shine she'd come to investigate, along with the little gate and the track at the side of the house. *Where had it been?*

She let her gaze roam the garden, sweeping back and forth, left to right, right to left, but found nothing. She'd have to check.

She pulled up the video on her phone and set it to play.

There! She hit pause, rewound a few seconds, hit play again, and paused it on the split second where the sun caught a glint of light in the briars. She checked the image against the wilderness in front of her, trying to match the location caught on film to the life-size thicket of brambles. *There?*

She moved carefully forwards, arms held high, trying not to snag her jeans on any thorns or brush her hands against nettles or thistles as she stamped a path through the brambles. As she neared the further edges of the garden space and the enormous rhododendron hedge, something else caught her eye.

She took another series of photos, then carefully pulled a green, paint-splattered canvas bag from the clutches of the brambles it lay on; its colour having provided a good deal of camouflage during yesterday's scan of the garden.

She set it carefully back on top of the brambles to free her hands, and focused instead on the gleam of shiny plastic her lens had found yesterday. As she closed in on the red-stained plastic bottle, she took more photos from different angles. The paint bottle had slid down, almost out of sight among the bushes, its smooth, slippery surface having allowed it to slip through the briars.

Jess tucked her phone into her jeans and pulled a pair of thick gardening gloves from one of the hoodie pockets and a pair of secateurs from the other. She pulled down the sleeves of the hoodie to fully cover her arms, slipped on the gloves, and carefully, painstakingly, cut away strands of bramble, holding each stem between thumb and forefinger to lift it aside, already sweltering in the early morning sun but grateful for the protection of the gloves and thick sleeves as spiny stems clawed at her arms.

Cut, lift, move to side, repeat, until she could finally stretch forward and pluck the bottle free from its thorny nest. A children's poster paint bottle, almost empty and missing its cap. No wonder the paint had washed off the windows so easily; where she'd expected to find a can of hard-wearing gloss, this was only the cheap, water-based kids' stuff. Holding the bottle and secateurs together in her gloved hand, she pulled off the other glove with her teeth, fumbled in the front pocket of her jeans for the large plastic bin bag she'd stuffed there, rubbed at it until she got it open enough to shake out fully, then dropped in the empty bottle. *Got it!*

She collected the canvas bag as she backed out carefully from the bushes, and dropped in into the bin bag with the bottle.

Behind her, someone coughed, and she almost dropped the whole lot back into the bushes in panic. The glove fell from her teeth and she spun around.

Marcus, glaring at her. Marcus, glaring, but the sparkle in his eyes showed held-back laughter, and as she swore, retrieved the dropped glove, and stepped cautiously over the brambles to get to him, he laughed aloud. "Oh Jess. I knew you were up to something!" He held out his hand, and she passed him the plastic sack containing the paint bottle and canvas bag. He took it from her and held out his other hand.

Still clutching the secateurs, she allowed him to help her clamber out of the thicket to stand beside him, her face burning with the embarrassment of being caught. "You followed me!" It came out angrier than she'd intended, but really, now she thought about it, how dare he follow her? "You *followed* me," she repeated, pulling her hand from his and giving the word the full weight of her accusation.

He reached for her again, dodging the secateurs, and clasped her gently by the wrist, pulling her back towards him. "Not exactly."

She glared at him.

"No, honestly. Well, yes, but not like you think. You went out in such a rush you'd left your lunch. I knew you'd forgotten it, because you didn't go back into the kitchen after you said goodbye. You *never* leave in such a hurry. You'd never make a spy, you know. I called after you as soon as I realised, but you were already in the car and pulling away. I tried to call you, too."

She tugged off the other glove and wrestled her phone from her pocket. He had. "It was on silent," she said. "So it wouldn't make any noise."

He rolled his eyes at her. "That's the thing with 'on silent'. It won't make noise."

She glared at him. "Don't be so infuriating."

His eyes crinkled in that way they did when he was laughing at her, or with her, and a million butterflies fluttered in her chest. *Damn you, Marcus Woo, with your crinkly eyes and that smile.*

"So I came after you. I thought I'd catch you before you got to the junction—" He tilted his head towards the Dublin road, where the traffic was notoriously heavy in the early mornings and it wasn't uncommon to wait there for several minutes before being able to pull out from the Ballyfortnum junction. "I did have a notion you might be stopping somewhere, as you'd left so early, and when I saw your car at the shop, which, Miss super-sleuth O'Malley, you know full well doesn't open till eight, well, then I guessed what you were up to. And here you are." He pretended to glare at her, but his deep brown eyes were full of amusement. "Here you are. Trampling over a crime scene." His gaze travelled to the secateurs. "Trampling over a crime and ... and cutting ... cutting pieces out of it." He began in his firmest policeman's voice, but by the end of the sentence, he was trembling with laughter, still holding her wrist so she couldn't escape, and the next thing she knew, he was pulling her closer and kissing her.

After a minute or so, she pulled away. "Dammit, Woo, you can't win me over with kisses." But by now, she was laughing too. He really should have been angrier with her, and if he wasn't, well, she could hardly stay angry at him, and besides, he was ... well, he was Marcus.

"All right," she said, trying to maintain her annoyance but betrayed by her twitching mouth. "I suppose you probably can. But, since you are here, and I'm here, and I'm finding the things your lot missed, I may as well show you something else I found, in case you missed that, too." She took his hand and led him to where she'd found the splash of paint in the grass beside the house. "Look. I took a lot of pictures of it all. I was going to send them to you as soon as I got back to the car but I may as well do it now."

She pinged him the pictures, along with those she'd taken of the paint bottle and paint-covered canvas bag before she'd fished them free from the briars. "Just tell me one thing, Detective Woo. Had Kev found that paint splash? Or that bottle? Or that bag? Had he?"

Marcus looked like he wasn't going to tell her a thing, but then he laughed again, and squeezed her hand. "No. No, Jessica O'Malley, he had not. But if you think for a minute I'm going to tell you he found a very clear track at the front of the house by those fruit trees—" He gestured towards the small gate. "—that was almost certainly made by someone pushing a bicycle through the grass, I'm not."

He looked at her through narrowed eyes, holding her back from getting any nearer to the road, and added in a low voice, "And I'm absolutely not going to tell you there were two such paths through this grass, and there is not a chance that I will carelessly leave my phone open later, and leave it where you might accidentally see some photos. Now," he said, letting go of her wrist and giving her a gentle shove, "don't you have to get to Kildare and learn some things about trees or something? Your lunch is on the bonnet of your car, and even though you were up and out ridiculously early, you are still going to be ridiculously late. Let's go."

He pulled open the small gate, held it for her, closed it behind them, and they walked hand-in-hand towards the shop and their cars. After one more delicious, gut-tickling kiss, she was on her way, knowing full well she would be late for her classes yet again, but with thoughts of Marcus still tingling in her belly and thoughts of bicycles and paint and poor, bashed Willie Keegan churning in her mind.

Chapter Nineteen

After an uneventful day spent not concentrating very well on the day's hedge-laying lecture at the horticultural college, Jess shared a rushed dinner of pasta with Marcus before heading over to the village hall's meeting room for what she and Lila had been calling the Afterparty and Henry had called the Dissection.

Maeve, however, had written ACCOUNT OF THE EVENTS OF THE JUDGING DAY OF THE TIDY VILLAGE CONTEST on her A4 notepad, and under that, the date, and under that, PRESENT, and under that, her name and the names of the other three committee members.

Jess, unsurprisingly, was the last to arrive, despite living the nearest to the village hall.

"Ah, here you are," Maeve said stiffly, looking up from the notepad with her customary frown. "We'll start, so." She printed Jess's name on her list below the others.

"I'm not late?" She knew she wasn't but it still came out as an apologetic-sounding question. Maeve did that to you, she thought; her face warm. She'd done nothing wrong. Nothing. And yet Maeve made her feel like she wanted to put her tail between her legs and hide in a corner like Fletcher had when she'd told him off for swiping a defrosting joint of meat off the kitchen worktop one Sunday when Eric and Alice and everyone had come for the weekend. They'd had to have sandwiches for lunch and go out later that evening for dinner, so it had worked out quite nicely in the end, but she hadn't told Fletcher that.

Henry cast her a sympathetic smile. "No, you're not." He made a point of looking at his watch. "It's only seven minutes to. You're nice and early."

Maeve humphed and shuffled her papers. She set her pen beside the notepaper and peered over her glasses at the committee in that way she had of taking charge. "We have a lot to get through."

Lila, across the table from Jess, caught her eye. For a worrisome moment, Jess tried not to laugh. Goodness only knew what Maeve would say if they started giggling like schoolchildren.

"I was just asking about Willie," Lila said, "but Maeve said it's on the agenda and wait until everyone got here." She, like Jess, seemed to be biting back amusement.

Jess stretched out her foot under the table and prodded her Lila's leg. "Stop it," she mouthed.

"But," Father James said, helping himself to what Jess guessed wasn't his first biscuit of the meeting, judging by the amount of crumbs on the table in front of him, "now that everyone *is* here, I heard from Mrs Harris who heard it from her goddaughter who work in St James's that there's no change. He still not woken." He met Jess's eyes as he looked around at his fellow committee members. "Which is a little worrying, but we're all praying for him."

"Marcus said much the same," Jess agreed, although Marcus had left out the praying part. "Did Mrs Harris's Betsy have any more to say about it?"

"Not about Willie, God bless him."

Maeve scribbled on her page, coughed, and moved her pen down to hover over her first bullet point. "I—"

Before she could speak, Father James went on. "She did say there was no news on Jim, either, though. Seems Betsy's quite the fountain of information—"

"So he's ended up in the ICU in St James's too? Where Mrs Harris's Betsy works. That's a bit of a coincidence." Jess held Father James's gaze steadily, and he inclined his head.

"Yes," he said. "I thought you'd think that. But Mrs Harris said Betsy hadn't come across anyone of that name. If we know Mrs Harris, I'm sure she set her to asking around. I've asked Patrick to keep us updated, and added Jim to the prayers, too."

Maeve gave a little sniff and shuffled her papers. "That's well and good. But now, shall we move on?" She tapped the paper with her pen. "We haven't read last week's minutes yet. We really do need to stick to the agenda. That really should have been in AOB, but I suppose there's no harm done." She glared at Father James over her glasses. She was probably the only person in the parish who would dare to openly glare at Father James.

He didn't seem to notice. "Yes, yes, but we were all worried about Willie and Jim, weren't we? Best to quickly update you all first so we could pay full attention without wondering, don't you think?"

Maeve nodded stiffly, just once, and said, "The minutes, then."

Jess didn't hear a word as Maeve read through the notes from the last meeting. She knew they were now largely irrelevant, as they'd detailed the plans and timetable for yesterday, and they all knew how *that* had gone. *Was there really any point?*

Maeve droned on.

Thoughts about Jim, even though she'd never met him, pulsed and grew and mingled with the image of Willie, lying in the tumbledown shed with his head bashed in, and the barrows full of uprooted plants, and the splashes of paint on the walls and windows, and the paint bottle, and Marcus kissing her in the tangle of weeds as if they'd fallen into a Ballyfortnum version of Sleeping Beauty or Rapunzel or any one of those stories where the prince batters through thorns—

"Jessica?"

She snapped to attention as Maeve spoke sharply into her daydream.

"Does anyone have any comments on that, or will we go on?"

For the next twenty minutes or so, Maeve took them line-by-line through the report she'd written about what the judges had done the day before, during their visit to the village, and everyone agreed it was accurate. Jess may have only been on the committee for a few weeks, but she'd quickly learned that no one ever bothered to correct Maeve's notes. To be fair, they usually *were* accurate, and any rare inconsistencies were always far too minor for anyone else to worry about.

The next part of the meeting involved speculating on the two-fold problem of how much the vandalism had affected their chances of winning in any of their entered categories, and how to go about ensuring such an attack didn't happen again.

"Armed guards," Henry suggested with a smile that said he was joking.

Maeve, of course, took him quite seriously, and wrote *Armed Guards* in neat cursive beside a bullet point, under the heading ACTION PLAN.

"Neighbourhood Watch, extra hours. Someone on duty twenty-four-seven in the week before the judging. On camping chairs." Lila said, so deadpan that Jess didn't dare look up, knowing for sure the giggles would get the better of both of them if they looked at each other.

"With flasks of tea, binoculars, and blankets," she added, and this time it was Lila who kicked out under the table while Maeve wrote *Neighbourhood Watch* on her notepad.

"We could leave all the planters locked away and ready to put out on the morning of judging," Henry suggested. "But that seems to defeat the purpose, somewhat. What's the point of having all those wonderful displays if no one can enjoy them?"

Maeve looked up, surprised. "To look their best for the contest, of course."

There was a bit of hubbub while they debated whether the main focus of the Tidy Village contest should be about winning it—Maeve's view—or about having a beautiful village for the residents to enjoy, which was the view tentatively shared by the others. They did, however, unanimously agree that the contest was the driving force in the community coming together to maintain the village, and even Father James shared their doubt as to whether anyone would bother if they weren't also aiming for the accolade of the prizes.

At last, they'd covered everything on Maeve's agenda and reached her final point: AOB. "Any other business?" she said, sitting a little less rigidly and a little further back in her chair as she looked at everyone in turn. Maeve always relaxed just a little once she'd done what they all called 'her bit' and reached the uncharted waters of AOB. It usually turned into a general chat about nothing in particular, over a couple more cups of tea and any biscuits that Father James had left them.

"I have some," Jess said. "I want to bring you all up to date with some things I discovered when I was thinking about who might have done it ... the paint, and Willie ... Me and Lila and the Dochertys were chatting about it at the farm yesterday, and then, well, obviously, Marcus ..." She tailed off, still a little awkward about publicly acknowledging her relationship with Marcus, even though it was no secret and the whole village knew he'd all but moved into her house in Orchard Close. To Jess, though, the relationship was still too new and she worried that by saying it out loud, she'd compromise it somehow. And she really, *really* didn't want to do *that*. She ducked her head towards her empty cup, trying to hide yet another bout of blushing.

"Pillow talk," Lila whispered across the table with a cartoonish wink.

Jess picked up her notebook and fanned her flaming face. "Stop it," she hissed back.

"Shall we get some fresh tea first?" Henry said, always quick to come to the rescue.

Jess shot him a grateful glance. "Good idea!" She got to her feet, picked up the teapot, and disappeared into the kitchen with Lila giggling like a child in her wake.

"Sorry, Jess, but you are so funny. Everyone knows you and gorgeous Marcus are together, so you really should stop acting like it's a big secret."

"I know …" She boiled the kettle, filled the teapot, and they went back to the table, still laughing. A warm, happy feeling lodged in her belly as she sat down amongst her friends to continue the meeting.

Chapter Twenty

Over more tea, more biscuits, and the sound of Maeve's pen scratching on the paper, Jess gave a summary of what she'd concluded so far: That the vandals may have come into the village on bicycles; may have waited at the side of the old cottage, hidden by the overgrowth, until they saw the judges go by, saw the children disappear into school, and saw the parents disperse. They may have either been disturbed by Willie before they went on a quick paint-throwing, plant-pulling rampage, or may have intended more damage but been disturbed by him as they returned to the cottage.

"It was in squeezy bottles, so that would have made it much easier, don't you think?" She glanced around the table but didn't wait for anyone to answer. "What we really need to know," she said, "is whether anyone saw Willie Keegan that morning, and what he was doing, and whether anyone aside from Siobhan's eight-year-old son saw anyone on bikes near that cottage yesterday morning. My guess is that they left their bikes at the cottage, walked to the shop, then did the damage as they came back towards the cottage. I think it would be too difficult to throw paint while pushing or riding a bike, don't you, even from a squeezy bottle?"

"Or to pull all the flowers out," Lila added. "They'd have had to drag the bikes up onto the pavement, negotiate around the pub tables to get to the window boxes, and reach up to get at the hanging baskets. I agree. You couldn't do all that and hold a bike; it would be really awkward."

"And slow them down," Jess said. "And the one thing we know for sure is that whoever did this wasn't *slow*."

"They probably climbed on the tables to get at the baskets," Father James said, helping himself to another biscuit.

"But how could they have done all that without anyone seeing them?" Henry crossed his arms on the tabletop and leaned forward onto them.

Jess shrugged. "I have no idea."

"I'd like to find the little hooligans. Ask them if their mammies know what they're up to. They should be banged up." Maeve narrowed her eyes at Jess. "Marcus will be onto it, no doubt."

"He is," Jess agreed. "But they haven't a lot to go on. Not that he's said, at least. I think if we could come up with any suggestions as to who might do it, that might help. I think that we—you—" She encompassed the group with a wave of her hand. "—could be giving some real thought to who might want to sabotage Ballyfortnum's chances of winning. I have a couple of ideas."

"Of course you do." Across the table, Lila laughed. "Who needs the Gardai when we have you? Isn't Marcus worried he'll be out of a job soon, with you around?"

Jess shot her a look but carried on anyway. "One. Someone from another village who thinks they'd have a better chance of winning if we weren't in the running. Two, someone from round here who's fed up with us all banging on about keeping everything tidy and wants out." She stopped, shrugged, and laid her hands on the table, face up. "And that's it. That's all I have. Anyone any other ideas?"

They hadn't.

"Does it matter?" Maeve said. "Does it really matter why? The damage is done."

"It's the motive that leads to the man," Father James said. "Right, Jess?"

She nodded. "Exactly. I think if anyone could determine a definite motive, it would help the Gards—Marcus," she added with a smile, "—discover who did it and, and as Maeve so eloquently put it, get them banged up, so we can get back to making our lovely little village lovely again and keep that trophy for years to come." She finished with a small laugh, and leaned against her chair back, hoping someone would produce a suspect like a magician producing a rabbit from a hat. "Someone must have an idea?"

"Maeve seemed to think it was kids." Lila raised her eyebrows at Maeve, inviting response.

"I didn't say anything of the sort."

"You said you wondered if their mams knew what they were up to, and called them 'little hooligans' as if you thought they were young."

Maeve looked startled for a moment. "Oh. I did say that, didn't I? Yes. I suppose if I think about it, I did imagine they must be young. I couldn't envisage a grown adult hurling paint about the place and desecrating the planters. Or coming on bikes. From wherever they came from."

Jess nodded. It was a fair point. "If they were schoolchildren, they'd have blended in with the school rush, I suppose. Not so noticeable ..."

"But if they were that young, they'd have been at school themselves! Surely you're not suggesting it was any of the kids from around here?" Lila's voice rose in disbelief. "*Why?*"

"I can call Mrs Byrne. Ask if any children were unusually late, or absent," Father James said slowly, mulling over the suggestion. "I think it's very unlikely, as they'd surely have to be the older ones, if any, to be able to reach the baskets, and get hold of paint, and be cycling to school alone? There are only a handful of children in Year Six and aren't they all nice enough, in those upper years?"

"Maybe ask her if any of the kids bike to school?" Lila suggested. "And if there's any paint missing from the art cupboard."

Father James pulled out his phone as if he were thinking of texting the principal immediately. He peered at the screen, then put it back in his pocket. "I'll call in, in the morning. Compliment them on their part yesterday. The judges were most impressed by the efforts in the playground. Most impressed."

"It would have been a lot easier for them to have spoiled the planters in the playground," Henry said, "if it was children from our school."

"Teenagers, then? Who are the local teens?"

"They'd have all been off to school by then ..."

"They wouldn't. They finished on Friday for the summer." Lila said.

"Bored already?" Henry raised one eyebrow. "Shouldn't think so, not yet!"

Although they batted around some more half-hearted suggestions, no one had any solid ideas. Maeve shuffled the notes into her bag and got to her feet, signalling that, as far as she was concerned, the meeting was over.

"I don't suppose," Jess said, as the others started to get up, too, "anyone thinks it at all odd that Frances is from Abbeydare? She knows Jim, too. And something made him ill at that dinner on Saturday. Was she there? I think she said she was? Is it *really* just a coincidence that all this happened at once, and that the replacement judge is from our biggest regional threat in the contest?"

There was a brief lull in the movement as everyone turned to look at Jess.

"No," Henry said firmly. "Frances has been involved in the contest for years. She's the national secretary. I don't think she would do anything except play fair. I really don't."

"Actually—" Maeve held open the door for them to exit past her, jangling the hall keys as if it might hurry them somehow. "I was the one who suggested she step in."

Everyone filed past her and she pulled the door shut and locked it, tugging firmly to check everything was secure.

"You did?" Jess said, unable to keep the surprise from her voice. Why ever would Maeve have suggested someone from their rival village join the judging committee?

"Not specifically for this time. About three years ago. Don thought he might not be able to participate last year. His daughter was getting married." Maeve encompassed Father James and Henry in a stern look, daring them to disagree. "Remember? And she was going to do it in June of last year. Don was worrying about it at the Christmas dinner we had with them in Dublin, in the Fairmount that year."

Henry stared at a point somewhere across the car park, rubbing his chin, his brow crumpled as he tried to cast his mind back that far. "Oh. Yes. That's right. You did well to remember that. Luckily she changed her mind. I think his wife must have stepped in. Had a word."

"They were discussing the options. Over dessert. You were there, too, Father." She tilted her chin at Father James as he swung his leg over his bike and leaned forward to unhook the helmet from the handlebars.

"Was I? I can't remember that long ago ..."

"You were. And Lydia and her husband and Jim and Helena and Patrick and his wife, and all the runners up for Champion Award. It was quite the do. Anyway, Don said he might not be able for the following year, not the upcoming one, and I said they could do worse than to consider Frances. She's been working behind the scenes for years and is very well established with the categories and rules."

"Yes! Weren't some of the newer categories her suggestions, now I think of it?" Father James paused his fiddling with the strap of the bicycle helmet. "I'd quite forgotten that. So you did, Maeve. So you did."

"She's a cousin of mine," Maeve said, "so I'd know her well enough."

Jess's mouth dropped open. She caught Lila's eye as the rest of the little group dispersed into the evening; Maeve setting off on foot in one direction, Father James and Henry in the other, one wobbling on his bike as he reached forward to put on the light, and the other pulling away smoothly in his car. It wasn't yet dark, but the sun was low and there were patches of grey cloud that threatened to bring the rain Maeve had predicted for the end of the week.

Jess and Lila stood beside Lila's Mini, watching them go.

"Well," Lila said, once everyone was out of earshot. "Fancy Maeve being related to Frances. Funny that neither of them said."

"I thought they didn't even know each other," Jess said. "Frances seemed like a fish out of water when they arrived yesterday, seemed quite nervous and new, like me. Wonder what that's about, then."

Lila laughed; this time a proper laugh that didn't need restraining in front of the committee. "If *you* were related to Maeve, would you admit to it?"

Jess gave a small inelegant snort. "Guess not. Can you imagine the fun at their family get togethers? I'll bet Maeve has a schedule for those, too."

Still chuckling, Lila slid into the Mini and drove slowly across the car park, chatting through the open window as Jess walked beside her, until Lila pulled out onto the road and turned towards the village. Jess crossed the street behind her, and, deep in thought, walked the short distance home to Orchard Close, where Marcus was waiting for her.

Chapter Twenty-One

O n Thursday, Jess begged a couple of bags of compost and several trays of bright bedding plants from Shay, her boss and friend at the Ballymaglen Garden Centre. She'd arranged with Lila and Anne that she'd call in at Lila's on her way home from work, and the three of them would spend as long as it took to redo all the spoiled planters. By the time Jess got there, Lila and Anne had retrieved the two barrows from the old sheds, and were sorting through the damaged plants. Most were ruined after all, as even those they'd thought might be salvageable on Tuesday had wilted during their few days in the dark shed.

"Good thing you got those," Anne took a tray of petunias from the boot of Jess's car and sniffed approvingly. The new trays of plants were a ragtag mix of colours and blooms, less coordinated than the previously coordinated displays, but they were cheerful and bright.

"Not usually one of my favourite flowers," Lila said, peering over Anne's shoulder into the car boot, "but they're colourful; they smell good, and they're free, so today, I love them!"

For a happy hour or so, the three women worked side-by-side, enjoying the early evening sun and the satisfaction of seeing the hanging baskets and pots come back to life.

By seven, their hands were stained brown from the warm, crumbly compost, and all the plants were used up; all the containers refilled.

"That'll tell them we're not a village to give in to bullies or disappointment," Lila said, sitting down on the edge of her patio with a swish of her long skirt. She stretched her legs out across the grass of her daisy-strewn lawn, leaned back against a large terracotta pot, and sighed in contentment. "Job well done, girls."

"Cheers!" Anne held her half-drunk, almost-cold cup of tea aloft for Jess and Lila to clink their mugs against in celebration. "Yes, well done, girls!"

Lila's husband Dom loaded everything into the back of his car—not his longed-for Harley Davidson but a generic hybrid something-or-other significantly larger than Lila's Mini or Jess's Corolla—and drove the planters the few hundred yards to the shop. With Dom's rear seats folded to fit the troughs and baskets, and one large planter balanced on the passenger seat, Lila and Anne bundled into Jess's car to make the same short journey.

Starting at the pub and working towards the shop, with Anne and Dom doing the high-stretching hanging of the baskets, and Jess and Lila setting the window boxes and table planters in place, the foursome worked efficiently together to reinstate the displays.

"Done!" Lila held up her hand and Jess smacked her a high-five.

"Done! Good job, everyone."

As the four stood back to admire their work, Mrs Dunne unlocked the front door of the shop and presented them with a handful of ice creams robbed from the freezer cabinet. "Dunno who likes what," she said, "but I'll say you deserve them, after your work."

Jess, whose hands the ice creams had landed in, extracted the Magnum from the pile and handed the rest onwards to Anne.

"You've done us proud. Again." Mrs Dunne stepped back into the road beside them and looked admiringly at the new arrangements. "They're even nicer than the first, I'd say. Can't beat a bit of colour." She sniffed and dabbed her eyes with the back of her hand. "You've done a mighty job, so you have."

"Well, ladies. And Dominic." Paddy's booming voice carried easily the short distance from the pub doorway. He strode along the pavement to join them. "I see Mrs Dunne has yous looked after, but I'll have a pint behind the bar ready for yous on top of tha'." He tipped his head towards the Cornetto in Lila's hand. "Fair play to you all." He nodded vehemently, up and down like one of those nodding dogs Jess used to see in the backs of cars when she was small. "Fair play."

After a quick discussion about whether they could run in now for a quick drink or if Paddy might hold off on his offer until tomorrow, when they'd have time to stop in properly and not be driving anywhere afterwards, they agreed to meet the next evening instead.

"Make a night of it." Lila said. "God knows we're ready for it. Bring Peggy? And Marcus, of course."

"Marcus'll be working," Jess told her, "I'll call Peggy. And Alice is coming." It hadn't taken much to persuade her sister to leave Dublin behind for the promise of another quiet, peaceful weekend in Ballyfortnum.

"Quiet, my arse," Dom said, smirking into his beard.

Jess clambered back into her car, leaving the others to bundle into Dom's now-empty seats. "I only had to tell her we had another mystery to solve, and she'd booked the train before I said another thing!" She pulled her car door shut, waved a final goodnight, and headed home.

Alice, it turned out, had arrived earlier than Jess expected. When Jess got to work at Friday lunchtime, Alice was sitting on the chair behind Shay's desk with a mug of tea in her hand, looking as if she owned the place.

"Al! You got in early! Where's Shay?" Jess looked around the stuffy portacabin as if he may be hiding behind the filing cabinet or under the paper-strewn desk.

Alice shrugged. "Polytunnel? Dunno. He went off somewhere about half an hour ago. Shouldn't think he's far away."

"What time did you get in?"

Jess wasn't the only O'Malley sister prone to blushing, and as her sister reddened to almost the shade of the poppies that poked up in the shabbier corners of the garden centre, behind the polytunnels and out of sight to the customers, Jess's stomach lurched.

Alice was hiding something.

And Jess was fairly certain she knew what it was.

Jess had first got to know Shay when she'd signed up for a gardening course last spring. It was during the course that she'd discovered her love of gardening—as much of a surprise to Jess as to anyone who knew her. She'd also discovered Shay. For a little while, Jess and Shay had thought they might have something going between them, and had shared a handful of passionate moments in the far reaches of the polytunnels, away from the eyes of Jess's course mates and Shay's staff.

She'd introduced him to her family, including Alice, when he'd come for Easter Sunday dinner that year. Unfortunately for Shay, that was also the weekend Jess realised her true feelings for Marcus. Nonetheless, after a short-lived interlude of awkwardness, they'd become close friends and Jess had settled into her job two afternoons a week she worked in the Ballymaglen Garden Centre with Shay her boss. Shay had also helped her get enrolled on her horticultural course, and while now and then they had a fleeting pang of 'what might have been', they'd managed to maintain an easy, bantering friendship.

Except, Jess thought as she watched her older sister squirm, there seemed to be something he'd forgotten to tell her.

Something Alice had also neglected to say.

"Alice! Did you come down *yesterday*? Have you been here all day? You sneaky cow!"

Alice hung her head, unable to look at Jess. "Do you mind?" she said quietly to the top of Shay's desk.

Jess considered the question for a moment. Did she? If she was completely honest with herself, she'd seen it coming. Even as far back as that Easter Sunday, when Shay had arrived for lunch about an hour after Jess confessed to Alice how she felt about Marcus. Shay and Alice had spent time together, chatting easily in the kitchen while Jess tried to avoid him by pretending her two nieces were demanding her attention.

And lately, now Alice came to Ballyfortnum more often, she usually got a Friday afternoon train to Ballymaglen so Jess could meet her at the station after she finished her Friday shift at the garden centre. Except Alice had frequently ended up getting the earlier train and walking to meet Jess at the garden centre instead. And hadn't she and Shay often holed up together in his office on the pretence that Alice could wait there away from the bustle of the shop after arriving on that earlier train?

Alice *always* got the earlier train these days, come to think of it, despite knowing Jess couldn't get away until five.

Yes, Jess had definitely seen it coming. But did she *mind*?

An image of Marcus, lovely Marcus, filled her mind. She shook her head. "No. I don't suppose I do." She threw a hard mock-glare at her sister. "But why didn't either of you *tell* me?" Another thought struck her. "Have you been down here sometimes without even telling me?"

Alice grinned at her, still pink-faced, but radiating a happiness Jess had never known from her sister. "This was the first time. I was going to tell you later, honest, but—" She shrugged. "I guess I don't have to now."

"Just don't go all boss's wifey on me." Jess waggled a finger in her sister's face. "You may be sat behind that desk like Lady Muck, but as I have to work, and you're using my favourite mug, you can go off and make me a cup of tea while I find something useful to do in the absence of my boss being around to tell me what's needed."

Alice got to her feet, came around the desk, and they fell into a fierce, tight hug.

"It's good to see you, Al. Go make me tea. I'll be out in the yard somewhere. I just hope you're not too loved-up to hear about the newest mystery in Ballyfortnum."

The garden centre was quiet enough, and Alice had refilled her own mug as well as making Jess the demanded tea. Ella had taken charge of the shop, and Shay and Jack were busy shifting plants around in the polytunnels, so Jess set to work tidying and restocking the large plant tables in the yard, where customers could browse for anything from bedding plants to herbs to vegetable seedlings to potted conifers and fruit trees.

Alice, chattering happily, followed Jess around like a faithful puppy, moving Jess's mug of tea from table to table while Jess lumbered about with armfuls of potted plants.

As Jess straightened pots, filled gaps with fresh supplies, and watered everything, she relayed the events of Tuesday's aborted Tidy Village judging and Willie Keegan's attack, interrupted by occasional customers: "Have you any starflowers, only I saw some in a magazine...?" or "Where will I find some sage?"

Alice, to her credit, mostly listened intently. She passed Jess her tea at regular intervals; took it upon herself to go off and find some tomato plants for a hopeful customer, and went off to fill the watering can whenever Jess asked, and only very occasionally talked about her blossoming relationship with Shay.

"Al, I really, really don't mind, I also *really* don't want the details. I've kissed him too, remember, so I know what it's like!"

"Eugh, so you have. That's weird. Right." She shook herself, just like Fletcher did after coming in from rain. "Eugh. So. The latest mystery. Tell me about the motive, means, method, murder. Who do you suspect? Why? Whose fingerprints are at the scene?"

"Mine, mostly! But there's no murder, don't forget. Not unless Willie doesn't pull through. Well, or Jim, maybe, if there *is* some kind of connection." Jess told Alice how she thought she'd been so smart, sneaking back into the garden at the crack of dawn to look for clues, only to caught in the act by Marcus.

"Red-handed, Alice. Literally. Red gardening gloves *and* red paint!"

"Is there anything you could have missed?"

"Wouldn't be surprised. It's so overgrown anything could've been tossed in the bushes and fallen out of sight where we'd never find it." She told Alice about the bicycle tracks Marcus's colleagues had found in the long grass, and the red splash of paint, and how even though there were plenty of old rusted tools in one of the sheds, none seemed to have been moved for decades. "Besides, according to Marcus, there were no traces of rust in Willie's wound. Just a bit of dirt from the ground, some leaves, some rose stems and ivy in his hair, and some of that paint. He had it on his hands, too, I saw it in the photo, so perhaps the bash hadn't knocked him straight out, and he'd touched his head with wet paint on his hands? I dunno."

"Or," Alice suggested, "He'd been whacked with the paint bottle?"

Jess stopped still, watering can poised over a tray of petunias, and studied her sister. "Hadn't thought of that, but I shouldn't think it would be heavy enough, just being a plastic bottle. I suppose Marcus's forensics lot will check though—oops! Shite!" Water cascaded from the edge of the table and ran onto her feet, soaking her trainers and legs. She put the watering can down and lifted the waterlogged tray of plants to a drier spot, staring at the growing puddle as something stirred at the edges of her memory. *Water. Was there something about the water?* If there was, it wasn't coming to her. She shook away the niggle and picked up the watering can to pass to Alice to refill, then changed her mind and headed for the tap herself.

"That's it!"

"What?" Alice called from across the yard.

Jess finishing filling the can and strode back to her sister. She set down the watering can and took her phone from her pocket. She fired off a message to Gary, then turned the screen to show Alice: *Hiya. Quick question. Did you USE the tap by the house, or did you see Willie first?*

Alice raised her eyebrows. "Why?"

"Because if he didn't actually turn on the tap to get water, which I don't think he would've, because I think by the time you got to the tap, you'd almost certainly have noticed Willie and then gone to him and not to the tap, don't you think?"

Alice shrugged. "If you say so. I mean, yes, if you saw him, you'd go to him first, but I don't know if you'd necessarily see him first? Not without knowing the layout."

Jess nodded. "It was right opposite him. I can't be quite sure, either, but let's say you didn't see him first and went to the tap?"

Alice looked at her with wide eyes and nodded slowly. "Then you'd—"

"—have definitely seen him when you turned away from the tap. You wouldn't have missed him. You simply couldn't have *not* seen him."

"What's your point though?"

"My point, Alice, is that when I was watching over Willie, just seconds after Gary found him, someone had used that tap recently. The ground was wet under it. Matty said, too, that he thought someone had got water from there, for the buckets and the plants and suchlike."

"And if that person wasn't Gary—"

"Then someone already knew Willie Keegan was there in that shed before Gary raised the alarm." Jess squinted at her phone screen, willing him to answer. It remained stubbornly blank.

"Or Gary bashed him? Then pretended to find him?"

Jess shook her head. "Don't think so. Firstly, I don't think he had time. Besides, Matty and the others were all around and no one seems to have seen Willie, even before Gary got there."

"Unless Gary bashed him earlier, then went back to help?"

"Hmm." Jess considered this idea for a moment, then shook her head again. "No. I really don't think so. He was at home when Linda went over to get him. There really wouldn't have been time." She peered at her phone again.

"Give it here." Alice held out her hand and took the phone. "I'll keep an eye while you crack on." She gestured to the yard. "Might as well do your job while we wait. Snap to it!"

Jess glared. "Boss's wife."

Alice scrunched up her nose in protest, then laughed. "Yeah, yeah. But you can still gossip while you work. I won't tell him. Tell me what else is suspicious. What else seems out of place so far?"

Jess straightened a tray of straggly pansies. "Well, there's the weird connection with the new judge being from the rival village. And Maeve being her cousin, too."

"Is Maeve from that other village too? Abbeywhatsit? Might she have divided loyalties?"

"Dunno," Jess said for what felt like the umpteenth time. "But no, I shouldn't think so. About the divided loyalties, I mean, because she's the heart and soul of Ballyfortnum's Tidy Village efforts, or at least the backbone ... not sure she has a heart!" Jess broke off with a laugh. "That's not really fair. Her heart's in the right place; she just has a funny way of showing it. But she's worked really, really hard on the committee for as long as anyone can remember, so no, I don't see that she'd have any motive to stop us winning. Especially when she's put so much into it."

"So that brings you back to whatshername? The new judge? Sounds a bit suspect, if you ask me. She gets roped in after another judge gets taken ill after a meal a lot of other people ate too and didn't get sick from—that's very suspicious if you ask me—then someone knows exactly what time to vandalise the village, then it turns out she's from the other village, and then it turns out she also forgot to mention she's related to Maeve."

"Maeve didn't say it either."

"I think," Alice said, as she trailed Jess around to the next table, "there are some obvious steps you're missing."

"And what might those be, if you're so clever, Detective Alice?"

Alice wrinkled her nose again. "I *am* in the Lollipop Club now, remember?"

"And still making up for lost time. After all those mysteries me and Eric solved, it's about time you did some of the work here." Jess waggled the watering can so a sprinkling of drops fell onto Alice's hand.

Jess's and Eric's childhood detective club had a different name back then, now long-forgotten. Enthralled by Enid Blyton's mystery-solving children, they'd determined to become equally proficient at snooping, sleuthing, and solving whatever crimes fell upon their neighbourhood. Alice, entrenched in the throes of an eating disorder, had no time or interest for her younger siblings' silly little detective games, and not much time for her younger siblings either. Only recently, with Alice apparently, hopefully, recovered, had the three siblings united. Alice, to her credit, was doing her best to make up for the lost years and be the big sister Jess had longed for throughout her childhood, her teens, and most of her adult years. She'd turned out to be quite good at mystery-solving, too, after helping Jess uncover who'd killed a local farmer only weeks before the Tidy Village contest had kicked off.

"I think," Alice said, "we should call in on Father James on the way home."

"Okay. Why? Not just for tea and scones and to say hello, I'm guessing?"

"All that too, of course, but mostly to see Mrs Harris."

"Okay." Jess nodded. "But why?"

"Because, you eejit, didn't you just tell me that Willie is still in St James's ICU, and didn't you just tell me that the judge who was supposed to come is also in St James's ICU, and didn't you tell me that there's some suspicion about what happened to him, with whatever it was he ate at the meal the other judges were at too, and—"

"And didn't I just tell you that Mrs Harris's Betsy, whoever she might be, works in the ICU in St James?" Jess said, as she caught up with her sister's train of thought.

"And might it be useful to find out if there is anything, anything at all that connects the two—the food-poisoning judge and the unconscious groundsman?"

"Ye-es," Jess said slowly, dragging the word out as she thought about what Alice was getting at. "Like what? Other than the Tidy Village contest; one not getting to Ballyfortnum, one being from Ballyfortnum ..."

"One knowing Maeve; one knowing Frances ..."

"I wonder," Jess said, passing Alice the watering can to refill, "if Mrs Harris's Betsy might be able to tell Mrs Harris who's visited, for example."

"In case the same person has been to see them both," Alice said, swinging the empty watering can back and forth. "But I think one crucial question is exactly how the judge got sick, and who might have been around when that happened, what he ate, and who might have had access to it to tamper with his, and only his, meal? Those, Jessica Marple, are the questions you need to get answers to."

"Okay Poirot. You go back to lover-boy's cabin and make a list. I'll finish up here, and we'll go detectiving at the parish house on the way home."

Chapter Twenty-Two

Alice's detecting plans were foiled by the absence of either Father James or Mrs Harris at the priest's house, much to her disappointment, and, unable to come up with an alternative way to find out more about Willie's condition or the cause of Jim's illness, they continued on to Orchard Close in thoughtful silence.

The plans Jess had made with Peggy earlier in the week had been adapted to fit around the decision to meet up with Lila and the Dochertys in the pub later that evening, to claim the promised free drink from Paddy. In lieu of the shared takeaway they'd originally intended, Jess had invited Peggy to join her and Alice for an earlier dinner of 'God knows what but you're welcome to join us', but Peggy had declined, saying she'd get her usual Chinese-meal-for-one from the takeaway in Glendanon and join them later for a drink or two.

Jess, meanwhile, threw together an easy meal of stir-fried vegetables and steamed rice, then the sisters tugged on their walking boots to take the dogs out for a good walk before leaving them shut in for the evening.

"We could bring them with us," Alice suggested, as they turned towards the farm track that led onto a stretch of bogland between Orchard Close and the village centre, walking side-by-side on the empty road. "They're allowed in the pub, aren't they?"

Jess stopped dead in the middle of the road and looked at Alice in amazement. "They are, and we could, but why would we? Fletch would be an absolute idiot and get tangled round everyone's feet, and Snow would just be miserable and wish he was curled up at home in peace and quiet. We've time to give them a good walk, and go without them, thank you very much. And if we're back in good time now, we'll walk to the pub, too, and Marcus can join us on his way home—he should get off around ten, I think—and then he can drive us home and we can get slaughtered."

They both knew Alice would not, in fact, get slaughtered. She would have one glass of white wine, two at most, and then spend the rest of the evening sipping slimline tonic water and sucking at the slices of lemon, or lime, or whatever fruit Paddy decided to play with that evening. He'd cut slices of apple, once, and fixed them to the rim of everything he served, but a string of complaints at the limp, rapidly-browning slices meant he'd never repeated that particular culinary aberration.

"You, however—" Alice told her sister in the tone their least favourite primary-school teacher had used whenever Jess got her maths wrong. Which was often. "You might very well drink a good deal more than is sensible, and spend the following day moaning about it. You'd better not. I'm only here till tomorrow night and I don't want to waste it with you complaining about a hangover."

They reached the rough earthen farm track. Jess stooped to unclip Fletcher's lead, and within seconds, he'd gambolled on ahead of them, wriggled under a strand of wire fencing, and away out of sight.

Snowflake trotted along the track, sniffing delicately at the edges, tail wagging happily.

"I won't ... I'll just have a couple. Probably."

Alice held up a firm hand. "If you get steamingly, stupidly drunk, I will pack up my toothbrush and go and spend tomorrow in the garden centre potting up plants with Shay." She tried for about half a second to keep a straight face as Jess tried and failed to picture her sister getting her hands dirty, then the two of them fell about laughing, clutching at each other, and giggling.

Fletcher, alerted by the noise, charged back down the track and jumped up and down between them like a defunct jack-in-the-box.

They walked on until they reached a strand of electric fence, pulled across the track and holding back a field of dairy cows who'd come to investigate. They hadn't been there the last time Jess had walked up this track, and while Jess knew that they wouldn't breach the electric, she was always a little unnerved when cows got this excited.

The curious herd edged closer.

She called Fletcher, who for once, came quickly, seemingly also a little concerned by the approaching cattle.

Jess and Alice clipped the dogs' leads on and turned for home, not letting the dogs off again until they'd walked far enough down the track for the cows to interest and mooch back to their grazing.

"We'll get a good long walk tomorrow instead," Jess promised. "By the river, perhaps."

"To clear your aching head," Alice said, shooting a sidelong glance at her sister.

Jess swung Fletcher's lead at her, missed, and called the Labrador to her to clip the lead to his collar instead as they rejoined the road. Moments later, Fletcher strained at the lead, tail thumping against Jess's leg, and began to bark.

Snowflake's ears pricked, and he too, began wagging his tail; shorter, stumpier, but with just as much enthusiasm about whatever it was they could sense or hear.

"What is it boys? Who can you smell?"

Fletcher and Snowflake didn't answer, but there was a burst of high-pitched yapping from ahead of them, and Henry and Elizabeth emerged from the park entrance with Stanley and Daisy.

With Fletcher tugging like a steam train, Jess let him propel her towards the other dogs, ready to haul him in close before they got near enough to rub noses. "He'll fight with Daisy. She's a brat. She'll have a go at Snow, too," she warned Alice. "Don't let them get close enough to touch. But we'll say hello to Henry and Elizabeth. Have you met them before? I can't remember."

Alice's reply was lost in the flurry of barking.

Jess reined Fletcher in tightly. "Be quiet, you idiot. You know full well it's only Daisy and she'll be as stupid as you if you don't stop."

Henry had similar words with Daisy, staring at her firmly until she, too, finally stopped yapping, and stood quivering beside Henry, hackles raised, emitting tiny whimpers and small growls.

Stanley and Snowflake, being of the better-behaved, well-trained kind of dog, sat panting at each other in a perfect embodiment of a pair of friends sitting down for a chat.

"Any news?" Jess asked after making introductions. "Any update on Jim?"

"Jess was telling me all about it," said Alice, as Henry shook his head. "Did they find out what caused it?"

Jess looked at her sister in admiration. She really was getting good at this Lollipop Club sleuthing work. She'd made it sound so natural; so casual. If Jess had asked, she was sure it would have come across as nosy.

"It was the salad, at the dinner," Henry said.

"Dinner?" Jess said, feigning ignorance.

"You know—the pre-launch dinner. They were talking about it on Tuesday."

"Oh! When they got together to go through the schedule? They did mention it. But no one else was sick?"

"Apparently there were beans in the salad, only some of them weren't cooked properly, or weren't small enough to be eaten raw—I'm not sure if they were cooked or not, to be honest. I spoke to Patrick yesterday afternoon. He'd been talking to Helena—Jim's wife?—and she'd said they'd tracked it to that chemical found in kidney beans. She was awfully confused at first, because she'd been at the dinner too, and no one had anything with kidney beans, but... well, most of them are gardeners, and most of them grow a bit of veg, and although Helena had no idea, Lydia suddenly realised it must've been the broad bean salad, although she'd had it too and was fine."

"Wow," said Jess. "I know kidney beans are dodgy, but I didn't know broad beans had the same thing in them. I don't like them much. We used to have them a lot as kids, and they were gross. Horrible big grey things."

Henry's eye's creased as he laughed. "I'll bet you mother didn't double-peel them. They're only good to eat young if you don't take off the skins. Not just the outer pods, but the bean's skin too. My mother was just the same. Try them again, but double-pod!"

Jess shuddered. "Now I know they made that poor man so ill? Don't think so, thank you."

"How come no one else got sick, if others ate the same?" Alice asked, repeating Jess's unanswered question.

"Bit of a mystery, that," Henry said. "Seems only his portion had the raw ones, or the big ones, or whatnot. Patrick couldn't answer that." Henry scratched his head. "Unlucky, I suppose. Poor man."

"Sounds like he's on the mend now anyway, so all's well," Elizabeth added.

"He is? I thought he'd got worse?"

Elizabeth's eyes sparkled with mischief. "Chinese whispers, Jess. Seems like poor old Donald got quite the wrong end of the stick, and it grew like bindweed!"

"Turned out his wife actually said he'd left hospital that afternoon and was on his way home. She was ringing to pass on good luck to them, and to say he hoped they enjoyed discussing the nature reserve. He was quite delighted when it turned out they hadn't got there, though, as he said now he'll be able to come with them another day. They can make a special outing out of it, he said, so a silver lining to the mix-up. All that worry! Don felt terribly silly, Patrick said."

"Poor Don," Jess laughed. "Easily done. We all heard the message and jumped to the same conclusion. Maeve said only last night about the dangers of speculation. Send him our best wishes, if you're talking to him or his wife—Jim, I mean, not Don. I don't remember him at all, but according to Lydia, Don, and Patrick, I might have met him. He knew Dad," she said, turning to Alice. "We'd better head on home; stop these dogs thinking about attacking each other." She cast a glare at Daisy and prodded Fletcher with the toe of her boot. "Come on Fletch, leave her alone."

"Beans," said Alice, as soon as they'd turned into Orchard Close and Henry and Elizabeth were out of sight. Earshot was in no doubt, as Daisy was still yapping, albeit getting steadily fainter as they walked further from the park.

"Beans," Jess echoed. "Beans and rumours. Who'd have thought. You know what we should've asked, though."

"What?"

"Exactly who else was at that dinner."

"Because if no one else got sick—"

"But others ate the same thing—"

"Someone *must* have tampered with his meal?"

"Exactly."

"I wonder," Alice said after they'd walked a little further, stopping for a second as Snowflake lifted his leg against the lamppost outside Number 4, "if they knew in advance what was on the menu."

"I wonder—" Jess added, tugging Fletcher away from the same lamppost. "Come on, Fletcher, don't be an idiot! I wonder where the meal was. Did anyone say?" Catching Alice's stare, she added, "I know you don't know. I'm trying to remember if anyone said on Tuesday. Remind me to ask Lila, later? But first, we need to call on Gary. He never did get back to me about whether he'd turned on that tap." She pulled a confused Fletcher passed the path to her own front door and knocked on the door to Number 8 instead.

Chapter Twenty-Three

"Jess!" Gary clamped a hand to his forehead. "Sorry, I forgot to reply. Come in?" Gary, barefoot and dressed in black jogging bottoms and a pristine white T-shirt, glanced down at Fletcher. "On second thoughts ..." He stepped out onto the doorstep, patted Fletcher on the head, and looked questioningly at Alice. "I'll come out. This your sister? You look alike. Hi, I'm Gary."

"So," Jess prompted, once the introductions were over, "about that tap?"

"Yeah," Gary shook his head. "No, I didn't touch it. I went around the back like your friend Matty suggested, and I saw there was a faucet there on the wall, all right, and I was heading over to try it, and I spotted that poor guy lying there."

"So you went straight to him, and *not* to the tap?"

He raised bushy eyebrows at Jess. "Sure."

"You're absolutely certain?"

"You think I'd see a man lying there on the ground and continue on over to see if a faucet had water before checking on the guy?" He held Jess's gaze and her face warmed under the scrutiny.

"No, of course not; that's exactly my point. No one would, would they? Anyone who saw someone lying on the ground would go them first, wouldn't they?"

"I'd think so."

"So then, why was the ground under the tap wet?"

Gary stared at her. "It was, wasn't it. I'd not registered that, but now you say it ..."

"Do you think there's any way at all that someone—whoever got the water for the buckets or the barrow, or whatever—could have got to that tap, got water for the buckets and those barrows of plants *without* seeing Willie lying there?"

Gary leaned back against his front door, quiet as he thought about the question. "No," he said after a long pause. "No Jess, I don't think they could. Even if they hadn't seen him right away, which I think they would've, they'd have seen him at some point, like when they turned around after getting the water, or when they came back to get more. There'd been water used for several buckets and for the barrow, so if that water didn't come from somewhere else, it'd have come from there all right. It might've come from some here else? Who got the water?"

"That," Alice said, "is exactly the question."

"Couldn't Willie have got it?"

"Everyone said he wasn't there, not when you were all cleaning up. No one had seen him."

"Perhaps he got water earlier, for something else?"

"But it was already getting warm. Wouldn't it have dried up already, by then? I'd think that water we saw under the tap hadn't been there very long at all."

"You can't be sure of that, though," Alice said. "If there'd been loads, what you saw might have only been what was left after some dried?"

Jess shrugged. "Possibly. We need to ask around a bit more. Matty seemed to think someone had got water from around the back of the cottage, because he told you to go there first to look, didn't he?"

"He did. I'd say you could ask him; see how he knew about that."

Jess nodded. "I'll add it to my list of things to ask everyone at the pub later. Want to join us? Everyone's coming; you can get to know everyone in more relaxed circumstances than the madness of Tuesday."

Anne, Matty, and Siobhan were already in the pub by the time Jess and Alice had finished dinner, changed, and walked back into the village. The evening was cool, with the threat of showers, so they'd commandeered a group of tables inside; pushing a few together to make space for everyone. Jess sat on the padded bench beside Matty, under the window, and immediately started to quiz the three Dochertys about who'd been involved in the clearing up on Tuesday.

"What I really want to find out," she said to Matty, "is how you knew the water wasn't disconnected, and that Gary would find a tap at the back of the cottage."

Matty looked at her blankly.

"You told Gary to check around the back." She tried to remember exactly what he'd said. "You said someone had got water and you thought it might have been from there. Something along those lines, anyway."

Matty took a swig of his half-drunk pint of Guinness.

"Had you got water from there already?" She stared at him, her eyes wide as she considered the possibility that Matty Docherty, who she barely knew but already considered a friend, could have been the first one to fill a bucket, and therefore already known Willie Keegan was lying there unconscious, and not said anything to anyone. "Before you told Gary to look there?"

Matty shook his head. "No, not me. I didn't know for sure; just that someone had filled those buckets from somewhere close by. Those old houses are mostly on well water, not the mains, so I'm not surprised the water hadn't been turned off. But no, I didn't know for sure. I don't know who filled the buckets. It was all a bit mad, with everyone rushing about trying to clean up, you know?"

Jess, suddenly grateful for the dim interior of the pub, felt her face flush with embarrassment. Of course it hadn't been Matty. How could she have thought such a thing, even for a second? "Sorry, yeah, I know. *Someone* must have an idea of who it was, though." She gazed helplessly at Anne, perched on a stool opposite. "Any ideas at all? Who else was there?"

Anne shook her head. "Us lot." She pointed to Matty and Siobhan, then gestured towards the publican. "Paddy came out in his kaks, but it was mostly done by then. Couple of the school mams, but they weren't much help as most of them had little ones to mind. Couple of the farm lads from round about. What're you drinking?" she asked Alice and Jess, rising to go to the bar.

The door swung open and Lila came in with a swish of her long, flowing skirt and a rush of cool air. Dominic, behind her, went straight to the bar. Lila plonked herself on a stool at the end of the table, beside Jess.

Jess mentally shelved the question of who'd got the water, and turned instead to Lila to ask the other question on her mind before either of them had a drink and forgot.

Lila, unfortunately, didn't have a clue about where the judges had met for dinner on that Saturday night, but she did have other news. Or, more to the point, Dom had news.

"Go on, Dom, tell them who you saw." Lila smiled soppily at her husband as he approached, his hands empty of drinks. "Where's my drink?"

"Paddy'll bring us that round he promised," Dom said, dragging another stool to the table to sit beside his wife.

"Go on," Jess said, after greeting Dom with a quick smile. "Lila said you've news?"

"He does. You'll never guess who he saw! Listen up, everyone."

Paddy drew up behind her, carrying a tray of drinks. "Here you are. First round on the—Oh shite!"

Lila, in her excitement at having news to share, had waved her arm to encompass all the gathered friends, knocking her hand against the tray of drinks.

One of the glasses crashed to the floor, shattering at Paddy's feet and spraying sticky lager across the room. He set down the tray as Jess grabbed at a precariously wobbling beer glass to catch it before it followed the first to the ground.

Lila leapt up, grabbed a bar towel from the bar, and fired off a garbled mix of apology and swearing as she dabbed frantically at the pooling mix of beer and wine on the tray, the table, and the floor.

Anne got a thick handful of paper napkins from the bar and Jess plucked the glasses from the spill, wiped their dripping bottoms with the napkins, and handed them round. "Sorry," she said to Paddy, even though it hadn't been her fault.

"Ah sure, these things happen. Back in a tick."

Once Lila had returned from the toilets, her skirt damp from washed-off beer, and Paddy had replaced the spilled beer—"Ah go away with you of course it's still on the house. I'll pop yous down a bill for the cleaning and the broken glass in the morning, eh Lila?" He winked at her, and she offered him a feeble smile.

"I really am sorry, Pad. Sit down and have one with us, won't you? Sláinte." She raised her glass to the pub landlord, who grinned, blew her a kiss, picked his own glass from the bar and pulled out a stool to join them.

"Sláinte."

"Cheers."

"To my clumsy wife," Dom said dryly, raising his glass to her.

Lila glared at him. "To the best pub in the village," she said to Paddy, "and to us saving the hanging baskets," she added to the rest of the table.

"And the scrubbing of paint." Matty lifted his glass again.

"To finding out who did it, perhaps?" Jess asked tentatively. "Any more news from anyone on that?"

The evening descended into chatter, and a fresh wave of speculations, most involving the identity of the culprits, but no one, it seemed, had anything concrete to offer.

"It's a bit of a dead end," Anne said, and then Lila got out her guitar and Matty pulled out a tin whistle, and Peggy arrived, and the evening turned to music and singing and more drinking and more laughter and by the time Marcus arrived at eleven, the pub was full and noisy and the Canadian couple had joined them, and Gerry the postman had come in, and Billy White and his wife, and the young couple who lived further down the pub lane had come in with their cocker spaniels, and even Gary and Sean had turned up for a quick drink on their way from somewhere to somewhere, and Jess, while not exactly slaughtered, was unsteady on her feet and the edges of the pub had become quite blurry.

They dragged out last orders until almost midnight and then Marcus and Alice bundled Jess in the back seat of Marcus's car and she thought she remembered something someone might have said but couldn't quite remember what, and hadn't someone come in and been chatting about something that might have been important, and perhaps Alice would remember and she'd tell her in the morning.

Chapter Twenty-Four

"Thought you agreed not to be hungover." Alice handed Jess a glass of orange juice, a cup of black coffee, and a couple of paracetamol. "Get these in you. Toast?"

Jess groaned and forced her eyes open. "What time is it?"

Almost ten. *Shite*. But still Saturday morning, at least. She downed the paracetamol with the orange juice and sipped at the coffee as she dragged herself from the bed and picked her jeans off the floor. "Ouch." She wasn't quite ready for bending over.

Downstairs, the smell of toast wafted from the kitchen, and Alice's and Marcus's chatter drifted through the house. A cupboard door clattered loudly. The fridge opened and closed, loudly. A car drove by outside the window. Loudly.

Jess groaned and stumbled into the shower, where she stood under the scalding water for long enough to wash her hair, then turned it to cold for a blast of energising, hangover-busting ice. She swore and turned it back to hot.

Ten minutes later, she joined Alice and Marcus at the kitchen table, where the three of them took turns to bemoan the turn in the weather and the state of Jess's head.

"There'll be no invigorating walk in that, anyway," she said, pointing to the drizzle outside the French doors with a twinge of guilty relief.

"We should make you go anyway." Alice and Marcus exchanged a look over Jess's pounding head that reminded her of her parents, way back when Jess was a teenager and Doreen O'Malley still loved her husband and George was still alive. Doreen had left George just as soon as they'd ploughed their savings into rural living in Ballyfortnum, and abandoned their retirement plans to run off to the Costa del Sol, where she now lived with an orange-hued, leather-skinned ex-pat called Alan.

"You sound like Mum," she said aloud. "We're not going anywhere. We can play Scrabble, if you like."

Alice and Marcus exchanged that look again.

"Jessica O'Malley." Alice shook her head slowly, feigning a look of disappointment Jess couldn't be bothered to rise to. "Firstly, you *hate* Scrabble. Do you even have a set?" She shook her head again. "Tut tut, Jess. Call yourself a mystery-solver? You really have no recollection of what Dom said last night, do you? Good thing one of us was sober enough to tell a policeman all about it over breakfast while you were snoring upstairs."

Marcus got up, came around the table to stand behind Jess, and patted her shoulder. Like someone would pat a child who'd got all their spellings wrong because they hadn't bothered to learn them. "Oh, Jess. See how much easier it is if you leave it to the professionals."

She groaned again, and leaned back into his hand.

He rubbed her shoulders, and kissed her head. "More coffee, dear?"

"Dear? You make me sound like your granny. Come on then, you two. Out with it. What did I miss?"

Lila's husband Dom, who worked as a bouncer, but was occasionally called to cover security guard shifts here or there, had, according to Alice, been called to one such job on Monday night. He'd been regaling the group with a story about catching someone on the CCTV monitors, not breaking or entering, or causing any trouble in the extensive grounds of the factory he'd been working at, but setting up a small camouflage tent, a comfortable folding chair, and a tiny gas stove, on which Dom had watched him boil a tiny kettle and make himself a large cup of tea, before sitting back in the chair, pulling his collar up and his balaclava down, and settling in for what, it turned out, was owl-watching.

Jess furrowed her brow, trying to keep up, wondering if perhaps she was still a little drunk. "What's that got to do with anything?"

"Nothing," Alice said. "But he came home at about quarter to nine on Tuesday morning." She leaned back onto her chair and narrowed her eyes at Jess. "And who do you think he saw, as he pulled into his driveway?"

Jess's ears pricked up, her fuzzy head clearing very slightly. "Who?"

"Willie Keegan."

"Willie?"

"Yep."

Jess sighed impatiently. "And? Did Dom speak to him? What was he doing? Where was he going?"

"He was on his way to do a last stroll around the village. One last check on things before the judging. He had a wheelbarrow with him; some garden tools—a strimmer, brooms, shovels, whatever a man like Willie Keegan takes out and about when he goes for a stroll ..." Alice tailed off and smirked at her sister. "A barrow full of clues, evidence, that kind of thing."

Marcus laughed. "Or a barrow full of the kind of things he might need to do any last-minute jobs to make sure the village was looking its very best before the judges turned up."

Alice wrinkled her nose at him. "Same difference."

Jess let her head drop onto her hands, the prickle of interest already waning. "Yeah, but that doesn't help much? We already guessed he'd been attacked between about nine and nine-thirty, so that puts him still un-attacked at eight-forty-five. No big surprise there?"

"It does help us piece together where he was and what time he got there, though," Alice said. "And that he was intending to do any last-minute tidying up, and—"

"Al?" Jess sat up with head-splitting jerk. "Ouch. Alice, you said about the tools in the barrow? Did you just make them up as random tools you've heard of, or did Dom *tell* you what was in the barrow?" She squinted at her sister through half-closed eyes, trying to concentrate despite the fuzz.

"Er ... What did I say? A strimmer? And a shovel?" Alice thought for a moment. "No, he definitely said those; that's why I remembered them. Dogs."

Jess looked at her blankly, rubbing her eyes as if that might help her make sense of Alice's random words. "What?"

Behind her, Marcus's hands squeezed her shoulders. "Dom said Willie was moaning about how once, about a decade ago, there'd been a pile of it in the middle of the pavement."

"A dog?"

"Dog shite, you idiot! On judging day," Alice said with a snigger worthy of a four-year-old child. "Dom did a great impression of Willie complaining. Well," she amended, "everyone who knows Willie was rolling about laughing and said it was spot on, but then they remembered he's still in hospital and sobered up—" She broke off and smirked at Jess. "Not you, obviously."

"He said he would never put the village in such jeopardy again," Marcus said, giving a low chuckle and resuming his gentle kneading of Jess's shoulders. "So, yes, Dom was absolutely certain there was a shovel in the barrow."

Jess stiffened. "But ..." She leaned forwards, her elbows on the table and her chin propped on her hands, running images of the scene through her foggy mind. "Where are all the tools? Some of them were in the shed, but ... Hang on; I've got a picture. A strimmer; some other things ... let me check." She reached for her phone and turned to Marcus. "So at least one of those barrows in the shed was his? And that strimmer I saw there?"

"Think so. Father James thinks the old tatty barrow is Willie's. Said it sounded similar to the one he uses in the churchyard. Couldn't be sure, of course, but let's assume—" He broke off as Jess jerked upright under his hands, wincing again as her head reminded her not to move so fast. "All right, all right." He dug his fingers lightly into her shoulders. "Don't say it. We don't *assume*. But in this case, we are confidently assuming. Yes. The strimmer and some of the other tools were his. Matty said someone took them out of the barrow when they used it to gather up the plants. Sit still, or I'll stop."

She turned back to face Alice across the table, and leaned back against Marcus's hands. "Carry on then. Both of you. Shoulder massage, you—" She wiggled a shoulder under Marcus's hand. "—and whatever else Dom had to say, from you, Al. Did he know where Willie was headed?" As she spoke, she swiped through the series of photos, looking for the one with the tools.

Alice shrugged. "No. But using those Lollipop-Club worthy brain cells, I'd say we could safely *assume*—" She threw Marcus a quick smile. "—that he was going from his house further up that lane, from which direction he was coming, into the village, in which direction he was headed when Dominic saw him. I think it highly likely, given that his barrow and tools were all stashed in that shed, that he was, in fact, going to that shed." She sat back in her chair and gave Jess a sickly-sweet smile.

"Hercule Poirot eat your heart out." She laughed, and Jess squirmed again under Marcus's shoulder-rubbing and glared at the pair of them in turn.

"All right you two, that's enough! If you can't see how helpful that is, then I will just have to solve the mystery myself. I'd think a policeman would be far more interested in finding out exactly where *all* Willie Keegan's garden tools ended up, given that if it was the same barrow that was parked in the shed next to him, it was full of nemesias and nasturtiums and creeping Jenny and although there was a strimmer and a rake and a bucket or two and a pair of shears, there was absolutely not a single shovel in sight. Look." She waved the photo evidence at Marcus and then at Alice.

"Good point," Alice said. "Why didn't we think of that, Marcus, while our Jess here was playing at Sleeping Beauty?"

"Beauty?" Marcus said, deadpan. "She was snoring like you'd expect from Shrek, and drooling across the pillow even worse than Fletcher."

"Oy!" Jess spun on her seat and swiped at his arm.

"Besides," he went on, dodging the swipe, "if only you'd been awake, oh, I dunno ..." He made a show of looking at the clock on the kitchen wall. "About two hours ago, you'd have heard me calling John to get onto it, and you'd have known that Father James, who had absolutely no idea, asked Mrs Harris, who did, and said of course Willie had been using those sheds as a handy place to stash his tools during the run-up to the contest, being both central and out of sight, and you'd also have heard me tell Alice that some of the other tools—a broom, another rake, for example, have already been identified as those used by all kinds of people during the clean-up. Willie Keegan, according to Mrs Harris, was the kind of gardener who marked all his tools.

"Put his name on them all, she said he did." Alice got up, went to the junk drawer, and retrieved Jess's notebook. "Only thing is, if Dom is absolutely certain there was a shovel or a spade or something similar in the barrow when he was talking to Willie, then no one knows where it is, not yet."

"Probably just got taken home by someone, or stashed somewhere, but even so, we'd like to track it down, in case it was used as the weapon that injured him." Marcus stopped rubbing Jess's shoulders and gestured at the notebook. "What's that?" he said, in the tone of someone who knew exactly what it was and thoroughly disapproved. "Jessica O'Malley, have you been taking notes on an ongoing crime investigation again? That's it. No more shoulder rubs for you." He pulled out a chair and dropped onto it with a sigh. "But since you *have* been making notes, I'd better take a look." He held out his hand.

"Hang on a min." Alice was scribbling furiously into the book, the pencil scritch-scratching across the page. "Okay, here you go." She closed the book with the pencil inside to mark the place, and slid it across the table.

Marcus and Jess reached for it at the same time, Jess marginally beating him to it and pulling it towards her, his hand on hers.

Alice had written *Where is the shovel/spade? Cottage's garden? Look? Ask around. List of people helping with clear-up?*

Marcus, leaning towards Jess so he could read it too, nodded. "Yes. Exactly the questions John and Kev will be out finding answers to." He picked his phone off the table and swiped a few times. "Already are, in fact. They're down in the village now. I'd better go and join them." He got up, wrapped his arms around Jess, kissed the top of her head, and nodded at Alice.

"See you later, my clever little sleuths."

Alice snorted. "What you really mean is, 'Thanks Alice for being sober and attentive while your girlfriend gets drunk and misses vital clues that could bust this case wide open'."

Marcus nodded slowly as she made each point, listening in mock seriousness.

"And," Alice said, "you also mean 'Thanks for telling me all about it while your super-sleuth mystery-solving-genius girlfriend snored away oblivious, despite knowing how annoyed she'd be that she had missed all the fun of finding a real-live witness, a missing link, and a potential weapon because she'd a had a glass or seven too many,' don't you?"

Jess put her head in her hands on the table and groaned. "My head hurts too much to be annoyed. Go. Go on and do the policeman stuff. I think I'm going back to bed."

"No you're not! The rain's stopped and the dogs need a walk. Give us a lift to the village, Marcus? And we'll walk back over the bog?"

Jess groaned again.

"Come on; I'll buy you chocolate from your wonderful Mrs Dunne to keep you going."

Chapter Twenty-Five

T he chocolate, it turned out, was a very good idea.

As Fletcher barked with indignation at being tied to the drainpipe outside the shop, and Snowflake sat quietly watching him with a doggy-glare and gently wagging tail, Jess and Alice stood open-mouthed as Mrs Harris shared the second piece of interesting news of the day.

Gerry the postman had, apparently, also seen the mysterious cyclists seen by Siobhan's son. Gerry the postman had been off since Tuesday afternoon, and hadn't been back into the shop since he'd completed his deliveries on Tuesday morning. As he tended to get to Mrs Harris good and early, he'd been and gone long before the vandalism, and been well into his rounds by the time the drama unfolded. Then he'd nipped home for a change of clothes and his fishing gear, and gone west to Connemara for the rest of the week.

"Using up a bit of holiday while the weather's good, so he was. Hadn't heard a thing about all the goings-on here, he hadn't, not till he came in this morning for a paper and a pint of milk on his way home. You haven't missed him by much, to tell the truth."

Gerry didn't live in the village, but somewhere out along the road beyond the Gun Club lands and onwards towards

Rathdowney. He'd pass through Ballyfortnum to get back from Connemara all right, although he could've got milk a good deal cheaper in the petrol station on the main road. *Checking in for gossip, most likely,* Jess thought. *Not milk.* Gerry liked a bit of gossip just as much as Mrs Dunne and together, they were quite incorrigible. She bit her cheek to stop a smile.

"He saw the bikes?" Alice said

"What?" Jess must have been more hungover than she'd realised; she'd totally missed the significance of what Mrs Dunne had just said. "Say that again. About the bikes, I mean."

Mrs Dunne said it again, and Jess listened properly this time. Gerry'd delivered the post to the shop at about eight-thirty on Tuesday morning, just as he always did, then carried on towards the Orchard Close end of the village. He didn't usually get to Jess's house until nine at the earliest, not that she got much mail these days, what with everything being done online. Come to think of it, she'd had no post for ages ...

"Jess!" Alice nudged her in the ribs. "Are you with us?"

"Sorry. Give me that chocolate, and a bottle of water. I need a sugar rush, I reckon. Sorry, Mrs Dunne. So he'd come from that way already, and got to the shop? So did he tell you then, that he'd seen the bikes? Who was on them? Did he know?"

Alice and Mrs Dunne sighed in perfect harmony, turning as one to shake their heads pityingly at Jess.

"No Jess, he did not tell Mrs Dunne anything about it on Tuesday because he thought nothing of passing two cyclists. He told her this today, when he called in for milk—"

"And a paper." Mrs Dunne matched Alice's tone perfectly, and a rush of heat crawled across Jess's face as the two of them spoke to her as if she was a particularly slow child.

"And when Mrs Dunne mentioned that the culprits might have been two people on bikes—"

"He kind of jumped a little like he'd just remembered something—"

"Which he had—"

Jess held up her hands and laughed, peeled back the chocolate wrapper and broke off a couple of chunks. "Okay, Laurel and Hardy, okay. I get it. So did Gerry know who they were?" She stuffed chocolate into her mouth and offered the packet to Alice, who shook her head, and to Mrs Dunne, who broke off a piece and handed back the rest.

"I'd say you need this more than I do. No, he didn't know who they were, but he did say he's seen them around before, and he did describe them. And," Mrs Dunne said with a distinct air of triumph, "I made him say it slowly and repeat it, so I could write it all down. Thought I'd give it to your Marcus, once the shop's closed for lunch and I'm done for the day." Mrs Harris usually took Saturday afternoons off, employing a girl from the next village to cover for her. "I was going to pop it through his letter box, but you'll be able to give it to him now. Save me a job. I expect you'll be giving it the once-over first, knowing you."

She leaned forward onto her bosom and smiled at Jess. "And the chocolate's on me. Can hardly be charging you for it now I've had a bite, can I now? Go on, go take that information to your Marcus. Hope you find the feckers." She tore a sheet of paper from an A4 pad and handed it to Alice. "I'll give it to you, since your sister seems to have a bit of a head on her still, eh love?"

The sisters left the shop under the tinkling bell. Fletcher jumped on Jess as if she'd been gone forever, and Alice clamped the piece of paper in her teeth so she could untie Snowflake from the drainpipe.

Jess, pushing Fletcher down and ignoring his demands to also be released from the drainpipe snatched the paper from Alice's mouth and read Mrs Dunne's list aloud.

"One red hair. One brownish hair. Maybe twenty, twenty-something, hard to say. Older than school. Old enough to be at work, should think. Dark coats or hoodies. Noticed that, what with it being hot. Big bag, both of them. Jeans, perhaps? Should think so. Looked a bit alike, could be brothers? Wouldn't like to guess it." She paused and looked at Alice. "That's all under a header saying 'Lads'. Then there's another: Bikes. Dark-coloured. Nothing out the ordinary. One had a carrier thing on back. Reflectery things in wheel. Then she's added in brackets: one, not both, he thinks." Jess laughed. "Great word, reflectery, and then there's one of those little arrows you use when there's a missing word, look, and she's added: one bike not one wheel. She's blooming good at this. Perhaps she really was a spy."

Alice took the paper back from Jess. "Untie that fricking dog before he has the whole thing off the wall, for goodness sake, will you!" She poked Jess with her foot, prodding her towards the frantic Labrador. "And then will we go and find Marcus? He can't be far away. Isn't that his car up there?" She gestured towards the cottage.

Jess untied Fletcher and spent the next few seconds trying to get him to calm down and walk sensibly.

Alice, displaying far more sense than the dog, and despite Jess's attempts to snatch it from her, kept the sheet of paper firmly out of Jess's reach until Fletch was settled. By then, they'd reached the pub and Jess plonked herself onto one of the picnic tables on the pavement and plucked the paper from Alice's hand.

"Okay, here's the last bit. Near Geraghtys. Farm workers, maybe? Talking to fella in black Toyota pickup. Driver, red

213

hair, bit older, Gerry thinks. Twenties, maybe. Chatting, not like strangers. Local plates on pickup."

Jess shook her head. "Means nothing to me." She read the whole list aloud again, slowly and thoughtfully. "No. No idea. Those descriptions ring absolutely no bells whatsoever, and even the pickup is no use. Every farmer in Ireland has one of those. I suppose you're right. We'll take it to Marcus. All right, Fletcher! I'm coming. Stop it!" She got up, then sat down again, smoothed Mrs Dunne's list out flat onto the table and snapped a photo of it on her phone. "Just in case," she said to Alice. "Because Marcus'll take this, won't he." She stood again, folded the sheet of paper and tucked it into her pocket.

"I wonder," Alice said as they walked towards the cottage, the Garda car parked on the pavement, and Marcus's car parked behind it, "if whoever was in the pickup could have dropped the bikes off?" She cast a sidelong look at Jess.

Jess stopped walking, turned to Alice, and frowned. "God, hope not! That would widen the search by miles, if they hadn't just biked here from somewhere close. Shite."

As they approached the cottage, voices drifted from around the back, and with no sign of either Marcus or whoever'd come in the Garda car—John and Kev, presumably—Jess and Alice went through the open gates and into the now very-trampled garden.

Not wanting to be accused of sneaking around a crime scene, again, Jess called out. "Hello, Marcus! Are you there?"

Almost immediately, he appeared from around the back, a puzzled expression on his face. "Jess, Alice. What's up? Aren't you going the wrong way?"

Marcus listened to the news about Gerry possibly having seen the vandals, made a phone call to the station, then agreed to dispatch Kev and John off to interview Gerry, "Just in case he remembers anything else. Although," he said, looking up from Mrs Dunne's notes, "she seems to have been thorough. Should be a Gard, that one."

"I reckon she's a former spy," Jess said, following him around the back of the cottage, where Kev and John were painstakingly and systematically poking at the brambles with long sticks. "They getting anywhere? Wouldn't it be easier to strim it back? I can't imagine they're making much progress, what with the brambles so thick."

John, who Jess had met often enough to sort-of know, stopped his search and grimaced at her. "I'd say I'll be putting in for a new set of uniform, after this." He lifted a sleeve and showed her a long tear. "And damages, too." He turned his cheek to show off a vivid red scratch.

Kev, behind the sheds and out of sight, gave a small yelp. There was a flurry of squawking and a frenzy of flapping, and a pheasant flew onto the shed roof.

Fletcher leaped up at the shed wall, barking hysterically, scrabbling to reach the panicked bird.

"Fletcher! Get down!" Jess tugged him off, unsuccessfully trying to quieten him, "Marcus, look." She pointed up at the roof, where she'd spotted something on the corrugated metal, overhanging slightly from the edge, nestled into the ivy and roses. "Fletcher! Will you shut up!" She yanked on his lead. "Stop it!"

Marcus stepped in, grabbed the lead, and used his firmest policeman voice, but for once, Fletcher took no notice.

Jess held up her hand in a 'wait' gesture as she tried to make herself heard over Fletcher's frantic barks. "Hang on." She hauled Fletcher away from the shed, and tied him to the gate, still barking and straining to get at the pheasant. "Shut up!" She turned her back on the dog and returned to where Marcus had, obediently, waited.

"Maybe tie Snowflake out of sight too?" he suggested to Alice. "Give the poor bird a chance to get down."

"Marcus," Jess pointed to the thing she'd seen on the shed roof. "Never mind the bird for the minute. Is that what it looks like? Is there anything to climb on?"

John, grateful for the distraction from picking through the brambles, was sent off to beg a ladder from the pub.

"Or," Marcus called after him, "failing that, try the parochial house? You can go on to talk to Gerry after that; leave the brambles for now. I'd say Jess is right. We'll need a strimmer to make any headway there."

"Hopefully you mightn't need it, if that is Willie's shovel," she said, craning her nek to try to get a better look. "I can't think of any good reason for it to be up there unless it was used to smack him over the head and someone wanted to hide it, can you?"

Chapter Twenty-Six

While waiting for John to hunt down a ladder, Jess took Mrs Dunne's notes from Marcus's hands and read them again.

"Well?" he said, watching her read. "Ringing any of those bells of yours that seem to go off anytime anything happens around here?"

She shook her head.

"Jess," he said, touching her cheek with his fingertips. "I know you won't want to hear this, but your idiot dog is going to have that gate pulled off the gatepost if you don't shut him up and take him for the walk you promised him. I'll let you know, I promise, but you really can't be here if we've something to analyse."

She started to argue but he held up a firm hand. "Jess, you know I can't compromise an investigation. You've already trampled far more of the scene than is sensible, over the last few days, remember. I'll tell you if you found something important, I promise, but Fletcher really will have that wall down in a minute if you don't stop him. Go."

With one final reluctant glance at the shed roof, Jess went with Alice to release the dogs from the gate, Marcus following behind them as if he needed to make sure they really did leave his crime scene.

He gave his little Westie a quick rub, ruffled Fletcher's ears, gave Jess a chaste peck on the cheek, whispered, "Later, when we're not surrounded." He stroked her hand gently, then turned away to greet John, coming towards them on the opposite pavement, bowed under an extendable ladder he had balanced on one shoulder. "That was quick." Marcus strode away from Jess and across the road to help with the ladder. "Good work. Here, I'll give you a hand. See you later." This last, he flung back over his shoulder to Jess and Alice, who still hovered by the gate to the little cottage. Marcus gestured with his head, directing them away. "Go on."

"Hmph," Jess said.

Alice tucked her arm through Jess's. "Come on. You'll only put him in a difficult position if you get in his way." She thrust Fletcher's lead into Jess's hand, looped Snowflake's lead round her own wrist, and dragged Jess towards home. "Besides, while he's busy there, we've got work to do."

"We have?" Jess turned to her sister; eyebrows raised. "What? What's more important than getting an assault weapon—maybe even a murder weapon if poor Willie doesn't come round soon—down from a roof?"

"Quite a few things, actually. Will we start by seeing if Mrs Harris wants to give two tired walkers a nice cup of tea?" Alice threw a surreptitious glance over her shoulder. "Okay, they've gone round the back. They'll be busy there for a while. They won't see us detour to the church. Come on." Her arm still tucked through Jess's, she steered them up the church driveway, walking fast, and casting the odd look back towards the cottage to check they weren't being watched by Marcus or his colleagues.

"Why the secrecy?"

"I think he thinks I was taking you home to keep you out of trouble. Not nosing around asking questions."

"I still have no idea what questions you're thinking of, to be perfectly honest, Al, so as far I'm concerned, we're just calling on a friend, saying hello, maybe stopping for a friendly cup of tea ..." She flicked a sideways look at Alice. "And maybe even a scone."

"That's the spirit," Alice said with a laugh. "Marcus will easily believe that much, anyway." She stepped forwards and rapped her knuckles sharply on the wooden door.

If Father James was surprised to see them, he didn't show it. "Good to see you Alice, how are you? I don't have another ladder, if that's what you want? Lucky I knew where that one was, to be honest. Willie usually has it locked away somewhere. Only that there was a bulb out in the church porch ... I was just about to have my morning coffee. And a scone. Coming to join me?" Without waiting for an answer, he swung the door fully open, and stepped back to let them pass.

Over a pot of tea and a scone—hot water for Alice, and only one scone each, as that was all he had left, he said apologetically—Alice admitted to Father James that it was really Mrs Harris's brains they'd come to pick, then carefully cut her scone in half, scraped a little jam across one side, and passed the other half to Jess.

"Her brains, or her ability to gossip?" the priest asked with a smile.

Jess, even though she still had no clue what her sister was up to, felt the warmth of a blush spreading across her face. She busied herself with smearing the half-scone with butter and jam, cut it in half again, and dropped one piece on Father James's crumb-strewn plate.

"Thought so," Father James said. "And is this gossip I want to be party to, or will I go and get on with preparations for the evening mass?"

Alice laughed. "It's not that bad. Jess mentioned that Mrs Harris might have heard how Willie is, and as we were nearby ... And of course it's always nice to catch up with you, too." She flashed a warm smile at the priest, who returned it, and topped up her empty cup with fresh water from the kettle and a slice of lemon from the fridge.

Mrs Harris, who despite her advanced age had the hearing of an owl, appeared in the kitchen doorway brandishing a vacuum cleaner and a duster. "Finished in your study, Father Jim."

"Jim?" Jess sent the priest a questioning look. "What's that about?"

He peered into his tea as if he hadn't heard, splashed a little more milk into his cup, and Mrs Harris gave a girlish giggle.

She's acting strangely, whatever's she up to. Jess was not at all convinced the housekeeper had, in fact, been hoovering, given that there had been no sound of it since she and Alice had come in, drunk a cup of tea, eaten a scone, and had time for Father James and Alice to indulge in a detailed "How are you, and how's Dublin?" conversation while Snowflake lay quietly at their feet and Fletch sniffed around hopefully for crumbs on the floor of the disappointingly spotless kitchen.

Mrs Harris parked the hoover in the corner and moved fully into the room, with a distinct whiff of furniture polish about her person. "You'll be wanting to know have I any news on old Willie?" she said, dispelling any notions Jess may have had about whether the housekeeper had been listening in or not.

Alice sat up straight and nudged Jess's foot.

Jess, laughing inwardly at the thought of Mrs Harris calling Willie old, given that she was the oldest person in the parish by several decades, if the rumours held any truth, nudged Alice back. "Tea?" Without waiting for an answer, she poured a cup for Mrs Harris, set it in front of her at the end of the table, and said, "Yes please, if you've heard? How is he?" She nudged Alice again, hoping her sister would understand that she'd guessed where Alice wanted to steer the conversation.

Sure enough, after a 'no change' update on Willie, Mrs Harris once again pre-empted their next question. "And you'll be wanting to know if she'd heard any more about that other fellow? Jim whathisname?"

"Yes please," Alice said, casting an overly-sweet smile at her sister. *See,* it told Jess, *I can do this sleuthing without even trying. Easy!*

"Our Betsy had a look at what he was in for, all right. Couldn't find any trace of him at first, as it weren't his right name, she said. James, he is, and she seemed awfully surprised about it. Only that they'd discharged someone with the same surname a few days ago and she did some more investigating and saw he'd been in for food poisoning, too. Gave me a right good chuckle, it did. Said it was the first she'd heard of Jim being short for James and asked did we ever call you Father Jim." Her beady eyes twinkled at the priest.

"You said," he said, encompassing Jess and Alice with an indulgent look. "And she's been calling me Father Jim ever since she spoke to Betsy last night."

"Ah." Jess snorted into her tea. "I did wonder what that was about."

Although Mrs Harris took a good deal longer to tell it than Elizabeth and Henry had, her findings were the same: Jim-the-judge had been poisoned by uncooked beans in his salad at the dinner with the other judges on the Saturday before they'd come to Ballyfortnum. Betsy, however, had one extra detail—the beans he'd eaten were definitely raw and the consequent alert to the hotel had confirmed that the beans in the salad were supposed to be cooked. Regulations, Mrs Harris explained, over yet another refill of the teacups, meant that if someone presented with food poisoning from a restaurant or hotel, environmental health got notified, and they'd be wanting to know if anyone else was affected and so on. Betsy, having asked around, had tracked down the doctor who'd been involved in the report, buttered him up on a tea break, and found out far more than Jess would have imagined a nurse should be able to.

"That's Our Betsy," Mrs Harris said. "Always could talk her way around anyone, so she could."

The gist of it, nonetheless, was that those beans Jim had eaten were added separately and deliberately and the hotel was under investigation from both Environmental Health and the local Gards.

"Blimey," Jess said.

"Blimey." Alice picked up her empty cup, took it to the sink, rinsed it, and set it on the draining rack. "Tea towel?"

Mrs Harris waved her off. "Don't be daft. I'll be doing that later, don't you worry. Now, I'd best be getting along, if there's nothing else you're needing from me.

"Mrs Harris," Jess said, suddenly remembering that there *was* something else. Something she'd almost forgotten in the excitement of the last few days. Something Mrs Harris had said the day the judges were here. You said you'd seen someone, that day?"

Mrs Harris turned shrewd eyes towards Jess. "I see a lot of people. Anyone in particular you're thinking of?"

"You said one of them had run away? One of whoever it was who'd done the vandalism and hurt poor Willie. What was that about?"

The white-haired housekeeper rested her hands on the table and closed her eyes for a moment. "Not running, as such. Lad on a pushbike. Older than a school child, not old, though, shouldn't think. Had a dark cap pulled over his face, black, I'd say, but with a flash of green ... yellow, maybe too. Hard to tell, from that distance. My eyes aren't what they used to be. Dark coloured top. One of them bags on his back."

"You only saw one?"

She tipped her head. "Just the one. Can't say if there was another ahead of him. Not after him, though. 'twere unusual enough to see anyone around that cottage who weren't the tidying-up committee or old poor old Willie himself, so I paid attention right enough for a minute or two before getting back to my cleaning. No one else followed him out, and I said to myself he'd just nipped in to relieve himself, most like. You know what fellas are like."

"Fair enough assumption," Jess said with a smile. "Where was he going?"

"Out the village, looked like. A tractor stopped out there by the school for a minute and he was gone by the time it moved on." She gestured through the window towards the Dublin Road. "And I'd say you'll want to know where he'd come from, too?" She turned her eyes from the window and studied Jess, her eyes sharp and clear amongst the wrinkles of her face.

Jess nodded. "Where had he come from?"

"Out the garden of that cottage."

"You can see it from here?" Jess moved closer to the large kitchen windows and peered out. "The trees are in the way."

"Can see it well enough from upstairs."

Jess swung from the window to face Mrs Harris. "You can?"

Father James sighed and got to his feet. "And now I suppose you'll want to see for yourself." He grinned at Jess. "Good thing it's not my room. It would hardly be appropriate to send you up there! Go on up to the landing. You too, Alice." He waved his hand towards the hall and followed the O'Malley sisters to the stairs.

"Fletcher, stay. Go back to the kitchen. Go on." Jess shooed the dog back into the kitchen, where he sat watching her dolefully, tail sweeping slowly across the floor, as she started up the staircase.

Sure enough, from the large sash window on the bright landing, there was a good view across the school playground and playing fields, taking in the pub's frontage, the derelict cottage, and some of the houses on Siobhan's road. Siobhan's house was hidden behind the school, and the odd taller tree broke the view, but overall, from the landing, Mrs Harris, would indeed have been able to see almost all the vandalised part of the village.

"Can you see the shop from any of the windows?" Alice asked Father James.

The only windows that faced in that direction were a small bathroom window with frosted glass, and a narrow window in a box room, but that outlook was obscured by a large and leafy beech tree and although they could glimpse fragments of the shop front, the door and window weren't visible at all.

"I guess you might see it better in winter," Jess said.

"Which doesn't help us now." Alice started back down the stairs. "You didn't see any of the attack?" she asked Mrs Harris, who'd waited at the bottom of the stairs, one crumpled hand resting on the newel post, and Fletcher at her feet.

"If only I'd been gazing out the window into space instead of cleaning them and doing my duties," she said dryly.

"If only," Jess said with a grin. "You'd have seen almost the whole thing—the paint on the pub, the paint on the cottage, the flowers being pulled up ... everything but the shop and Willie being bashed."

"I do keep telling her she shouldn't work so hard. Shouldn't be working at all, should you?" Father James followed Jess and Alice down the stairs, speaking to the housekeeper over their heads as they descended. "Can't get rid of her, we can't." The affection in his voice said he liked having her around, despite his disagreement with her insistence to work. Her loyalty to Ballyfortnum's church and clergy was second to none, and the general consensus amongst the villagers was that her ghost would continue with the dusting for centuries yet.

Mrs Harris tutted, and returned to the kitchen.

Jess gathered her plate and cup from the table, stacked them with Father James's, and added them to the pile beside the sink. "Mrs Harris? *Were* you a spy?"

The elderly housekeeper swished a towel at Jess but her eyes twinkled. "That'd be telling. Go on, get off with you both, and leave me to bake a fresh batch of scones for the week, in case you're up this way again."

"One last question, then we'll get out of your hair, honest. Didn't you notice the paint all over the cottage, if you were looking out the window at it?"

"Aye, but I can't say it registered 'til after I'd seen the fella off on his bike, to tell the truth. I went back to my window-washing and thought to myself something else weren't right neither, and I looked over at it all again, thinking something was out of place, and when you're my age you wonder if your mind plays tricks on you because wasn't I so busy scanning for movement that I didn't see hadn't the whole front wall had gone and changed its colour!" She chuckled and plunged her hands into the soapy water to wash the teacups.

"And what kind of time was this? Was anyone else around?"

"That's another question, so?" Mrs Harris turned to face Jess again, dripping suds onto the floor.

Jess smiled. "Sorry. But ..."

"Just as I were turning away, thinking I'd best let Father know, and on my way down to the phone, that dark-haired Docherty girl and that Heron one and Geraldine Brady all came on over the road in a bit of a rush. They ran over to the cottage and got all of a fluster and pulled out their phones and I said to myself that'll do, sure won't they be alerting all who needs to know about it, and I went back to the dusting, glad I'd been saved a trip downstairs and back again."

"So about nineish?"

"After, I'd say. Father'd been gone a while as I'd time enough to get round his rooms. Maybe quarter after, more likely."

Jess nodded. That tied in with what Siobhan had said. Sounded like she'd only missed them by a minute or two. Whoever it was, they'd been lucky not to get caught, by all accounts. How had they managed to get away with it?

After another round of goodbyes, Father James accompanied them to the driveway, where he turned right towards the church and Jess, Alice, and the two dogs turned left.

"Goodbye Father Jim! Thanks for sharing your last scones."

"Ah, sure, there's no one I'd sooner share them with."

Chapter Twenty-Seven

At the cottage, both the Garda car and Marcus's car had gone. Jess and Alice turned in the opposite direction, towards home. As they walked, Jess pulled out her phone to check for messages.

Gone to station. Willie's shovel on roof. Well done you! Back for dinner xx

"Well," said Jess, "looks like we're getting closer. Deliberate poisoning. Hidden weapon. Sightings of suspects. Not a bad day's work, so far."

"Not bad at all," Alice agreed, stopping at Marcus's gate as Snowflake sniffed at the path and looked up inquiringly as if to ask if he was going to this home or Jess's home. "Come on Snow. Other home tonight." She jiggled the lead and Snowflake trotted onwards, little white tail wagging happily.

"Actually—" Jess stopped abruptly on the pavement, causing Alice to almost trip over a bemused Fletcher, who'd been jerked to a stop by Jess's sudden halt. She spun around, to face back the way they'd come. "I just want ask Mrs Dunne something before we go. Come on."

"These poor dogs are beginning to think we are going to do nothing but walk up and down this short stretch of the road all day long," Alice said, bending to rub Snowflake's head, then striding after her sister, who'd set off at a pace fast enough that for once, Fletcher paced along beside his mistress with all the smooth synchronicity of a dog competing at Crufts, tail wagging and tongue lolling, not tugging on the lead like he usually did. "Want to tell me?" Alice called after them.

"In a min." Jess darted across the road in front of an approaching car, causing the driver to slow to the speed he should have been doing through the village centre to start with, and shooting Jess a glare. She waved an apology, and carried on.

Her rush was impeded by Alice, who'd waited for the car to pass before crossing the road at more sedate pace.

"Here." Jess thrust Fletcher's lead at Alice almost before Alice had set foot on the curb. "Won't be a min." She ducked inside the shop, leaving the bell tinkling in her wake as the door closed behind her.

"Mrs Dunne," she said, as she crossed the shop floor in three long strides, "I just had a thought, and wanted to double check something."

Mrs Dunne glanced up from her novel. "Jess," she said, and returned her gaze to her book, marked her place with her finger, and looked up again.

"I was thinking," Jess said, pulling her phone from her pocket and opening up the picture of Gerry's description of the two cyclists.

Mrs Dunne muttered something that sounded a lot like, "always a bad sign," and turned her still-open book upside down, the finger-place-holder abandoned as she leaned forwards on her arms.

"Well, you said you'd not seen anyone unusual in the shop that morning, not counting Lydia, and that everyone else was a familiar face, and I was thinking that maybe you did see those two cyclists but didn't realise it?"

Mrs Dunne raised her eyebrows, her lips clamped together as she waited for Jess to go on.

"Hear me out. So when Gerry saw them, he described one with red hair and one with dark hair, and even around here, I'd reckon you'd notice red hair and have remembered that, right? So you probably didn't see anyone red-haired—"

"The Hegartys were in all right, and I'd sure as eggs notice them, with or without that hair of theirs." Her chins wobbled as she held back a laugh.

Jess didn't know the Hegartys, but they were well-known around the village: a large family of tousled redheads; all the children in the primary school and all within a year of the next one's age.

"—but when Siobhan's son saw the cyclists, he said something about them having hats on, so my question for you is, did any of the people who came in that morning have hats on? You'd surely have noticed that, with it being so hot?"

Mrs Dunne's lips set into a thin line; her brow furrowed in thought.

"I don't know if he meant bike helmets, or caps, or what kind of hats, but a redhead in a hat stops being an obvious redhead, right?"

"There were them two lads who come in once in a while. Caps. The pair of them wearing caps, so not so peculiar, with all that sun we had. Most of the lads round here would put a cap on, working out in the fields and the like. Wouldn't think nothing of it, so I wouldn't. Brother works for Geraghty, if I'm remembering right."

Jess gave a quick snort of laughter. "You *always* remember right, so that means there *are* two lads who come in sometimes who *do* have a brother who works at the Geraghty farm. And that, Mrs D, is really interesting, given that Gerry saw two boys with bikes beside a farm truck up at Geraghtys', don't you think? So what I'm thinking is that maybe the two boys Gerry saw, who had bikes but weren't on them because they were talking to someone? Well maybe they—"

"Were maybe the two same boys who got themselves onto those bikes, pulled hats over their heads, and came on down to the village to throw paint all over us?"

"Exactly. But at some point between Gerry seeing them and them doing the paint-throwing, is it possible that they left the bikes somewhere, and then come into the shop?"

Mrs Dunne straightened fractionally; her eyes wide. "You think that pair of hooligans came in and bought bars of chocolate and a packet of Taytos before going off on their merry way to destroy the whole fecking village?"

"I don't suppose you'd remember either if anyone else was in the shop when they came in, or how soon after they left the paint was thrown over your window?" She looked hopefully at Mrs Dunne, who was fiddling with something at the till, pressing buttons and squinting at the screen.

"Here we are ... bottle of coke, Mars, KitKat Chunky ... Taytos ... That'd be them. Eight-fifty-eight."

"Money or time?"

"Eh?"

Eight-fifty-eight. Money or time of day?"

"Oh, time. Total was five-fifty."

"You sure that was them? No one else had anything similar?"

The shopkeeper frowned at the screen, peered at it for a minute more. "Thought so. That was them all right."

"Do you remember anything else about them? Did they say much?"

Mrs Dunne turned away from the till and slouched over the counter again, one arm folded over the stack of papers under the over-turned paperback, and the other hand propping up her chins. "They were here a few minutes, should think. A good few of the school kids were in, so I'd have been busy enough. They bantered a bit about what to get." She stared at a point somewhere beyond Jess's head. "Seriously, Con, it's frigging breakfast time innit."

"Huh?" Jess looked at her in confusion. "Who's Con?"

"That's what one of them said. Called the other one Con."

Well, Jess thought. *We've got a name.* "Anything else? Think?"

"I'd say the timing's close enough, eh love? Close enough." Mrs Dunne's voice had risen, and her eyes darted around the shop as if the two lads might still be lurking behind a shelf. "But there were plenty of others around about, at that time. Busiest times of day, 'fore and after school, so I'd say it's mighty odd no one else saw them about."

"I think," Jess said softly, "that's kind of the point. I think people did see them, but didn't think about it, because they weren't proper strangers. You said yourself they're in often enough, and you hadn't thought anything of it. Well, I'm guessing you're not the only one who didn't pay them a second glance. Thanks, Mrs D. You've been very helpful."

Outside the shop, Fletcher scrabbled at the window, pressing his nose to the glass and scratching at the sill with his front paws.

"Oops, sorry, better go, before he sends that window box flying and we have to redo it all over again." She rushed from the shop and grabbed the lead from Alice. "Get down, you idiot! Get down. Al, I think we've got a name! Well, half a one, at least. I'll tell you the news as we walk; come on!"

They had just started away from the shop when Jess froze, thrust Fletcher's lead at Alice, and dashed back towards the shop door. "Be right back!" she called to Alice as the shop bell tinkled and in she went.

"Sorry, forgot to get a paper." She tugged one of the weekly papers from under Mrs Dunne's arms and confused look.

"You don't usually get the paper, love."

This was true, but as Jess had said the word 'news' to Alice, a black and white image had flickered in her mind. A black and white image of an unloved, derelict cottage in Ballyfortnum surrounded by a crowd of onlookers on Tuesday morning. An image that she'd glanced at and away from as Mrs Dunne had turned to the till and uncovered the pile of newspapers.

Back outside the shop, Jess ignored Alice's efforts to return Fletcher to the charge of his owner, and instead, quickly scanned the article beneath the paper's headline: **LOCAL TIDY VILLAGE ENTRANT IN BIG MESS**, with Deiric Shaugnessy's byline. Obviously cobbled together from the chaos of the morning, it gave more questions than answers, and Jess found nothing she didn't already know. She studied the grainy image.

"There's a lot of people in this. When we get home, we'll try to put names to everyone ..." She held the paper closer, then turned it towards her sister and pointed at a detail in the photo, mostly hidden behind the cluster of people. "What do think that is, there, behind that pushchair?"

Alice screwed up her eyes, squinting at the object Jess was pointing at. "Maybe a bike?"

"I think so too. Now, let me tell you what else Mrs Dunne said about it all."

Under an overcast sky and the looming threat of more rain, Jess and Alice walked quickly as they headed for Orchard Close.

"I'll have walked off those scones in time for lunch," Jess said, panting a little as they sped along. "Think there's a couple of Linda's brownies left in the tin."

"Never mind that." Alice glared at Jess. "What did Mrs Dunne say that's left you so excited?"

As Jess relayed the information Mrs Dunne had given her, Alice listened without saying much other than occasional "Go on," noises, until Jess ran out of steam.

"You know what?" Alice said, pausing at a farm gate.

"What?"

"Something else Anne said last night. She said some of the farm lads had helped with the clearing up."

Jess stopped beside her and leaned on the gate, gazing over the field towards the distant mountains. "She did, didn't she."

"So ... what if Mrs Harris only saw one of them running away because one of them didn't run away?"

"And stayed to help?" Jess squinted at the sister. "Why would he do that?"

"Loads of reasons ... He felt guilty? He hadn't meant Willie to get hurt? He hadn't time to run off? I don't know."

"Hmm. So what if ... what if he, whoever he is, bashed Willie, dragged him into the shed, tried to help him, then the others all arrived and he hadn't time to get away and didn't want to be caught so he just started to help? And he was the one who got the water, to keep everyone else away from that tap opposite where he knew Willie was lying?"

"I think," Alice said, "that does sound kind of plausible. You said someone had put something under Willie's head, too. That doesn't sound like the actions of someone who wanted to hurt him, does it?"

"I think," Jess said, "that we're getting close to putting it all together. I think I can see *how* it was done in such a short space of time, and I think we're getting closer to finding out who did it, too."

"Well," Alice said, pushing herself off the gate as Snowflake snuffled towards the hedge, "I'd say if you have the *how* part figured out, the rest might fall into place. There'll be something in the *how* that tells you what you're missing, and once we know what's missing, we'll know where to look for it." She waggled Snowflake's lead. "Maybe."

Jess laughed. "I loved how philosophical and confident you sounded until that 'maybe'. We need paper. I'd say if we can get it written out, we may see something." She sent her sister a sidelong grin. "Maybe."

Chapter Twenty-Eight

I n the sunshine-yellow kitchen of Number 7, Orchard Close, Jess rustled up two plates of sandwiches—cheese and mayo and salad for her; salad and salad for Alice—while Alice doodled in Jess's notebook.

"You said you think you know the *how* part?"

"Have you written everything we found out so far? And looked through what I already had before today?"

Alice flipped back through a couple of pages, scanning the notes. "Think so ... Want to check?" She pushed the notebook across the table to Jess, who turned through the same pages, skimming for the details.

A thin slice of cucumber slid from her sandwich and landed on the notes with a feeble splat. "Oops!" Jess retrieved the cucumber, put it in her mouth, and blotted the mayonnaise-splattered page, leaving the penned note about the boys seen at Geraghtys' farm smudged and blurry. "Geraghty ..." What was it about Geraghty that was niggling at her? It wasn't just that whoever these lads were, they may work for Old Man Geraghty. Labourers, at his farm, she guessed, but it wasn't just that. Where else had she heard his name in relation to all this? "Al? Did you see Geraghty written somewhere else in our notes?"

Alice shook her head. "Don't think so—not other than there, anyway. Who would know if he has a pair of labourers matching those descriptions? There must be someone you can ask?"

"Mrs Dunne said she thinks their brother works there. Wouldn't she know if they did too?"

Alice nibbled at her sandwich, her nose twitching rabbit-like as she chewed. "Probably. She knows—"

"Everything. True." Jess tipped back on her chair, rocking it back and forth with its front legs a little off the floor. "I'll text Anne. Matty would probably know. Don't all these farmers know each other's workers? I'm sure they share them around, half the time." She pivoted her chair towards the worktop and stretched to get her phone from where it lay beside the sink.

She righted the chair, typed out the message—*Does Matt know Geraghtys workers? Ask him?*—hit SEND, and picked up her sandwich, managing only one large bite before jumping to her feet and rushing from the room.

"What's up?"

"Back in a mo!"

In the living room, Jess stood still in the centre of the floor. "Where is it?" she muttered quietly to herself. "Where is it?" She lifted a couple of the sofa cushions, and ran her hand down the spaces between them all, finding only a two-euro coin, a crumpled tissue, and a bookmark. "Think, Jess, think ..." The scrap of paper wasn't there. *Where else could she look? Coat pockets?*

Her coat pockets produced a haul of tissues, loose coins, and three hairbands, but not the piece of paper she'd suddenly remembered. *What had she been wearing the day she'd sat in the farmhouse conservatory and taken notes? When even was that?*

"Tuesday!" It seemed like weeks ago, and somehow disconnected from the day of the judging by several days, not the same afternoon. "It was Tuesday afternoon and I was wearing ... no, I wasn't, I came home and changed ... what into?"

"Jess?" Alice appeared in the kitchen doorway, an amused smirk on her face. "Have you gone completely mad? Who are you talking to and what are you telling yourself? You know what they say about that, right?"

Jess, too distracted by her frantic search to retaliate, glanced up at her sister, frowned, and said, "I just remembered something, only I can't find it."

"What?"

"A piece of paper with the notes about what Siobhan's son said."

"And what did he say?"

Jess stopped rooting through coat pockets—a fruitless effort anyway since it had been blazingly hot that day and she knew full well she hadn't been wearing any coat, never mind the one hanging under the one she'd already checked. "Alice, if I knew what it said, would I need to be looking for it?" She let the coat fall back against the wall under the row of hooks and ran up the stairs, Alice following behind.

She cast her eyes around her bedroom, looking for the pair of jeans she thought she'd changed into after changing out of her blood-stained, bramble-torn, dirt-smeared judging-day clothes, expecting to find them tossed over the back of the chair.

"Wash basket?" Alice suggested, a hint of laughter in her voice. "I doubt you've actually washed them yet ... you're not that organised."

Jess nudged her out of the way and Alice sidestepped from the doorway back onto the landing. Jess pushed the bathroom door shut to get to the laundry basket behind it. Alice was right. Tangled amongst a bundle of other dirty clothes were the jeans, and in their pocket, the list.

"Damn you Alice," she said, holding the list out as if it was well-presented homework she was handing to an impatient teacher. "I can't even be infuriated with you for being right. And smug. Stop it!" She glared at Alice's smirking face, and poked towards Alice's leg with her toe.

Alice neatly dodged the kick, swiping the list from Jess's hand as she moved, and stepping backwards into the room she often slept in when she visited Jess; the bigger back bedroom overlooking the garden that used to be their father's room. She flopped onto the bed and lay on her back, holding the list above her to read it.

"It's the list of cars?"

"Yes."

"So what'm I looking for?"

"Is Geraghty on that list?"

"No ... yes. But no."

"What is it? Yes or no?"

"You've written Geraghty tractor but not OMG. What the heck does that mean?"

"OMG? Let me look ... why would I write that?" Jess snatched the list form Alice and peered at it.

"Oh! *Oh. Em. Gee.*" She dragged out the letters. "Oh my God, but not oh my God. Old Man Geraghty. But also, oh my God because that helps it all fall into place, so it's quite fitting, really, that I wrote it like that!"

"You're making no sense at all, Jessica O'Malley. Anytime you want to explain in plain English, go ahead." Alice sat up on the bed and swung her feet back onto the floor. "What?"

"I need to ask Ryan if he can describe the driver. Come on!" With that, Jess ran back down the stairs, leaving a still-bewildered Alice to follow if she wanted to know more.

Jess snatched her phone from the table and started to text Siobhan, then changed her mind and called her instead.

"Siobhan? It's Jess. I'm glad you answered! Is Ryan with you? Can you ask him something?"

There was a moment's silence while Siobhan went off to find her son, punctuated by the occasion sound of her calling his name emanating from a muffled mouthpiece.

"What are you asking him?" Alice said, while Jess waited for Siobhan to return.

"Hang on," Jess mouthed as Siobhan spoke again.

"Okay," Jess said into the phone, "well can you ask him this? Who was driving the Geraghty tractor on Tuesday morning? Remember he said he saw it, but it wasn't Mr Geraghty?"

Siobhan relayed the question to her son.

"He's not so good at people as he is at cars. He just says it wasn't Mr Geraghty."

Jess thought for a moment before speaking again. "Okay, so ask him how did he know it wasn't Old Man Geraghty driving his own tractor?" She jiffled on her feet while Siobhan relayed this question.

"You'll be pacing like Marcus does in a minute," Alice whispered, her lips twitching as she held back laughter.

"Shh," Jess hissed, and turned her back on her sister. "I'm trying to listen."

Siobhan spoke away from the mouthpiece to address her son.

Jess couldn't hear Ryan's side of the conversation, but Siobhan, carefully phrasing her questions, was clearly getting somewhere with the boy.

"So you know he wasn't Mr Geraghty because he was taller? Good. That's really helpful. What else was different?"

More muffled replies.

"Mr Geraghty does always wear that tweed cap; you're quite right. You have great eyesight, so you do! Not sure I'd see that from here."

Muffle muffle muffle.

"No, I don't mean exactly here. Not here in the kitchen! I meant I don't think I'd see that far from the gate, where you were when you saw him."

Jess pictured the boy solemnly nodding to his mother as he processed the likelihood of his mum seeing through the kitchen walls.

"So, you know the driver wasn't wearing Mr Geraghty's hat. Can you remember how you know that? Like was he wearing a different hat, or could you see his hair, or what?"

Muffle. Muffle.

"Well done, that's great. Fair play to you, Ryan. Aren't you great at details. Let me tell that to Jess, hang on a minute."

Jess thought she was telling her son to wait a minute, but there was more muffled talk, and Siobhan didn't say anything more into the phone, so perhaps she'd been telling Jess to hang on.

"You know, Jess who is helping Marcus ... Yes, go on now. Sorry Jess! Ok he's gone. Sorry, it's easier sometimes to just make it sound like you're official!"

"Not just a nosy cow, you mean?" Jess laughed, hearing the truth in her words. "Can we at least agree it's a bit of both. I mean, I will tell Marcus, if I find something useful, so that's kind of official, right? What did Ryan say?"

"The driver wasn't Mr Geraghty because he was much taller, and maybe had ginger hair, by the sound of things. I'd say it was that farmhand of his, what's his name ... something stupid, they call him. No, sorry, can't remember. And also, apparently, not driving like Mr Geraghty drives, but honestly, Jess, I wasn't even going to try to get into what he means by that. Geraghty does drive a bit like a doddery old fellow, come to think, so maybe this guy wasn't weaving all over the road like a drunken duck—Goose!"

"Goose?"

"His name is Goose. Nickname, I s'pose. Don't ask me."

Jess imagined Siobhan shrugging. She gave Alice a thumbs up. *We're getting somewhere.* "Siobhan? Can you ask him one last thing? Can you ask him was the tractor going towards the farm or towards my end of the village? And what colour it was? And did it have a trailer?"

"That's three things," Alice muttered from the sofa.

Jess ignored her.

"Will do," Siobhan said. "He's gone off outside, so I'll text you in a bit."

They disconnected the call and Jess sat heavily onto the sofa, a great gush of air squooshing from the cushion.

Fletcher, hoping his mistress might finally keep still for a minute, jumped up beside her, scrabbled at the sofa cushion, turned round three times, and flopped his head onto her lap, sighed, and closed his eyes.

Jess fondled his ears. "Okay, okay. I guess that's me pinned down. Make a cup of tea?" She raised her eyebrows hopefully towards Alice. "And bring the rest of my sandwich? Then I'll tell you what I think might have happened. That *how* part I said about."

Chapter Twenty-Nine

"I think," Jess said, studying Alice over her of her steaming mug of tea, "the tractor might be a clue."

"Jess," Alice said in the patronising tone of an older sister teaching the younger one something very obvious, "you live in the country. In a farming community. There are a lot of tractors."

Jess glared. "Yes, but haven't you noticed that a tractor has cropped up at exactly the wrong moment throughout the whole mystery?"

"But Jess, you live in the country. In a farming com—"

"*Alice!* Don't you dare say the same again. I'm not a complete idiot. Listen. Ryan saw Old Man Geraghty's red tractor—Ryan was quite indignant about it, she said—" Jess waved her phone at Alice for emphasis. Siobhan had called back while Alice obediently made tea in the kitchen, saying it was easier to just call than get it all in a text. "A Massey Fergusson—he said that before, didn't he? On that list? And they, apparently are red. Who knew different tractor makes are certain colours? Not me, anyway."

"John Deeres are green," Alice said, straight-faced. "Everyone knows that."

Jess shrugged. "Shut up. That really isn't the point here. It was red and it was towing a trailer—the kind they might use for getting turf in, or something, not a really big silage trailer, apparently."

"Is this important?" Alice rolled her eyes and sipped at her mug. "What is your point here?"

"Actually, it is, because, on Tuesday morning, I also saw a red tractor, with a trailer, stopped between the village hall and the end of the close." She gestured with her mug towards the living room window, in case Alice had forgotten where Orchard Close might be. I thought—think—the driver was on his phone and had just stopped there to answer it, but Alice ..."

Alice's eyes lit up as the penny started to drop. "Ah. So ... maybe he hadn't stopped there because he needed to answer a call, but because—"

"He needed to make the call, and he needed to make the call from exactly outside Orchard Close because—"

"It's exactly outside the village hall!"

"Exactly." Jess leaned back against the sofa cushions and took a large slurp of her tea, smiling as her sister worked it out. "Go on."

"And he was watching for something, and he only made the call after that something happened?"

"I think so. I also suspect that if we asked Mrs Harris, she'd tell us the tractor she saw stopping by the school—"

"—was actually stopping by that old cottage."

"Exactly. And I think she'd tell us it also had a trailer. And I'll bet you anything that the reason it stopped was so someone could throw a bike or two into the trailer, climb up into the cab, and get a lift out of the village." Jess sighed and wriggled enough to shift Fletcher off her lap so she could tuck her legs beneath her.

He huffed, got to his feet, turned around twice, and flopped back into almost the exact position he'd started from.

"So first the tractor went through the village not very long before the vandalism, when Ryan saw it. I wouldn't be at all surprised if it hadn't dropped off two bikes then, come to think ... although maybe not." Hadn't Gerry seen them beside a farm pickup that morning? "No, I think ... I think the one who Mrs Dunne knows works at the farm brought the boys and the bikes from somewhere else; unloaded them at the farm gates, continued on down to the farm, collected the tractor and trailer and went on out through the village, turned round somewhere, and parked up beside the village hall to wait until the judges arrived." Jess watched Alice, waiting for her to show agreement, or to offer a contradicting idea.

Alice nodded. "Okay, I'm with you so far, but how would the tractor driver know who he was looking for?"

Jess raised her eyebrows, throwing Alice an unspoken question.

"I mean, would he know your car, and Henry's and Lila's, and whoever else? How would he know which one was the judge's car, or which people were the judges, or whatever?"

Jess thought about it for a moment. "I think it would be obvious, to be honest. Firstly, the judges' car probably had Dublin plates—" She held up a finger to stop Alice's interruption. "Yes, I know! That alone wouldn't be conclusive, because it might not, and you couldn't be sure no one from round here might have Dublin plates too, although I don't think any of us do, but that's not the point. Because, he only really had to look for the car that spilled out four smartly-dressed Dubs holding clipboards and looking like they'd been in the car for an hour or two. I don't think it would be hard to work it out, really?"

"S'pose," Alice said, nodding slowly. "Guess that makes sense."

"And then he phones the lads he'd left in the village, gives them the go-ahead, and drives up to the village to collect them. He'd drive slow enough, with a tractor and trailer, to give them time to run from the shop to the cottage, doing their damage, then climb into the tractor and get out of the village far quicker, or at least less obtrusively, than on bikes."

"Especially if they were covered in red paint or mud."

"So now we think there were three of them, not two. One in the tractor and two on bikes."

"And we are fairly certain that at least one of them works for Geraghty? Does he actually *have* a first name?"

"Dunno. Everyone always calls him Old Man. Can't believe I never clocked those OMG initials!"

"Jess?"

"What?"

"It's also possible, don't you think, that they knew which car was the judges' car because they knew the judges?"

Jess turned her mug in her hands, staring into it as if it held all the answers. "I guess. Would that make a difference?"

"I guess it would eliminate doubt. They'd want to be pretty sure they'd got it right, I'd think."

Jess shrugged. "So is there any other reason to think they might know one of the judges?"

It was Alice's turn to stare silently into her cup. "Remember," she said after a long pause, "how I said if you worked out *how* they'd done all the damage in such a tight time frame without being seen, it might lead you to who had done it—which we do kind of know except we don't actually know who the three lads are—but what we're really still missing is *why* they did it."

Jess looked at her in surprise. "But we do know, don't we? To stop us winning the Tidy Village contest."

"Yes, but *why*? *Why* did they want to stop you winning?"

Jess pulled her legs back out from under Fletcher and got to her feet, pushing him to the far end of the sofa. "No, don't get up, I'm just getting one of those brownies. Stay there. Stay." She held up her hand in 'stop'.

Fletcher thumped his tail softly against the sofa, but didn't get up.

Snowflake, curled in a tight white ball on Alice's sofa, opened one eye, decided all was right with his world, and closed it again.

Chapter Thirty

While Jess got the brownies, Alice turned to a new page in the notebook and wrote <u>WHY?</u> in small, neat handwriting. She underlined it twice and began a bullet-pointed list below.

Jess passed Alice a brownie and perched herself on the arm of the sofa to peer over Alice's shoulder as she wrote. "I kind of did that already."

Alice put her finger on the page to mark her place, then flicked back through the pages. "You didn't though, not really. Look." Sure enough, Jess had written <u>SABOTAGE</u>, and drawn a few arrows pointing to empty space, and a new heading saying WHO? but added no further motives for the sabotage. "And the more I think about it, the more I think we're missing something."

"We're missing quite a lot, I'd say."

"Perhaps Marcus'll know more when he gets back. Any news from him?"

Jess checked her phone for the umpteenth time, but Marcus still hadn't texted. "No. What are we going to do now? I'm stumped."

Giving up on the notebook and the mystery and the whys and whos of it all, Jess flicked through the television channels as they searched for something they agreed on. "House of

Games? Bake Off? Old film ... think I've seen that one recently ... News? God no. Who wants to know all the depressing stuff? Harry Potter?"

"Again? I swear that's on somewhere at any time of any day. Is there anyone in the world who hasn't seen it, who still wants to?"

"Shouldn't think so." Jess hit SELECT, and the Weasley twins filled the screen, the pair of gangly redheads laughing at something in their joke shop. "Oh, I love this bit!"

"We are *not* watching Harry Potter. What? What are you looking at now?"

Jess had frozen the screen and was staring at the twins as if she hadn't seen the entire series a hundred times, or had never seen the Weasley twins before. Her mouth hung open as something clicked into place with such force she was certain Alice must have heard the clicking.

"Jess? Earth to Jessica ... Jessica ..." Alice clicked her fingers and Jess stood up, turned off the TV, and tugged her gaze from the fading screen.

"I've seen a picture of red-haired boys."

"Fred and George Weasley? Yes ..." Alice shot Jess the kind of look that suggested she thought Jess had finally turned completely mad.

"Fancy another walk? The dogs will be happy. Let's go see Maeve."

Alice huffed and muttered something Jess couldn't quite catch but got the gist of.

"No, really, come on. I'll go without you, if you don't want to come, so it's up to you. I'll have to ask Eric if you can stay in the club if you don't come, though."

That did the trick. Alice, having been admitted into Jess's and Eric's childish detective club a mere twenty-five years after they'd first started it, was clearly unwilling to relinquish her hastily-drawn, Sellotape-covered badge, wherever she'd stashed it, and got to her feet with a groan. "Okay, okay. But only because Marcus will never forgive me if I let you go off snooping on your own. Somebody has to keep you out of trouble while he's at work—ouch!" Alice caught the cushion Jess had thrown at her, sidestepping into the low side table and bashing her shin. She threw the cushion back with an aggressive chest pass worthy of her long-ago position as Goal Attack on the school's netball team, and Jess staggered backwards onto the sofa.

Fletcher already on his feet at the first hint of a second walk, bounced onto the sofa, jumped over Jess's lap, flung himself across the space between the two sofas, and then completed the entire circuit again without touching the floor, while Jess and Alice dissolved into giggles.

"Stop it, Fletch, stop it," Jess said feebly as she tried to regain her composure. "This is serious. I think those boys are Maeve's cousins."

Alice stopped laughing. "Maeve's cousins?"

"Frances's brothers." She pushed Fletcher to the floor, got up again, and went to the hall to pull her trainers out from under the narrow table. "And we are going to ask Maeve to confirm it. So get up, get your shoes on, and let's go see her." Her trainers in one hand, Alice's shoes in her other, she stepped back into the living room and dropped the shoes at Alice's feet. "Here you go."

Fletcher, delighted by the unexpected thrill of another walk, walked with all the direction of a balloon released without being tied first; twining around their legs and making it generally impossible for any of them to walk straight.

Snowflake, his patience finally running out, bared his little white teeth and let out a low growl. "Fletcher O'Malley," he seemed to be saying, "if you can't walk sensibly, I'm going to drag Jess all the way back to the house and nip her ankles until she shuts you inside so the rest of us enjoy this lovely extra walk. Just stop it."

"Look at his little stern face!" Alice bent to rub the Westie's head. "Honestly, Snow, if Jessica can't control her dog, I think you and I should walk on the other side of the road. Come on." She untangled Snowflake's lead from Fletcher's and crossed over, throwing a smug look at her younger sister as she did so.

By the time they reached the end of the close, Fletch had settled down, and the four of them walked onwards in a far more orderly fashion, towards Maeve's and hopefully towards the answers to the 'who' part of the puzzle.

Maeve was in her garden, on her knees and bent over a flower border, a small pile of tiny weeds in a trug at her side. She looked up at the sound of their approach, and frowned. "Hello, Jessica."

"Wish my weeds were that small," Jess said. "Hello Maeve. This is my sister, Alice. Alice, this is Maeve. She knew Dad."

Alice held her hand out to Maeve. "Everyone round here knew Dad," she said with a smile.

Maeve wiped crumbs of soil from her fingers and shook Alice's outstretched hand. "George O'Malley was an asset to Ballyfortnum, so he was. What do you want?"

Jess, by now becoming used to Maeve's abrupt way with words, smiled. "I think you might be able to identify the people who did the damage to the village." *And put Willie in hospital,* she added silently. She'd decided as they'd walked, that by focusing on the less serious issue of the vandalism, rather than on Willie's life-threatening attack, Maeve might be more willing to drop any notions of family loyalty and expose the culprits. Although Jess had seen that Maeve was truly upset about Willie's condition, she couldn't help but suspect it was the mindless destruction and sabotage of all the committee's hard work that had riled Maeve more. Nonetheless, she felt uneasy at the thought of interrogating the woman, and a prickle of heat was already creeping up her neck under Maeve's cool gaze.

Maeve blinked at Jess. "And how exactly do you think I might be able to do that?"

"When Frances and I were walking back from the Dochertys' farm on Tuesday, she showed me a photo of her family. On her phone. We were chatting about our siblings, and she was telling me she's a lot of them, and how rare it was they all get together these days." She looked at Maeve to check she was following.

Maeve nodded. "Nine of them altogether."

"Frances is one of the older ones?""

"Second one. Where are you going with this, Jessica?" She said the words in her usual flat tone, without hint of defensiveness, and Jess relaxed a little.

"Gerry—postman Gerry—described a couple of lads he saw on bikes on Tuesday morning, and another man who might have been with them, up at Geraghtys' gate. I think he may have been describing Frances's brothers." Jess pulled out her phone and found the photo of Mrs Dunne's list. She zoomed in to enlarge the writing, and began to read. "One with red hair. One with brownish hair. Maybe twenty, twenty-something, hard to say. Older than school. Old enough to be at work, should think." She stopped and looked at Maeve. "There's more, but it's about their clothes and bikes."

"There's plenty around here with red hair," Maeve said.

Jess skimmed down Mrs Dunne's notes. "Oh, yes, and this bit—the guy in the pickup truck Gerry saw them with before was red-haired too. A bit older."

Maeve nodded; her mouth set in a thin line.

"One of the boys in the shop was called Con."

"Yes," Maeve said, her expression unchanged. "Conor and Chris are the younger set of twins. Conor has red hair. Chris's is dark. The older boys have that same red hair too. Only Chris—"

"—and Callum," Jess and Maeve said together, Jess suddenly remembering what Frances had said as they'd stood waiting to cross the road.

Maeve inclined here head again; one small dip of acknowledgement.

"Only Chris and Callum missed it. That's what Frances said, about their hair. Maeve," Jess asked, as the other woman avoided her gaze, "does one of them work at Geraghtys' farm?"

Maeve nodded again. "I wouldn't be surprised. All the lads are all into farming, all right."

"Is there one called Goose?"

"Gavin." Maeve nodded again. She stooped to pick up the garden trug and a pair of gloves she hadn't been wearing. "I suppose you'll be wanting a cup of tea," she said, turning towards the back of house. "You'd better come around this way. Tie those dogs to the gate again, and come on around. I'll put the kettle on."

Chapter Thirty-One

"Now, what is it you're wanting to know about Gavin?" Maeve set three mugs of strong tea on a round wooden garden table. "Sit down there and then it won't matter about shoes." She frowned at the ground around Jess's feet as if Jess's shoes might be covered with several gallons of slurry from the short walk along a country road between their two houses.

Obediently, Jess and Alice sat. Jess immediately pulled her back straight and put her feet primly together, tucking them back on themselves to hide any traces of dirt from Maeve's critical eye. "I think," she said carefully, "it might not just be Gavin. Tell us about all of them?"

Alice nodded; a tiny almost imperceptible movement that Jess interpreted as "Go on."

Maeve repeated some of what Frances had already told Jess: Frances's family was large and loud, with nine children. "All adults now, mind." Maeve gave a small shudder at the thought of this noisy, boisterous family Jess imagined gathered around an enormous kitchen table, jostling for space, and all trying to be the one that got heard, each shouting louder than the next.

She imagined raucous board games and a gaggle of red-headed children charging around a large, untidy garden with hurleys or a football, and, for not the first time since she'd met Frances, was grateful for being one of only three.

Maeve was still talking. "Even wee Callum's eighteen, since March."

"What do the younger ones look like? From Goo—Gavin downwards?" Alice said at the same time as Jess asked the altogether less useful "Why's he called Goose?"

Maeve answered Jess first. "I have absolutely no idea." She turned her head fractionally to address Alice. "Gavin and Conor are two of the redheads. Chris and Callum the darker ones. They've Frances's colouring, the two of them. My father used to say the red ink had run out by the time it got to the youngest ones."

Jess laughed. "That wouldn't explain why it missed the girls, though."

"It wouldn't," Maeve agreed, her mouth set in its usual serious line.

"What do they all do?"

The other two girls—one each side of Frances—were both teachers, one in a Dublin secondary school and one more locally in the Ballymaglen Primary school. The eldest boy—one of the other set of twins—was working his way up through the ranks of a prestigious hotel in Dublin, aspiring for *Maitre d'* but so far stuck at waiter. "He's good at it, mind, by all accounts."

Jess and Alice exchanged a smile. "Doesn't tip soup in laps?" Jess said.

Maeve rewarded her with a thin chuckle. "That kind of thing. I don't really know."

Jess, however, had remembered something Maeve probably *did* know. "Which hotel?"

"That fancy one, in Dublin. The Fairmount."

"The one the judges went to for the pre-launch dinner? Someone said that, didn't they? Back at Christmas time? Did you go?

"Of course not. We only go the prize-giving dinners."

"But Frances went?"

Maeve's brow furrowed a fraction. "Perhaps. I don't know. Why exactly are you asking, Jessica?"

Jess shrugged. "I'm not exactly sure ... I wonder ... I ..." She tailed off, having absolutely no idea where she was going with this train of thought, despite the faintest of niggles that it could somehow matter.

Alice, who hadn't said much since they'd arrived in Maeve's garden, poked Jess with her foot. "Maeve," she said slowly, leaning forward onto her elbows, her chin propped on the backs of her fingers, "do you know if the other dinner, the one on Saturday, was also at the Fairmount?"

And there it was; the niggle that had been tickling at Jess. A connection between the suspected vandals and Jim's mysterious reaction to the salad. Another of Frances's brothers, hovering on the edges of the judging process. She cast an admiring glance at her sister. *Alice is earning her place in the Lollipop Club for sure.* She stretched her foot towards Alice's, below the garden table and out of sight from Maeve, and returned the poke. *Nice one, Al!* she silently transmitted through the toe of her walking boot. *Nice one.*

Maeve, unfortunately, didn't know.

Jess got the distinct impression that Maeve wasn't particularly close to her large family of cousins, despite living only a few miles away from most of them. Perhaps when there were so many in the immediate family, it was inevitable they didn't need to make time for Maeve. Jess didn't see her own cousins very often, not that she had many to start with.

Families, she thought, with a small shake of her head. "Do you have any siblings?"

"Two brothers," Maeve got up and gathered the mugs. She turned towards the house, and Jess took the cue to get up too. As Maeve reached the back door, she turned back. "I'd have a liked a sister. Your father would be proud of the pair of you, you know. Thank you for calling in. You'll come again, I hope."

A rush of warmth and a slight pang of sadness thrummed in Jess's chest. Maeve, she realised, was lonely, despite her involvement in the community. For all her abruptness and bossy tendencies, Maeve was lonely. "We will. Thank you for the tea, Maeve."

"You know what we need to find out," Alice said as the O'Malley sisters walked back along the narrow road, Fletcher twining around their legs as he sniffed at clumps of dandelions or tufts of grass first on one side and then the other. "Oh do stop it, Fletch!" She untangled Snowflake's lead from Fletcher's and stepped further away from Jess and Fletch.

"We need to find out," Jess said, tugging the Labrador away from a gatepost before he could pee up it, "whether the dinner last Saturday was in the Fairmount, and whether Frances's brother was there—"

"And if he has access to that salad—"

"—to tamper with it."

"Exactly. How are we going to do that?"

By the time they approached the opening to Orchard Close, they'd decided the only way to find out was to enlist Henry's help.

"Will he do it?" Alice asked.

Jess shrugged. "I don't know. Let's walk up that way later and ask him. Fletcher! Stop it! What now?" She yanked him towards her with a sharp tug, but he continued to strain at the lead, hackles up, and a growl rumbling in his throat. "What is it?"

A familiar figure rounded the bend, heading towards them from the village, and Fletcher erupted into a volley of frantic barking.

"Shut up, Fletcher!" Jess said in her firmest but still ineffectual voice, at the same time as Alice said, "It's Elizabeth. That's handy."

Elizabeth, now propelled towards them by a pulling Daisy, battled with the bad-mannered whippet for a moment, got her back under control, wrapped the lead around her wrist several times to bring the dog in close, and raised her other hand in greeting—the one holding the lead of the far more sensible Stanley.

As the dogs approached one another, Fletcher's barking was punctuated with the odd growl; his hackles up as he watched Daisy with suspicion and dislike.

Jess mirrored Elizabeth's movements by wrapping Fletcher's lead around her hand a few times to keep him tight against her leg.

Alice thrust Snowflake's lead at Jess and went to relieve Elizabeth of Stanley so the older woman could give all her attention to restraining the bad-tempered Daisy.

Once the four dogs were under control, Elizabeth, Jess, and Alice moved off the road to stand beside the wild flower patch at the entrance to Orchard Close; Jess and Elizabeth taking care to keep Fletch and Daisy well apart.

"We were just talking about you," Jess told her friend. "We wanted to ask Henry something, but to be honest, you might be better at asking him than me." She took in Elizabeth's pale face and realised her friend was exhausted from the efforts of dealing with Daisy, who was far more difficult to manage than lovely little Stanely. She wondered, not for the first time, whether Elizabeth regretted having taken in her neighbour's dog when she'd had to leave her home the year before. Henry, Jess knew, certainly did. "Do you want to come in for a cup of tea?"

Elizabeth seemed visibly relieved by the suggestion, and while Jess kept Fletcher on the opposite side of the road to Elizabeth and Daisy, and Alice walked Stanley down the middle of the empty street, Elizabeth told them she rarely brought the two dogs out by herself. "She's quite difficult, you know. She really does miss Breda, I think. I feel quite sorry for her, when I'm not cross with her. But Henry's gone up to Dublin to see Jim, and I thought I'd cope."

Jess started, momentarily breaking stride as she turned to stare at Elizabeth. "Well," she said, "that's a bit of a coincidence, as that's exactly what we wanted to ask him about. Jim, I mean. Not you or Daisy."

Elizabeth raised her eyebrows. "You'd better ask me about it over that tea, so."

Chapter Thirty-Two

With Daisy and Stanley shut in the garden; Fletcher and Snowflake shut in the house, and tea made, Jess, Alice, and Elizabeth settled onto the kitchen chairs.

"The thing is," Jess said to Elizabeth, as she passed a mug of tea across the table towards her friend, "we would very much like to know if the dinner last Saturday was at the Fairmount hotel, and we hoped Henry might be able to find out."

Elizabeth poured milk into her mug. "Oh, it was." She looked up from the tea to meet Jess's eyes. "Why?"

Jess set down her tea without taking a sip. "It was? Are you sure?"

Elizabeth, it turned out, was quite sure, because she'd been chatting to Lydia about it over lunch on Tuesday, as the two women had discussed the merits of Mrs Harris's scones. Lydia, Elizabeth relayed to Alice and Jess with a smile, had said that Mrs Harris could easily supply the Fairmount, as her scones were far better than those served with the Fairmount's very extortionately-priced afternoon tea, and Elizabeth had asked Lydia if she often had afternoon tea at the Fairmount and Lydia had laughed and said not for ages as it was so expensive and the scones weren't all that good, not for the price, but that they had been there for dinner that Saturday and it had been perfectly lovely until Jim had taken sick from it.

Only once Elizabeth had finished relaying all this to Jess and Alice did Jess take up the abandoned mug of tea and take a large swig, her eyes still on Elizabeth as she processed the news.

"I don't suppose you happen to know," Alice said, "firstly, was Frances with them? And secondly, if she was, did she know any of the staff?"

Jess nodded at her sister, then turned her attention back to Elizabeth. "That," she said, "is exactly what we need to know." She looked hopefully at Elizabeth.

"Should think so," Elizabeth said. "It would be common enough for the secretary to attend those meetings. Would you like me to text Henry?" Without waiting for an answer, she shuffled in her chair to remove a basic Nokia phone from the pocket of her trousers. "I'll ask him first; you can tell me why while we await his answer."

She typed for a minute or so, squinted at the little screen, jabbed at another button, and set the phone down on the table, face-up. Almost immediately, the phone bleeped, causing Jess and Alice to jump in their seats. Elizabeth laughed. "Not yet! That's the message to tell me the message has gone."

Jess and Alice exchanged a look, and relaxed back against their chairs.

Beyond the French doors, Daisy scrabbled at the glass, a determined look on her thin face.

"Sorry Daisy," Jess told her, "I'm not letting you in. You'll only pick a fight with Fletch."

"Sit down, Daisy, for goodness sake." Elizabeth waggled a stern finger in Daisy's direction and she obediently sank to her haunches.

Stanley came to lie beside her, his head resting on his front paws as he turned soulful spaniel eyes on his owner, watching her through the glass.

"Someone else who knows how to properly train a dog." Alice smirked at her sister across the table.

Before Jess could retaliate, Elizabeth's phone jangled on the table—a quite different tone to the previous bleeping—accompanied by a wild dance across the table as it vibrated violently.

Elizabeth peered at the display. "Yes," she said, raising her eyebrows at Jess. "Yes, Frances was there, and yes, she knew one of the restaurant staff. Why are you asking?"

A flutter rose in Jess's belly. She glanced at Alice, wondering if she felt the same frisson of excitement; a sense of edging ever-closer to solving a mystery.

Alice shot her a small smile and gently tapped her chest, in roughly the spot she'd fastened a small, badly-drawn, hand-made badge featuring what looked a little like a lollipop but may have been a magnifying glass, just a few weeks ago when Jess had made it for her.

Jess tipped her head the tiniest fraction—*Yes!*—before turning back to Elizabeth. "I think—we think—" She gave Alice an apologetic glance. "We think we might know who was responsible for the mess in the village and attacking poor Willie."

Over a second cup of tea, Jess and Alice filled Elizabeth in on their thoughts about Frances's brothers, and how it seemed likely that three of the younger ones had worked together to sabotage Ballyfortnum's attempts at securing the trophy for yet another year.

"But," Jess went on, "what we're also beginning to wonder is whether they also had a hand in Jim being ill."

"Another brother, that is," Alice said.

Elizabeth set down her mug. "I hate to say it, but you could be onto something. I'll have a chat to Henry when he gets home. Ring you if he says anything else that may interest you."

She got to her feet and picked up the two dog leads from where they lay on the doormat. "I'd better get these two home, get the dinner on."

"I'll run you back in the car, if you like?" Jess said.

Outside, the two dogs leaped eagerly to their feet, tails wagging like flags on St Patrick's Day.

In the living room, Fletcher whined and scratched at the kitchen door.

"You're not going out again," Jess told the door, as she stepped out onto the patio slabs in her socks to walk Elizabeth to the gate, before coming back in for her car keys and shoes.

Over dinner that evening, Jess and Alice filled Marcus in on their latest sleuthing.

"Gossip, you mean," Marcus said, but the crinkles around his eyes gave away his amusement. Nonetheless, the serious set of his mouth implied a level of professional interest as Jess explained how she and Alice had discovered a clear link between several members of Maeve's family and the events surrounding the sabotage of the Tidy Village contest.

"So," he said, setting his fork down onto a plate cleared of a large helping of chilli and rice, "you think Maeve is behind it all?"

Alice sighed softly. "Well, that's what we're really not sure of, to be honest. Maeve? Frances? Neither seem entirely likely, if you ask me, but Frances at least has a bit more motive, what with being from ... whatever that village is called?"

"Abbeydare. Yes, I'd say she has more reason than Maeve to stop us winning." Jess got up and stacked the plates in a neat pile by the sink. "Although Maeve had been moaning a *lot* about all the work she puts into it ..." She pulled three bowls from the cupboard; took a shop-bought apple pie Marcus had brought home off the kitchen worktop, and retrieved a pot of cream from the fridge.

"More cake?" Alice wrinkled her nose. "Really?"

"Take it or leave it. More for me and Marcus. Besides, it's not cake; it's fruit." Jess set the pie in the centre of the table and offered Alice the knife, before picking up the thread of her conversation. "Although from what I already know of Maeve, moaning is her default setting, so I'm not sure that tells us anything. And I really *don't* think Maeve would put all this effort in to the contest just to sabotage it at the eleventh hour. What would be the point?"

Alice cut herself a thin sliver of the pie. "I agree. I know I only just met her but I really can't see it being her."

"Besides, she certainly wouldn't wish Willie Keegan any harm." *Would she?* Jess shook her head, dismissing the doubt. *No, she wouldn't.* "She's pernickety and bossy and fussy and single-minded but she doesn't seem to be *nasty*. I do think her heart's in the right place ..."

"What about Frances?" Marcus frowned at Jess. "What was your impression of her? You're the only one of us who's met her." He splashed a generous helping of cream over a generous slice of apple pie.

Jess shrugged. "A long-term campaign of working her way up until she got to be a judge, so she could guarantee winning the trophy for her village?" She laced her words with a hefty dose of scepticism. "Maybe, but why go to all that trouble?"

"It's at odds with being on the committee, too, don't you think?" Alice said, carefully picking pale yellow chunks of apple from the pie and chewing each spoonful slowly.

Jess shrugged again. "Seems very vindictive ..."

"And far too much hard work," Marcus added.

"Her family acting off their own bat, then?" Alice said.

"But using her inside knowledge to do it ..."

"We're going to call some of the brothers in. See if they can answer a few questions about where they were on Tuesday." Marcus shot a stern glance at Jess—his Serious Policeman look. "But I didn't tell you that."

"Is it worth you talking to Frances, too? She might know a bit more, especially about the dinner the Saturday before the judging? You know; about Jim?"

"Dublin," Marcus said. "Not our area."

"But—"

Marcus held up a hand to cut her off. "But yes, we've spoken to them. Environmental Health are on it, of course, but we are also looking into what has all the indications of being a deliberate poisoning."

"Did you—"

"Yes." His eyes creased into the laughter lines Jess adored. "Yes. I told them that someone, who I didn't name, had discovered there was a strong possibility that raw beans had been added to a salad, and that the same somebody was quite certain there should not be raw beans in that salad ..." He gave a Jess a wry half-smile. "Which, of course, they already knew. From Environmental Health."

"But you won't have told them about the connection with yet another of one of the judge's brothers," Alice said. "Because we only told you that tonight ..."

Marcus nodded. "And that's why, as soon as I've finished off this pie, I'm going to relay that information to Dublin. But I'm not risking losing a slice of apple pie to anyone else who might decide to finish it off." He shot a meaningful glare at Jess, who scraped the last of her own cream-smothered pie from her plate and into her mouth.

Before Marcus could make the call, Fletcher leaped up from where he'd been lying across Marcus's feet and ran to the living room, barking. He flung himself at the window, jumped off the sofa to run to the front door, then back to the window, still barking.

"What now?" Jess said to no one in particular, trying unsuccessfully to hush Fletcher as someone walked down Jess's short driveway and rapped sharply on the door.

Chapter Thirty-Three

"Maeve?" Jess couldn't hide her surprise at seeing Maeve standing stiffly on the doorstep of Number 7, her satchel over her shoulder, and clutching a folded umbrella. "Is it raining?" Jess looked first at the dry ground and then skywards. "What brings you here?"

"Is Marcus here?" Maeve nodded at Marcus's car, pulled up on the pavement outside the house. "That's his car, isn't it? I would like to speak to him, if you don't mind. I've been thinking about what you said. I've been speaking to Frances."

"Would you like to come in? Hang on. I'll just put the dogs outside so they don't jump all over you." She opened the living door just wide enough to call to Alice and Marcus to shut the dogs in the garden, closed it again, and ushered Maeve into the small hallway.

Maeve sat stiff and upright on the single armchair. She refused the offer of tea, and pressed her fingers together, twisting them nervously as she spoke. "The thing is," she said, tilting her head in Jess's direction, "I believe you may be correct. So I phoned Frances. We don't speak very often on the telephone.

She's quite a bit younger than I am although we do share some interests."

Jess nodded. "Gardening."

Maeve squeezed her hands together. "And the contest, of course. We like each other well enough. Our paths have crossed more in recent years, and when I suggested her as a judge, I was quite confident she would be well-suited to it. I wouldn't have suggested her otherwise."

Jess nodded again. "Of course not."

"Maeve—" Marcus leaned forward and spoke gently. "Is there something troubling you about Frances?"

Maeve studied her hands for a moment then looked up towards Marcus, not quite meeting his eyes but fixating on the wall just beyond his head. "Not Frances, no. The lads. It's like Jessica said. So I took it upon myself to ask a few pertinent questions."

Alice shifted slightly on the smaller sofa.

Jess caught her eye.

"Lollipop Club," Alice mouthed, out of Maeve's line of sight.

Jess flashed her a quick smile. *Yes. She's been sleuthing!*

"Go on," Marcus said.

"In the event, I didn't need to ask. She volunteered the information anyway, you see, so I suspect she was troubled by it, too. She said she'd been pleased to see me and what a shame it was about Tuesday's upset, and I asked after the family. Her parents are in good health and she said the judging in Abbeydare had passed pleasantly and without incident." Her eyes flickered towards Marcus. "I hadn't asked that, of course. We've been jeopardized enough without being seen to extract information about other contestants from the judges."

"Of course," Jess said, wondering where this was going.

"But then she became quite irritable and said her brothers were up to something and Chris seemed to be troubled but wouldn't say by what, and Con and Gavin were being secretive and she was worried Chris had either done something terrible or was sick, but she suspected if he was sick, surely one of them would have said something about it." Maeve stilled her hands and met Marcus's gaze for a fleeting moment. "I asked her was it since Tuesday."

"And she said yes?" Jess guessed.

"Yes. She had to think about it, but then she said she thought it probably *had* started on Tuesday, because after they'd had dinner together, her ma had taken her aside and said had she seen the boys after she'd left the house on Tuesday morning, what with them all being in Ballyfortnum together that morning, and did she have any notions of what had got into the boy?"

Jess and Alice simultaneously leaned towards Maeve; ears pricked.

"Frances said she'd been confused at that, as she hadn't realised they were all working in Ballyfortnum, and wasn't it great the lads had found summer work so easy—they'd both be up in Ballyhaise, in term time. And her ma—my aunt—said no, the twins weren't working. They'd just come along with Gavin that day as they'd notions of going on a bike ride, what with college off for the summer and it being fine weather."

"Ballyhaise?" Alice asked.

"The agricultural college?" Jess only knew this from her time in the horticultural college she attended, as the colleges had occasional overlaps and shared interests. Ballyhaise was in County Cavan, up towards the border with Northern Ireland, and about an hour's drive from Ballyfortnum.

Maeve nodded. "Gavin and Adam both went there, too. All the boys have the farming blood, our grandfather always said, except Michael, of course. He's Adam's twin. Has notions of running a hotel."

"The one who works at the Fairmount?" Alice asked.

Maeve's eyes widened as she turned to Alice. "That's right."

"And he was working there on Saturday night—someone said Frances knew one of the waiters."

"She didn't say."

"And he'd have had access to the food, and the menu, and known who'd ordered what." Alice said.

"And been able to slip a handful of uncooked beans into a salad without anyone questioning it." Jess glanced at Marcus; his forehead lined with concentration as he followed the conversation. She inched her fingers towards him, but he was out of reach.

Maeve studied at her hands, curling and uncurling her fingers. "I suppose he most probably would, wouldn't he."

"But," Marcus spoke softly; firmly. "That still leaves one problem."

Jess and Alice turned to look at him. "What?"

"Someone must have told him they were going to dinner, in advance. Just like someone must have told the others what time the judges were arriving, and on which day, and all that other information. Did you—" He encompassed both Maeve and Jess in the question. "—know which days the judges were going to any other town? Or what time they would get there?"

Maeve looked up from her hands and stared at him.

Jess, who'd already thought of this, shook her head.

"No," they said together.

"Exactly. It wouldn't be the kind of thing people would know. So the real question is, who told them?"

"That's easy," Alice said. "Frances. But probably only in casual conversation. For example, didn't you say Frances had come down early; spent the night in her family home? Caught up with her family since she had to come this way anyway? She'd have told them why she was coming; that she was judging, and which villages she would doing."

"Yes," Jess said. "And that's why the judges met her at the junction, because she was almost here already; not in Dublin."

"Did they? I wouldn't know about that." Maeve said. "I suppose I presumed she'd got a ride with Gavin. Silly girl." Maeve sniffed. "I can't imagine why she wouldn't have come with her brother, or driven all the way here if she'd come as far as the junction anyway."

Jess was silent for a moment, remembering how she'd assumed Frances hadn't known any of them, and how Maeve had barely acknowledged her when she'd arrived. It probably wasn't personal; Maeve was like that with everyone, but she could understand how Frances might have preferred to come in with her colleagues. "Maeve? Had you and Frances agreed that you'd act like you didn't know each other?"

Maeve's eyebrows shot up.

"You never said you knew her, either before, or when they arrived, but you didn't show any surprise when she came in, so did you know she was coming before the judges got here?"

"After you called up on Monday evening to let me know there'd been a change of plans, I wondered might it be her coming, so I phoned her, to ask. We talked briefly. Said it would be lovely to see each other but we'd keep it professional until after the judging. She might call in that evening, we agreed, and we might share dinner. Or I might meet up with the family over in Abbeydare. We hadn't made firm commitments, and as it turned out, no one felt up to being very sociable after the day's events, so she went on back to Abbeydare. And I didn't."

"Maeve," said Alice, "I don't suppose you have a photo of your cousins? The boys, I mean. Particularly the two we think might have been in the shop on Tuesday morning."

Maeve took a phone from her bag. "I don't. I'll ask Fran to send me one." She typed something into the phone then set it on the arm of the chair as the screen faded to black. Within seconds, the screen lit up again. Maeve picked it up, looked at it, and passed it to Alice. "Conor and Chris. Chris is the darker one."

Alice looked at the image. "Would you mind sending it to Jess?"

"Why?" Marcus asked, holding his hand out for the phone. "Perhaps—" He looked at the image then passed the phone back to Maeve "—you could send it to me, though. I think it might be very helpful." He leaned sideways to retrieve his own phone from the small table beside the sofa.

"How about," Jess said, careful not to look at Marcus as she addressed Maeve, "as you already have my number in your phone, you send it to me and I will forward it straight to Marcus for you." She kept her voice level, interjecting as much 'this is a very reasonable and sensible suggestion that Marcus cannot possibly object to' into her voice as she could. Beside her on the sofa, she sensed Marcus stiffen, but he didn't object.

Maeve pressed a few buttons and Jess's phone beeped to announce the arrival of a message.

She opened the photo and forwarded it straight to Marcus. And Anne. And Matty. She quickly typed a short message to send to both the Dochertys: *Were either of these two helping with the clean up?*

Within seconds, her phone bleeped again. She felt Marcus's glare as opened Anne's message. *Think dark one there. Helping with plants. Not 100% sure.* Wordlessly, she handed her phone to Marcus.

He looked at the message, nodded, and handed back the phone. "Maeve, do you or Frances have any idea why her brothers might have decided to do this? If it was them."

Maeve sat up straight and focused on the spot on the wall again. Her face was set firm but her eyes were very slightly damp as she spoke in her usual flat, calm manner. "I think," she said, "it may have been something I said." She faltered and flicked her gaze at Marcus for a split second.

"Go on," he said in his gentle, reassuring tone.

Jess longed to reach out for him, touch his leg, or his arm. He was so good with people.

"Frances's father told me once, after Ballyfortnum had won that third Champion of Champions, how much it annoyed them that Ballyfortnum always did so well in the contest. He was unkind about it, I think." Maeve's voice shook just a little and she took a small, sharp breath. "I haven't forgotten it, either. He said they all got fed up with my ... my *up-myself-smugness* about it all and who did I think I was telling them about all the work I'd done as if I was solely responsible for the success of the village each year and one day I'd get my comeuppance."

A bright spot of pinkness flushed Maeve's cheeks. She kept her gaze levelled at the spot on the wall, just beyond Marcus's ear. "I didn't know what he meant, not really. I asked Frances's older sister about it once. We'd be a bit closer, being the oldest female cousins. She said I sometimes come across as if I think I'm better than everyone else, but I don't mean to. It's just the way I'm built. I was proud of the award, and always thought that with their interest in the contest and their interest in keeping their own gardens and village nice, it was something we had in common and they'd like to talk about it."

She looked down at her hands again, neatly folded in her lap. "I'm not always very good at making small talk. Don't see the need." She sniffed, glanced at her phone as if it might explain the world to her, and glanced back towards Marcus without making eye contact. "Their da, my uncle Fred, he said pride comes before a fall, so it does, and I'd see if it didn't. I think," she said, in her flat, low voice, "that the lads saw to it that he was right. Always did want to please him, they did. He's a hard man to please, by all accounts."

"Do you think Frances was part of it?" Alice said softly.

Maeve was silent for a moment. "No," she said, glancing towards Alice. "I don't think she was. I do think she maybe talked about it, when they got together, and that was what gave them the ideas."

"And the information," Jess said. "Would she have said in advance about the pre-judging dinners, too, would you think?"

Maeve turned her face towards Jess, but kept her eyes averted. "You wouldn't think it from Tuesday, but when she's in at home, she's quite the talker. They all are. Most likely she'd have chattered about the contest, and she'd have known she would step in as the substitute judge, if one of the others couldn't do it for some reason. She probably would mention the dinners, what with Michael working there in the Fairmount. It does seem they used the same hotel for all their dinners, doesn't it? Or perhaps he asked her, having seen her there a few times. She'd have no reason not to tell him. Family chitchat, I'd say."

Jess got to her feet. "I'll make us a cup of tea. Sounds like your family aren't very nice to you, if you ask me. I think it's amazing what you do for the village and the contest and we're all very proud of you, around here." Even as she said it, she realised it was true. Maeve may be abrupt and bossy, but without her, the village wouldn't be half as beautiful as it was, and without Maeve, Jess was quite certain there'd have been no awards given to Ballyfortnum, ever. Some of the others were great at gardening and all that, but without

Maeve's determination and organising, they'd never have come together to work as a team.

Maeve rewarded her with a flicker of a smile. "You're very like your father, Jessica. Thank you. And I think I *would* like that cup of tea now. A little milk and no sugar. Not too strong."

Jess nodded. "I know. I've seen how you take it, at the meetings. I'll bring the milk separately. You can add your own."

Maeve tipped her head in acknowledgement. "That'll be grand."

Chapter Thirty-Four

Marcus followed Jess to the kitchen.

Hoping the sound of the kettle would muffle their voices, and that Alice would have the sense to make some kind of smalltalk with Maeve, however hard the other woman found such banal chitchat, Jess pulled Marcus towards the French doors to whisper her thoughts.

"I think she's right. I don't think it was Frances. I think the two younger boys came with the older one—the one who works for Geraghty—with the intention of causing trouble. I think he was in on it too, and was the one who drove the tractor around. He got them to the village in the first place—Frances knew their bikes were in the back, didn't she, once her mum said about it. But that's not really important; it's not as if she knew what they were planning. They've two sisters who work as teachers, so getting hold of that paint would be easy, or anyone can buy poster paint in any art or toy shop, anyway. I think the two younger ones biked down to the village from Geraghtys', or got a lift with the tractor, and waited in the cottage garden while the older one—Goose, Gavin, whatever you call him—drove the tractor down to watch for the judges to arrive. I'll bet that when Frances left their parents' house, they followed her, so they knew exactly what time she'd get picked up. Or they went on ahead ... that doesn't matter, does it, because if it was one of Frances's cousins watching for the judges to arrive, they wouldn't even need to know the car, or anything, because they'd recognise Frances."

The kettle rumbled loudly towards its boil.

"So Goose, or whatever his name is, he sat in his tractor opposite the park, waiting, and as soon as they arrived, he called the other two, who had already casually walked down to the shop so they were in place. No one would have thought anything of two farm lads standing by the shop chatting, eating crisps, especially if they are fairly local. Once they got the call, they only had to wait until there was no one around, then run back to the cottage squeezing out paint and yanking the plants down. They'd have had it ready in their bags—the green one I found, and Mrs Harris said the other one had a bag too. They were lucky not to be seen, but I'd say they could have managed it in less than two minutes, all in."

Marcus nodded. "I agree. But what about Willie? Where does he come in?"

"This is where we start speculating, I'm afraid. You okay with a little bit of assuming for a minute?" She glanced at the kettle as it burbled to a stop. "Dammit." She went to the fridge and got out the milk, then rummaged loudly for mugs, spoons, and a tray.

"Jess, I can't actually hear you either if you make all that noise." He took her hand and pulled her back towards him. "It's okay. Go on. Give me those assumptions and I'll see what I make of them. After all—" His eyes creased as he smiled at her. "—you *have* had the odd correct assumption, once or twice."

She batted his arm with her free hand. "You will never be able to tell me off for making assumptions again, right? Okay, so, here's where I start guessing, but remember, they are educated guesses, based on evidence. I think what happened is that the two boys ran into the cottage garden, pulled down all those roses and the like from out the front; squirted the rest of the paint over the cottage, then went round the back to hide and wait for their brother to come back with his tractor." She sighed, and he stroked her arm.

"Go on."

"I think it *was* probably just meant to be a prank, not real malice ..." She trailed off, thinking about the mess and the upset, and poor Willie. "I think, perhaps, they are young and hadn't quite thought it through." She shook her head, not wanting to get distracted with worrying about whether or not they had really just thought it was a harmless joke. "Where was I?"

"Round the back, waiting for the tractor."

"I think Willie was there. It seems he used that little shed to store his things in the run-up to the judging anyway, and I think he'd arrived while they were in the shop. No one seems to have seen him since about eight-thirty, but equally, if the boys were waiting at the side of the cottage, or in front of the orchard bit, Willie could have gone in through the double gates, and around the back without them seeing each other—I know it sounds unlikely, but the timing does work. I'd say it's far more likely he was somewhere else for that tiny window of time between Dom passing him and the boys going off to the shop. They may even have passed each other, for all we know. I also think Willie Keegan is such a regular sight around the village, some of the school mums might have seen him after Dom did, but not really noticed him, if you know what I mean. He's like part of the furniture, always out with his tools."

Marcus nodded.

"Like how no one noticed two farm lads they've seen before. Not even Mrs Dunne, at first." Jess dropped a tea bag into each mug and poured hot water over them. "So the boys go running round the back of the cottage, laughing about what they'd done, and Willie sees them and they have some kind of confrontation, and one of them ends up bashing Willie with his own shovel and knocking him out. I think Mrs Harris only saw one of them because only one of them left. I think one of them ran off, threw his bike in the tractor, or cycled away, but the other one stayed to help Willie."

"The one who moved him and put the sweatshirt under his head?"

"Probably, yes. I think he probably tried to help, and was in a bit of a panic, and then Siobhan and her friends raised the alarm and suddenly there were loads of people there, and the lad panicked even more, dragged Willie into the shed, made him as comfortable as he could, and then went out past the fruit trees, grabbed his bike from wherever he'd stashed it—there's a bike in the photo in the newspaper; did you see it?—leaned it against the wall as if he'd just been passing, and offered to help with the clean-up. I bet he offered to get the water, so he could make sure no one saw Willie. I'd guess he was desperately hoping Willie would come around."

"So why didn't he stay around? Or even pretend he found Willie lying there? Where did he go? *Why* did he go?"

Jess shrugged. "I don't know. Maybe he got really scared when Willie showed no signs of waking up. Maybe he was just waiting for the first opportunity to get away. I don't know."

"No one saw him leave?"

"Did anyone see anyone leave, really? Was *anyone* able to tell you exactly who was there and what time they got there or what time they left? I imagine with all the confusion, there were so many people coming and going, you'd not have noticed anyone specifically."

Marcus nodded, kissed Jess on the forehead, and opened the French doors, blocking Fletcher and Snowflake with his body as he stepped out into the garden to phone his colleagues at the Garda station. "I'll send a car to pick up the three boys. Dublin can look after the other one—the waiter." He flicked his eyes towards the brewing tea. "Leave mine there; I could be a while."

Chapter Thirty-Five

"Well?" Jess greeted Marcus when he met her at the door on Monday evening.

"Well," he said, holding out his arms for a hug. "Don't you want to get in, first?"

She kicked off her shoes and followed him into the living room. The scent of something delicious wafted from the kitchen. A scrabbling at the glass of the French doors told her the dogs were shut outside.

He tipped his head towards the noise. "Sometimes I just want a chance to fling myself on you without him getting to you first." His eyes crinkled in that way they did when he smiled, although there was tiredness in his face, too.

"What time did you get back?"

"About an hour ago. Linda's been great. She let Snowflake and Fletcher out a couple of times, spent some time with them. Left us a cake."

Jess followed him to the kitchen, where she ignored the doleful sight of Fletcher; nose pressed against the glass as he watched her with his huge chocolatey eyes, and prised the lid of the Quality Street tin in the middle of the table. "Victoria sponge! Yum."

Beside the tin was a white envelope, hand-addressed in neat cursive that Jess immediately recognised. "I wonder what she wants." She ripped it open to reveal a couple of lines of Maeve's careful handwriting. "Emergency committee meeting. She wonders if we can meet tonight at her house—that's unusual! Guess it was too short notice to book the meeting room." She glanced at the clock on the kitchen wall. "She says eight. Have I time?"

Marcus peered through the oven door. "It's just about ready. Ten minutes? I guessed you'd want to go, even if you are wrecked, because you'll be thinking she has some gossip from her cousin and where else would you find out what happened to them all?"

"You knew what the note said?"

"Linda was here with the dogs when she dropped it in. She asked Linda to be sure you got it, as she needed to call an emergency meeting, and it was short notice but she hoped you'd be able to go. I knew you'd want to. Like I said; gossip."

Jess moved closer to him, wrapped her arms around his waist and gazed straight into his dark eyes. "I have no idea who else could tell me anything," she said, mock-serious. "It's not as if I know any good-looking policemen I could bribe with a large slice of Linda's Victoria sponge, after all."

He kissed her nose, then gently extracted himself to pull on an oven mitt and open the oven door. A rush of steam filled the kitchen, along with the smell of melted cheese. "Lasagne. And jacket potatoes. That okay?"

In the garden, the sun still beat down on the patio, despite it being almost seven o'clock. It had been another scorcher, and there wasn't a cloud in the sky. Jess nodded towards the French doors. "Good winter food, huh?"

"Add a salad, then?"

"I'll get stuff for it." She rooted in the fridge for cucumber, lettuce, and red peppers, and grabbed a dish of cherry tomatoes from the worktop and a large bowl from the cupboard. "Here. How about you tell me everything you know, while we eat, and then I'll go to Maeve's, where she'll tell me everything she knows, and I'll report back to you when I get home? We'll eat outside?" She nodded to the garden, grabbed cutlery from the drawer, and opened the French doors.

Fletcher, delighted to finally gain her attention, flew up at her, and the knives and forks clattered across the patio.

"You big idiot! Get down!"

Behind her, Marcus laughed and rummaged in the drawer for replacement silverware.

Jess dropped to her knees to embrace the dog. "Eugh, no licking, stop it! And let me say hello to Snowflake, too. Budge over."

Marcus set the bowl of hastily-thrown-together salad in the centre of the table beside a pile of small jacket potatoes. He returned to the kitchen and came back out a moment later with an oven dish filled with lasagne; the cheesy top a bubbling golden-brown.

"You spoil me."

"True. But you've had a long day, too."

That was also true. Jess's college days were long and often physically tiring, and by the time she'd driven home, she was usually half-asleep. The thought of going to Maeve's for a committee meeting was hardly appealing, but Marcus was right about that, too. She *did* want to know what Maeve had to say that couldn't wait until their next scheduled meeting. She checked the time on her phone. "Thirty minutes, give or take. Did you get any further with any of her cousins?"

Marcus had been busy since Maeve had called to Orchard Close on Saturday afternoon. They'd tried to round up Frances's brothers that same evening, but they'd all been out at various football matches, pubs, or whatnot, and no one seemed entirely sure how to get hold of any of them. On

Sunday, they'd brought them all in for preliminary enquiries. Conor, Chris, and Gavin had been summoned to the station in Lambskillen, while Michael had been interviewed by Marcus's counterparts in one of the Dublin stations.

"No one," Marcus said, "was detained overnight, but the questions resumed first thing this morning. They were all back in by nine." He didn't know yet where they'd got to in regards to Michael's involvement with causing Jim's illness, and the inquiries with Conor, Chris and Gavin would be ongoing, depending on whether Willie recovered or didn't. Marcus, used to that kind of thing, delivered the possibility that Willie could yet die in a matter-of-fact, even tone, but Jess shivered at the thought of yet another unnecessary, violent death in the neighbourhood.

"I do hope he wakes up soon," she said.

He met her eyes with a steady, serious gaze. "It will be so much better for those boys if he does."

"Did any of them tell you what actually happened? How much did we get right?"

"Lots, I'd say. But we've a way to go yet. They're all trying not to drop each other in it while not taking the blame themselves, either. The older one, Gavin, claimed he was nothing to do with it at first. He admitted giving the other two a ride, but swore blind he didn't know what they'd planned."

Jess raised her eyebrows. "I find that hard to believe."

"Then the twins both tried to cover for each other, but that tripped them up, in the end. You were right about Chris—he'd hung around, terrified about what they'd done to Willie. Tried to help, but then got even more scared when people started to show up. He wouldn't say who out of the pair of them had hit Willie, only that it was an accident. Over and over: 'It was just an *accident*. An accident.' Poor lad. He was quite distraught."

"They're only young, those two? Twenty? Something like that?"

"Twenty-two. Old enough to know clonking someone over the head with a shovel isn't going to end well." Marcus's tone was brusque and at odds with his sympathetic 'Poor lad' comment of just seconds before. "There's every chance he won't wake up. Reminding Chris of that set him off all over again. We told his brothers he'd confessed to hitting Willie. That got them talking."

"And had he?"

"It seems more likely it was the other one. Conor. Piecing together their accounts, it seems almost everything you and Alice suggested happened—don't look so smug!" He waggled his fork at her, eyes crinkling as she tried to put on a serious 'I'm listening' expression.

Even though she did, indeed, feel a bit smug. *Right again, Alice, right again!*

"They insisted they'd only intended to scupper the contest. Not meant to hurt anyone or cause any permanent damage. They'd run in behind the cottage to catch their breath and sort themselves out—put the bottles in their bags, tear off their paint-splattered clothes—and yes, Willie was there with his barrow and his tools."

"He confronted them?"

"He confronted them. Asked them what they'd been at, and they didn't answer, but he saw the paint, and guessed they were up to something, and they tried to run off, get their bikes, get away, but he grabbed Chris's arm and Conor grabbed at Willie, and it escalated. Willie was already holding the shovel. Both boys said that. They got a bit muddled after that. And if Willie *does* wake up, he may say different."

"But one of them bashed him with it."

"Yes. We think Conor thought Willie might swing for them, and tried to wrestle it from Willie and somehow managed to hit Willie with it. They both swear it was an accident, but when Willie fell to the ground bleeding, Conor grabbed his bike and ran. Gavin was already parked up waiting for them, so Conor flung his bike in the trailer and got in the cab. Chris didn't follow, and Gavin didn't wait for him."

"That padding under Willie's head?"

"Chris's sweatshirt. He was sure Willie would come round at any moment, he said. He didn't know what to do."

"Called for help, perhaps." Jess stared at Marcus, torn between horror that the boys *hadn't* called for help, and sympathy for the young lad who had at least stayed behind. Until he hadn't. "Who hid the shovel?"

Marcus shrugged. "They both say it was them. Conor says he threw it up there after Willie got hit. Chris says he threw it up to hide it after Conor ran off. The bag you found seems to be Chris's though; Conor had his with him when he went off in the tractor, if Mrs Harris's eyes are reliable."

"Spy," Jess muttered.

"What?"

She shook her head, laughing. "Never mind. Go on. The bag?"

"We'll fingerprint it and the bottle if we need to, but I doubt it'll come to that."

"Will that help? Don't twins have matching fingerprints?"

Marcus laughed. "No, Jess. They don't."

"So what happens next?"

Marcus looked at his phone. "Next, my nosy little sweetheart, you get yourself round to Maeve's committee meeting, because you wouldn't like to be late for Maeve. Imagine her disapproval. You'd better drive, or you'll definitely not make it on time."

She pulled a face. "I meant with the boys, but yeah, I'd better get moving." She sighed. "I really don't want to go. I bet it *could* wait."

"To answer your question, though, it depends. It's not a murder investigation yet. And the boys aren't telling us all the details. Conor will almost certainly be charged for assault, although exactly what level remains to be seen. And of course, that'll escalate if Willie doesn't pull through. Chris will be charged with vandalism, at the very least. Gavin? Aiding and abetting if nothing else. We'll see what else will stick. You'll be late, you know?"

Jess scraped her chair backwards over the patio slabs, shoved a last forkful of lasagne into her mouth, plucked another tomato from the salad and ran upstairs to get changed.

At the door, Marcus passed her the car keys. "Maybe do more listening that talking? If Maeve knows already, fair enough, but if she doesn't ... it's not public knowledge yet."

Chapter Thirty-Six

J ess hadn't been inside Maeve's house before. The kitchen
was bright, airy, modern, and spotless. Jess would've
predicted 'spotless' if she'd given it any thought beforehand,
but certainly not 'modern'. A bright floral print hung on one
wall, and a group of botanical drawings hung on another.
The countertops were a sleek marble effect, and the cupboards
a fresh cream. Maeve had laid out a plate of chocolate chip
cookies and a set of matching mugs adorned with birds that
Jess recognised as a popular Shannon Pottery design. It was
most welcoming.

Maeve, however, was her usual stiff, zipped-up self. She
gestured to Jess to take the chair beside Henry, already seated
with Father James at the cloth-covered kitchen table. "Thank
you for coming at such short notice. I know you've been at the
college all day. I expect you're tired. We'll just wait for Lila and
then we'll make a start. I have something I must say to you all.
I'm afraid it couldn't wait." Her face, as usual, was serious and
sombre, and her tone gave nothing away as to what this news
might be.

A car pulled into the drive, and a moment later, the doorbell
rang.

Lila gushed for a moment about the botanical prints,
oohing and aahing over each one until Maeve coughed and

inclined her head towards an empty chair. "Do sit down. Lila."
Once Lila had done as she was told, Maeve consulted her A4
notepad, cleared her throat again, and said, "I'll get straight to
the point. I must submit my resignation from the committee."

Everyone started to speak at once, but she held up her
hand and spoke firmly. "My family have disgraced the contest.
I cannot, in good conscience, remain involved in the Tidy
Village proceedings. It has come to my notice that several—"
She faltered briefly and the paper fluttered in her hands. "Yes,
several. Several members of my family conspired to interfere
with the proceedings, resulting in jeopardising our position in
the contest; decimating our village, and putting Willie Keegan
in hospital. I cannot apologize enough for their misconduct
and I remove myself from the committee with immediate
effect."

She set the papers onto the tabletop and sat rigid in her chair.
"I trust you will do me the courtesy of drinking your tea before
you leave, and I suggest that Jessica here fills my position as
secretary forthwith. She will be quite capable."

There was a silence around the table, then, once again,
everyone spoke at once.

"Don't be so silly."

"None of this was your fault."

"You couldn't have known."

"Oh, Maeve ..."

Father James held up a hand. "I think—" he said, looking
around the table at each of them in turn, waiting until
everyone fell silent before he continued. "I think I speak for
us all when I say we do not accept your resignation." Lila, Jess,
and Henry nodded in agreement. "We will, however, accept
your offer of tea. I, for one, will also accept a chocolate chip
cookie, and I have absolutely no doubt that Jess, at least, will
join me."

Jess helped herself to a cookie and held out her mug for Maeve to fill with tea. "Maeve," she said, "I know how difficult this must be for you, but none of us think for a second that you were involved. We couldn't possibly manage all this without you."

Two small pink blotches on her cheeks brought a splash of colour to Maeve's pale face, but her voice remained steady. "I'm not sure you know it all. Let me tell you what I know before you decide."

She gave a version of events that largely echoed what Marcus had already told Jess. The three boys had worked together, using information gleaned from Frances, to 'play a prank' on Ballyfortnum. Backing up what the boys had told the Gardai, Maeve and Frances were united in their belief that this 'prank' had, indeed, intended only to knock Ballyfortnum off the leaderboard; give Abbeydare a fighting chance at the prize, and cause no real harm.

The oldest of Frances's brother, Michael, had also pried information from Frances, and done his bit to help the plan run smoothly.

Jess's ears pricked up as Maeve talked about Michael's involvement. *Here's what Marcus doesn't know!*

Michael, in his position as a waiter in the Fairmount, had served the judging team on several occasions. "They always hold their dinners at the Fairmount, as it turns out. I wasn't aware of that." Maeve stared at the pattern on her mug. "Not just the prize-giving ceremonies and Christmas celebrations. The pre-launch dinner, too, and the weekly planning meetings during the judging period. Funded by the sponsors, Frances said. Terribly extravagant." Maeve huffed her disapproval. "Could be put into the prize fund." She turned the mug in her hands but didn't drink from it. "Michael knew they would be there on that Saturday. Fran had told him to expect them. She always let him know when they'd be in, she said, and he tried to arrange his shifts to make sure he was on duty. She thought it was because he was pleased to see her; a natural thing, being family." Maeve's voice tremored, and Jess reached across the table to pat her arm.

"I'm sure it was, at least most of the time. I imagine he just saw an opportunity; that one time. Encouraged by his brothers, too."

Maeve nodded stiffly. "I'm sure you could be right. Nonetheless, he's lost his job. Been let go with immediate effect. As soon as there was the hint of a misdemeanour," Maeve said, "they asked him to leave. He's brought disrepute to the establishment, and they can't show any tolerance of such. He's back in Abbeydare. Came home last night. There will probably be charges."

"I suppose that will be up to Jim?" Henry said. "Is that how it works?"

No one knew the answer to that, but they did all agree that they would not allow Maeve to step down. Nor, they agreed, should Frances.

"She can't be held responsible for her family," Father James said. "I'll testify for her, if it comes to it. I expect she feels bad enough over it all."

Again, the others agreed.

"But," Lila said, "we can't control that either; only give her our support. We can, however, decide here and now that whatever the outcome this year, we will *not* be beaten and we will make sure that Ballyfortnum holds onto that trophy for many years to come. Let's meet next week to draw up the agenda for next year's entries and show Abbeydare why we *deserve* our title."

Jess groaned. "Can't we take a week off first, to get over *this* year's efforts? I've got to admit it was far more dramatic than I'd expected it to be." She laughed; only half-serious.

Lila glared at her. "No. So, here's to the All-Ireland Champion of Champions, last year, next year, and with any luck at all, this year too." She raised her mug and Henry, Jess, and Father James clinked theirs against it.

"To the Champion of Champions," they echoed. "Maeve?"

Slowly, grudgingly, and somewhat rigidly, Maeve inched her mug into the mix. "I suppose so."

At home, yawning, Jess sank into a bubble bath.

Marcus stood in the bathroom doorway, a cup of tea in each hand. "Do you think," he said, eyes crinkling at the corners as he smiled at her, "we could have a quiet life from now on? Please?"

"Marcus?"

"What now?"

"Do you think you might bring me a slice of that Victoria sponge we didn't have time for earlier? And yes. A quiet life. That would be *lovely*." She sank down into the bubbles as Marcus smiled at her, set down her tea, and left the room.

Acknowledgements

NOVEMBER 2024

A Deathbed of Roses has proven to be my most difficult book to date. Not because of the content or the story—I've got to know the residents of Ballyfortnum well over the past few years, and the Tidy Village contest idea has been brewing in my head for ages—but because I've had a particularly tough year. With several bereavements, a change of job, a bout of sickness, and some eye problems, to name just some of the drama, I've struggled with finding time to focus on writing, and have had to snatch fragmented moments here and there, wherever and whenever I was able. As usual, my husband has been a tower of support, and my readers have cheered me on with lovely emails and messages. I couldn't have got here without that encouragement and support, so as always, my biggest thanks are for you: Readers and husband, thank you.

I'd also like to thank my fellow mystery writers in the Cozy Crime Collective (you can find us on Facebook: https://www.facebook.com/groups/cozycrimecollective). I've dropped the ball in terms of my engagement this year, but they've been supportive and kind. I hope to up my game again, now I've finally got this book done!

Thank you also to the wonderful Gladstone's Library and all the staff there. You gave me well-needed sanctuary twice this year, and neither this book nor this year's other book, *Claude, Gord, Alice, and Maud,* would have made it to print without that oasis. I'll be back soon!

About the author

Jinny was first published in Horse and Pony magazine at the age of ten. She's striving to achieve equal accolades now she's (allegedly) a grown-up. Jinny has had some publishing success with short story and flash competitions and has been placed in the prestigious Bath Flash Fiction Award, Flash 500 and Writer's Playground contests, published in MsLexia Magazine and Writing Magazine, among other publishing credits. She holds an MA in Creative Writing for which she was awarded a Distinction.

Jinny also teaches English as a foreign language to people all over the world and finds her students a constant source of inspiration for both life and stories. Her home, for now, is in rural Ireland, which she shares with her husband and far too many animals. Her two children have grown and flown, but return across the Irish Sea when they can. If you follow her on Facebook, you'll see many photos of the settings of her novels. *A Deathbed of Roses* was inspired by the very real SuperValu Tidy Towns Award, which keeps so many Irish villages and towns well-maintained and blooming.

For up-to-date news and exclusive content including your own map of Ballyfortnum and extra short stories about the characters in this series, please sign up for Jinny's newsletter by popping over to her website:
www.jinnyalexander.com
Say hello at facebook.com/JinnyAlexanderAuthor
To help other readers discover this series, please leave a review on Amazon and Goodreads. Thank you.

Also by Jinny Alexander

The fifth Jess O'Malley mystery, *A Snapshot of Murder*, will be coming soon.

Jinny is also the author of the Mrs Smith's Suspects series. Book 1, ***Claude, Gord, Alice, and Maud***, was released in summer 2024. Book 2, ***Carrie, Gary, Bel, and Harry,*** will be released in late 2025. A non-fiction account of Jinny's work as an online ESL (English as a Second Language) teacher was released in summer 2025.

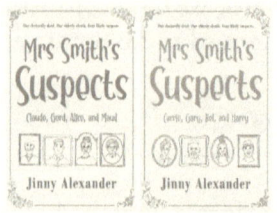

Jinny also has stories and flash fiction in anthologies and magazines. A more comprehensive list can be found on her website at www.JinnyAlexander.com

Dear Isobel (March 2022, Creative James Media) is currently out of print following Jinny's reversion of rights.

Praise for *A Diet of Death*

This is a light-hearted cosy that will delight fans of
M C Beaton's Agatha Raisin. [...] Highly
recommend it to those looking for a frothy,
enjoyable read that is low on violence and high on
feel-good entertainment!

MAIRI CHONG,
The Dr. Cathy Moreland Mysteries

Well-written and intriguing, this mystery
revolving around members of a weight-loss
group is one that will keep you turning the
pages until the very end.

KELLY YOUNG,
The Travel Writer Cozy Mystery Series

A classic British style whodunnit.
With an engaging and believable heroine - Jess O'Malley - and
set in rural Ireland, this is a fun mystery with lots of heart.
An enjoyable read leading to a satisfying solution, already
looking forward to the next book.

GERALDINE MOORKENS BYRNE
The Caroline Jordan Mystery series and *On
the Fiddle! The Music Shop Mysteries*

The whole book was a warm, comforting read for
anyone who loves mysteries. Highly suggested for
fans of *The Thursday Murder Club.*

ALISON WEATHERBY,
The Secrets Act

Jinny Alexander's outstanding cosy mystery
A Diet Of Death is a real treat.
(And not the kind with calories!)

J. IVANEL JOHNSON,
The JUST (e)STATE Cozy Mysteries

This tale is a homage to those much loved
classic detective authors, and is perfect for
escaping the worries and stresses of the world.

LOUISE MORRISH,
Operation Moonlight

Jinny Alexander embeds her murder mystery with the satisfying
atmosphere of rural Ireland. [...] Cozy mystery readers who enjoy stories
of friendships and murder possibilities will find *A Diet of Death* unusually
strong in its atmosphere, which does equal justice to both the murder
mystery component and the entwined lives of a small village [...]

MIDWEST BOOK REVIEW

Praise for *A Hover of Trout*

A warm hug of a book; a literary mug of cocoa with a dash of murder for spice. Jinny Alexander once again captures village life with her quirky cast of characters. I'm already looking forward to Jess O'Malley and the gang's next outing.

AMANDA GEARD
The Midnight House, The Moon Gate

A Hover of Trout is an excellent second book in the Jess O'Malley Mystery series […] as well-written as the first, with intriguing characters, plenty of suspects, and some interesting character dynamics.

KELLY YOUNG,
The Travel Writer Cozy Mystery Series

A Hover of Trout, the second in the Jess O'Malley Mystery series, is an absolute joy for those who love classic detective mysteries. Sprinkled with a little romance along with the comfort and familiarity of Jess's rural Irish village, this expertly-crafted page-turner of a whodunnit had me guessing until the end. An excellent addition to the series!

ALISON WEATHERBY,
The Secrets Act

Fabulous characters and witty dialogue as more mysteries are revealed and solved by Jinny Alexander. I guarantee you will go back and read Book 1 in this charming mystery series.

MIKE MARTIN,
Award Winning Author of the Best Selling Sgt. Windflower Mystery series

The story is satisfyingly twisty with plenty of red herrings, coupled with likeable, believable characters. There's plenty of fun, and a lot of heart. The Jess O'Malley series deserves to become a firm favourite with mysteries lovers everywhere.

GERALDINE MOORKENS BYRNE
The Caroline Jordan Mystery series and *On the Fiddle! The Music Shop Mysteries*

Lyrical, atmospheric, Alexander's words lure you alongside amateur sleuth Jess O'Malley into the tangled webs of Ballyfortnum village. Very soon, you're too caught up to leave, nor do you want to. If you need a cosy weekend escape read, this is your ticket.

DAMYANTI BISWAS,
The Blue Mumbai series

This, the second in Alexander's Jess O'Malley series, is an incredibly satisfying read.

Jess O'Malley is the perfect companion on a wintery evening with the curtains drawn and a steaming mug of hot chocolate! A frothy mystery sprinkled with just the right amount of intrigue and a healthy dollop of romance, what's not to love?

MAIRI CHONG,
The Dr. Cathy Moreland Mysteries